Rhett

A Walker Brothers Novel

Seven Sons Ranch in Three Rivers Romance™
Book 1

Liz Isaacson

ISBN-13: 978-1-63876-362-8

Rhett

1

"It's totally fine," Evelyn Foster said to the woman on the other end of the line. "Not every first date goes well." She often had to counsel her clients through a few dates before they could see what she saw.

Being a small-town matchmaker, where ninety percent of the men were cowboys, wasn't an easy job. But Evelyn loved it, as she could make everything line up on paper like a dream. The women knew what she was doing, but the men...well, sometimes men just needed to get out of their own way.

And Evelyn provided a way for them to do that—and conveniently run into the woman of their dreams. They just didn't know it yet.

And obviously, Tina didn't know it yet either. "He's perfect for you," Evelyn assured her. "What happened that rubbed you the wrong way?"

"For starters, he wanted to take me to the big box store for a date."

Evelyn could hear the eyeroll in Tina's voice.

"But you persuaded him to do something else, right?" Evelyn asked, shuffling a couple of pages on the desk in front of her. The wind shook the windows of her office, and she glanced outside to see a dust storm had kicked up on the farm where she lived with her sisters.

Granted, they didn't really use the two hundred acres they had, as that was a lot for three women to manage by themselves. Their father had retired a few years ago, and they mostly planted as much as they could and sold the hay to other farms and ranches surrounding Three Rivers.

"I did, yes," Tina said. "But is that going to be my whole life moving forward? Me trying to persuade this guy to do what I want?"

"Let me look through a few more candidates," Evelyn said, focusing on her papers again. May was an exceptionally busy time for her services, as well as around the Shining Star Ranch. While her oldest sister, Callie, ran most of what happened on the ranch, Evelyn had plenty of chores to do too. "And I'll get back to you in a couple of days, okay?"

"Okay," Tina said. "What should I do if Gideon calls?"

"You get to decide that," Evelyn said, looking at Gideon's one-sheet. "He really does seem perfect for you. Maybe he just didn't want to commit to something as long as dinner."

"I don't know how that's a plus," Tina said dryly.

"Well, he's met you once, for what? Five minutes at the dry cleaner? Somewhere I only knew he'd be because we got a last-minute phone call." Evelyn never revealed her sources, but she had spies all over the town of Three Rivers.

With a population of almost seventeen thousand now, she certainly couldn't be everywhere at once, or know where every eligible bachelor would be at any given time.

"And that was the first time he'd been there," Evelyn reminded her. "So maybe give him a little slack?" She spoke as kindly as she could. After all, Tina was paying her, and she didn't need to lose a client because the cowboy Tina had her eye on was out of his element.

"Okay." Tina sighed. "But still look at a couple of other guys for me."

"Anyone in mind?" Evelyn asked, because no one else on her list stood out for someone like Tina. She liked a through-and-through Texas cowboy, with a big hat, and the biggest belt buckle possible. Rodeo experience a plus.

While there were plenty of cowboys in Three Rivers, Tina wanted Cowboy Extreme.

"I've seen a man at church the last few weeks," Tina said. "He looks new in town."

Evelyn repressed a sigh and looked out the window again. She couldn't see the trees she knew were only ten feet away. Alarms started sounding in her mind, and surprise darted through her that she hadn't lost cell phone reception yet.

"I don't know his name or where he lives," Tina said.

"All right," Evelyn said. "I'll put out some feelers to find out who this guy is." With that, the line crackled, and Tina's words broke up. In the next moment, the service cut out, and Evelyn looked at her phone to see the call had indeed been severed.

"Great," she muttered. Now she had to hunt down a mystery cowboy who was new to town. Maybe Patrick would know. Her boyfriend worked the meat counter at the grocery store, and he saw a lot of people—especially single cowboys coming to buy their steak dinners.

Of course, a lot of the cowboys around Three Rivers worked on farms and ranches, and they often got plenty of beef for free from their employers. So maybe Patrick wouldn't know. But it couldn't hurt to ask him.

He knew what Evelyn did for a living, and he often sent her texts with information on men she needed to know about. She couldn't send him a text right then, as it seemed her provider had gone down with the crazy windstorm.

She left her office at the same time a horrible, glass-shattering sound filled the whole farmhouse. She screamed, hers matching her younger sister's in the living room.

Callie burst in the back door with the words, "There's a tornado headed this way. Come help me with the animals." She spun away before either Evelyn or Simone could answer.

Thankfully, Evelyn already had shoes on, and she hurried after her oldest sister, saying, "The sirens haven't even gone off. Maybe it's just a windstorm."

The moment she finished speaking, the chilling, distinct wail of the tornado siren filled the air.

She ran after Callie, who handed her a grease pen and a handful of fly masks. "Put our phone number on their sides. Put on the fly mask, and we'll set them in the pasture."

They didn't have the hurricane clips or reinforced beams needed to tether the horses securely in the barn, and their horses were used to roaming in pastures.

"Maybe it'll go north," Callie said, her voice panicked. "Like that last one."

The last tornado had been over two years ago, and it had indeed turned north before inflicting too much damage on Three Rivers. She handed Simone the same items she had Evelyn, and the sisters got to work.

"We have to go next door, too," Callie said. "We'll put our number on the animals at Fox Hill for the new owner."

"Who is it?" Evelyn asked, glancing east though she couldn't see more than five feet in either direction. Even Callie's voice coming through the swirling dirt and dust felt eerie and otherworldly.

"Some guy," Callie said vaguely, which meant she didn't know either. "Last name's Walker, I think. Mason texted a couple of days ago and said he'd be here this week, and that we could turn the keys over to him then."

Mason Martin had lived and cultivated Fox Hill Ranch next door for years and years before deciding to up and move to Hawaii, of all places. He'd put the ranch up for sale, and contracted with the sisters to take care of the few animals he'd left behind. He had a staff of four still on the premises too, and Evelyn wondered why they couldn't take care of their own horses.

"What about Orion?" she asked. "Can't he turn the horses out to pasture over there?" It was at least a half-mile to Fox Hill, though their properties touched one another along a fence line on the east side of the ranch. Evelyn did *not* want to get caught out in the storm.

"They went into town this morning," Callie said, finishing with her last horse, smacking it on the flank and saying, "Go on. Stay safe."

With their own livestock numbered and protected as much as possible, the three sisters piled into Callie's pickup truck and rumbled down the road. If anything, the wind blew stronger at Fox Hill, but Evelyn kept her head down and her fingers moving as she marked the eight horses Mason had left behind.

He also had two pigs, six goats, and a whole herd of chickens. The tornado would likely pick them up and carry them off, and she certainly didn't know how to hold one long enough to write a phone number on feathers.

With all the animals marked that could be, Callie shouted, "We have to go inside!"

Exactly what Evelyn didn't want to do, at least not here. But one look at the sky, and she knew she didn't have a choice. Panic filled her, though she'd lived through tornadoes before. They weren't super common in this area of

Texas, but she'd had enough experience with them to know what to do in case of an emergency.

"Where's Daddy?" Simone asked.

"He's with Granny," Callie yelled, holding her hat on her head as she ran for the back door of Mason's homestead.

It felt strangely quiet inside, with the three of them panting as they sucked at air that finally wasn't filled with debris.

"Come on," Callie said. "He'll have a tornado shelter."

Evelyn had been to Mason's house several times, and she knew right where it was. As Callie turned to go down a hallway, she said, "It's over here, guys. He showed it to me once." She hated that she wasn't in her own home, protecting it and herself.

But just inside the living room off the front door, she swept aside the rug and pointed to the hatch door there. "Goes down into a cement foundation."

"Get in," Callie said as glass broke somewhere in the house. The tornado might not strike Three Rivers directly, but this wind was definitely wicked and causing some real damage.

Evelyn went first and turned on her phone's flashlight. Callie followed and did the same, with Simone bringing up the rear. No sooner had Simone closed the door above them and come down the steps did it open again.

Callie shone her flashlight on the man sliding down the steps, pure fear in every line on his face. "Who are you?" she asked as Evelyn swung her light onto him too.

He bore a strong jaw and dark eyes—exactly the kind of man Evelyn would be interested in. You know, if she wasn't already dating someone.

The stranger drew in a deep breath and spoke in an even deeper voice. "I'm Rhett Walker. This is my ranch." He dusted himself off with a pair of big hands and added, "You must be the Foster sisters from next door."

"Guilty," Callie said, lowering her light so it wasn't shining right in Rhett's face. But Evelyn couldn't do the same. His good looks and bass voice seemed to have frozen her to the spot, and all she could do was stare while her heart pounded wildly in her chest.

"Can you stop shining that in my face?" he asked, his voice a touch colder than before, and Callie put her hand on Evelyn's arm to make her put the phone down.

"So," he said with only the soft glow on his features now. He was somehow sexier and more beautiful than in the harsh light, and Evelyn wondered where in the world all these thoughts and feelings were coming from. "I guess the tornado is welcoming me to the Texas Panhandle." He laughed, and Simone and Callie joined him.

Evelyn simply reveled in the sound of his laughter, thinking that if she weren't with Patrick, she'd definitely be setting herself up with one cowboy Rhett Walker.

Callie started to detail what they'd done for his animals and why they'd come in his house instead of theirs, and Evelyn shied behind her sister so she could continue to simply stare at her new next-door neighbor.

2

Rhett Walker could not believe his rotten luck. It seemed like he'd run into a string of it, and he wondered when it would end. Just like this blasted tornado. It seemed to go on for a long time, and not only because he was trapped in his own storm shelter with three strangers.

Women, sure, but they chatted more with each other than him. He'd switched on the flashlight on his phone and currently stood in front of a long shelf with dozens of cans on it. At least they wouldn't starve down here.

"How do you know when the tornado is over?" he asked, thinking he needed a camera that showed the weather outside so he wouldn't have to risk losing his hat to check. He felt six eyes on him, but when he turned, only one woman still stared at him.

"Evelyn, right?" he asked, taking a step closer to her.

"Right," she said, her voice hoarse. She coughed, and

Rhett watched her. "Sorry," she added. "We were out in the dust and dirt for a while before coming in." She cleared her throat and bent down to a lower shelf.

She straightened and held two bottles of water in her hand. "Do you mind if I have one of these?" She extended the second one toward him, and he took it.

"No problem."

"Where are you from? Have you been in a lot of tornadoes?"

"I grew up outside of Austin?" Why he phrased it like a question, he wasn't sure. He found himself clearing his own throat, as if this woman made him nervous. Everything about coming out to a ranch made him squirm a little, and three of his brothers were supposed to be with him. But there had been some problems at the office a couple of days ago, and he'd ended up coming north himself.

"I know where Austin is," Evelyn said with a small smile. She hid it behind the water bottle as she drank.

Of course she did, and suddenly the storm shelter felt a little too hot. He returned his attention to the shelves in front of him. "My father owned a technology company there," he said, glancing at her. "This shelter needs one of his cameras, then we'd know when the tornado has passed."

"You'll be able to tell," she said. "Even without a camera."

"You think so?" He wasn't sure how, as it wasn't like there were any windows in the shelter.

"A camera would get knocked around in a storm," she said, cocking her head at him, the questions clear.

Rhett shuffled his feet, but he kept his eyes on hers. "My dad had contracts with the military and government," he said. "The cameras were tiny."

"Tiny? How tiny?"

"Pinhead tiny," he said. "The wind wouldn't knock it off." As if the world had been holding its breath and had just released it, something changed. He looked up to the ceiling, the lack of groaning evident. "I think the storm is over."

"It's passing," one of Evelyn's sisters said, and Rhett couldn't believe that she could tell without visual proof. "Let's give it a few more minutes," the other woman said.

"Callie," Evelyn said, providing Rhett with the name he'd forgotten, though they'd only been in the shelter for maybe ten minutes. "She's the oldest," she added in a mock whisper, and Rhett got the message.

A chuckle started in the back of his throat, and he ducked his head as he tried to quiet it. "A little bossy, is that what you're saying?"

"She has moments," Evelyn said, and Rhett met her eyes again. She had a beautiful smile to go with that long, dark hair and those sparkling eyes. He couldn't really tell what color those were in the glow of flashlights, and he told his heart to stop skipping beats.

He hadn't bought this ranch out in the middle of nowhere to get his heart broken again. He'd managed to do that in Austin, thank you very much.

"I'm the oldest," Rhett said. "Six younger brothers."

"Wow," Evelyn said, those eyes still shining at him. "I thought some of them were coming with you."

"They are," he said. "The twins got held up in Austin, tying up loose ends, but I had to come up for the job."

She cocked her head again. "The ranch is fine."

"Oh, Jeremiah is going to mostly be doing the ranch stuff," he said. "I'll help a little. The twins are technology dudes, but they insisted on coming." He shrugged, because Tripp and Liam didn't even own plaid shirts.

"So what's the job?" she asked.

"I'm a forensic veterinarian," he said. "There's a case up here that's expected to take a while. My dad's company was selling, and this place was for sale...." He let the words hang there.

Evelyn's eyes narrowed. "Have you ever lived on a ranch?"

Before he had to answer that, Callie said, "I'm going up." That caused movement, and while Evelyn watched him for an extra moment, she too moved toward the ladder. He let them all go up first, feeling like perhaps he should've done so to make sure no one got hurt.

Thankfully, the house still stood at the top of the ladder, though there were several windows broken.

"Looks bad," Callie said, walking over the dirt that had been blown in through the broken windows.

"This is bad?" Rhett asked, not quite the house and ranch tour he'd been expecting. The weight of the clean-up felt like tons and tons, and he couldn't shoulder it. He stood in the middle of the kitchen, turning slowly.

The appliances were still there. Countertops. Even the kitchen table and barstools.

The women had gone out the back door, and Rhett went out onto the deck as well. He had so many questions, and he'd been hoping he could ask the four men who supposedly lived here on this ranch he'd bought.

Only Evelyn paused at the edge of the lawn and lifted her hand in a friendly wave, and Rhett returned it. Then she turned and followed her sisters, their red pickup firing up and rumbling down the road to the west, where their ranch obviously was.

He sighed and looked up into the still angry sky. "Really, Lord? A tornado? What am I supposed to do now?"

He had the very strong feeling that he better get to work, so he went into the garage and found a broom. After all, God had led him here, and he couldn't leave now.

———

Rhett had most of the main floor swept out when his phone rang. "Hello?" He didn't recognize the number, but he had a feeling he'd be answering a lot of calls from people he didn't know in the near future.

"Mister Walker?" a cowboy drawled.

"Yep, you got 'im," he said.

"I'm Orion Goldberg," the other cowboy said. "We got

stuck in town and wondered where you ended up during the tornado. Maybe you're not in town yet?"

"I'm at Fox Hill," he said, pushing the huge pile of dirt out onto the deck. Everywhere he looked, there was more work to do, as evidenced by the patio table and chairs his eyes caught on. The umbrella was still there, but bent, and a sigh passed through his whole soul.

"Arrived just before the tornado. Good news," he said, trying to find the silver lining in this situation, the way his mother had always done. "The storm shelter is stocked with food and fits four people." With room for more.

"Four people?"

"The women from down the road were here," Rhett said, thinking immediately of Evelyn. He consciously switched his thoughts to how he needed to rename the ranch now that he'd finally arrived.

Just another thing in a long to-do list.

"Well, we're still in Three Rivers," Orion said, his voice fading for a moment. "What do you need us to bring back? How'd the windows fare? The animals?"

Jeremiah was supposed to be here to run the ranch, and Rhett had paid little attention to the type and number of animals on the ranch.

"Uh...." He looked out over the land behind the homestead and found several outbuildings. Barns and stables and coops. He turned away from them, over-whelmed and thankful for the four men who would be back soon. Hopefully. "There are several broken windows. Dirt and stuff everywhere. I'm sweeping out the house now."

"We'll bring back lumber and some cleaning supplies. What about groceries?"

"Can I call something in?" Rhett asked, turning back to the house. He'd bought the ranch a couple of months ago, but he and his brothers hadn't made the move immediately. The owner had said his neighbors and the crew at Fox Hill could manage for a while, and they obviously had.

"To where?" Orion asked, and that answered Rhett's question. It only took fifteen minutes to drive into the town of Three Rivers, and it was a bustling place. At least Mason Martin had told him it was. Rhett had come straight to the ranch when he'd seen the windstorm kick up and the sky turn an ugly shade of green.

"Never mind," he said.

"We can bring out some food, boss," Orion said, and Rhett wasn't used to being the boss. He worked for the state as a forensic veterinarian, and while there were only a few people who did what he did, he wasn't the boss.

"That would be great," he said. If they wanted him to be the boss, he could do it. "I'll pay you back." He outlined a few grocery staples for Orion, and the call ended. As he swept the dirt back onto the ground where it belonged, he supposed things at Fox Hill could be worse. He could be the only one here, with no money to pay for anything.

As it was, he had a crew coming back with the supplies he needed, and his brothers on their way. Oh, and plenty of money, as when his father had sold the company he'd built, he'd gotten billions for it.

All the Walker brothers now had billions too—which was how Rhett had gotten this ranch in the first place. It was the second-biggest one in the area, and well-maintained. At least it had been.

"And it will be again," Rhett vowed. "But it needs a new name. A fresh start." Just like him and his brothers.

"So what do we call it?" he mused aloud to himself, not quite used to so much country stillness and silence. He and three of his brothers would be living here. "Four...." The only word he could think of was men, and that sounded stupid.

Plus, once Wyatt finished with the rodeo circuit, he'd probably come to the ranch too. With Rhett's parents retired and living in Grand Cayman now, there was no "home" for the rodeo king to return to.

"Seven Sons," Rhett said, the name popping into his head. It fit. It was perfect, and while Rhett certainly hadn't appreciated all of the rotten luck that had brought him to this part of Texas, he tipped his head back and looked up into the clearing sky.

"Thank you, Lord," he whispered, because he at least had a place to stay, money to fund the rebuilding of this place, and family coming.

He didn't need a wife, despite what his mother said. Oh, no, he did not.

3

One year later:

Evelyn gripped the steering wheel of her sedan as it moved from the asphalt of the highway to the dirt lane that led out to Shining Star. Hot tears gathered behind her eyes, but she willed them back.

She'd lost another client, and things were seriously starting to look dire. "Why couldn't things just work out with Patrick?" she asked the blue sky in front of her. The huge gate and arch for the Seven Sons Ranch loomed ahead, and Evelyn turned toward it as she always did.

She and her sisters had come to the unveiling, where Rhett had stood beaming with the other three Walker brothers that had moved into the homestead a year ago. They were as frustrating as they were friendly, as Evelyn had tried—quite unsuccessfully—over the past twelve months to get one of them into a relationship with one of her clients.

But she couldn't just come out and tell them what she did. If too many people knew, the whole operation would be blown wide open. Thankfully, while Patrick had broken up with her, he hadn't told a single soul what she really did for a living.

"Doesn't matter anyway," she muttered, looking darkly at the huge Texas star on the closed gate. The name WALKER sat beneath that in big, bold letters, with seven smaller stars, one for each Walker brother.

Evelyn had met them all over the months, though Skyler, Micah, and Wyatt still didn't live permanently on the ranch. Jeremiah mostly ran things, while the twins, Liam and Tripp, helped on the farm but worked from home on some techy stuff Evelyn didn't really understand.

She maintained her own website, but she knew one of the twins could probably help her set up a killer one that would bring in much more business. Of course, then she'd have to tell him what she really did in her office.

Which would be fine if only Liam or Tripp knew. Even Jeremiah. But she did not want Rhett Walker to know what she did. She'd had a Texas-sized crush on the man since he'd moved in, but he was colder than the North Pole when it came to dating. Stronger than gravity in his conviction not to get involved with anyone.

She'd only tried once to set him up with someone else, and since then, she'd simply tried the brothers. But those

Walkers...they were definitely as frustrating as they were friendly. Because she hadn't been able to get even one of them a serious girlfriend, the women in this town had started to doubt her abilities.

After all, she had such easy access to them. She knew them so well. They lived next door to one another, attended the same church, and she even had breakfast every Tuesday with Rhett, on the back deck at the newly named and christened Seven Sons Ranch.

Fine, she'd done that for herself, hoping that Rhett might warm to the idea of being her boyfriend.

Which was another reason she'd just lost another client. Patrick had broken up with her four months ago, and Evelyn was currently single herself. No one trusted a single matchmaker who couldn't even get a date with any of the four delicious, dark, mysterious cowboys who lived right next door.

Scoffing, she turned away from that huge arch that probably cost Rhett ten thousand dollars. Not that it mattered. The man was made of money, and if ever there was something he didn't want to pay for, one of his brothers would.

Callie had taken advantage of their generosity more than once, though the Walkers didn't throw their money around—at least not where normal people could see.

But Evelyn, Callie, and Simone had seen the new barns go in. Seen the tornado preparations—and accepted Rhett's offer to beef up their barns and security measures too, should another twister decide to touch down in Three Rivers.

She saw the fancy farm equipment. Saw the whole homestead get completely remodeled, right down to the latest and greatest technology in terms of appliances, computers, and televisions. The brothers certainly liked their technology, and she knew that all came from their father.

Pulling into the slummier house where she still lived with her sisters, she saw Rhett's ATV parked along the side of the house. Perfect. She'd have to face him with tears still in her eyes, and it wasn't even Tuesday.

Sure enough, she found the man in her kitchen, a coffee mug at his lips while Simone stirred something on the stove for lunch.

"What are you doing here?" she asked as she plunked her purse on the built-in desk.

Rhett's gorgeous eyes moved to hers, filling with surprise as he looked at her. "What am I doin' here?" he drawled in that voice that kept her awake sometimes. "You told me to come at eleven-thirty so we could go over the case one last time."

Instant humiliation filled Evelyn. "That was today?" Of course it was today. He'd been working an involved case for a farm a few miles outside of Three Rivers, and he had to be in court tomorrow.

"I'm so sorry, Rhett." She moved over to the couch and sank onto it, cradling her head in her hands.

"Her business isn't going well," Simone said, sympathy in every word.

"I can see that." The barstool scraped as he stood up. He joined her on the couch, his leg pressing right into hers. If she had to name three best friends, they would be Callie, Simone, and Rhett Walker himself.

Still didn't keep her heartbeat from accelerating, as it did every time the man got too close to her. Had his pulse ever sped at the sight of her?

She looked up into his eyes. Those kind, deep brown eyes that seemed to know exactly what she was thinking. He smiled at her, such a tender best-friend smile, and kissed the top of her head like he was her father not the star of her fantasies.

Still, she leaned into his touch, because it was nice to be taken care of by Rhett Walker. "What can I do to help?" he asked.

"I don't know." She wiped her hair back out of her face and tried to put on a smile. She did know what he could do, but telling him would require revealing so much more, and she just wasn't ready to do that. He wouldn't look at her with such soft eyes then.

Would he?

"It might help if I knew what your business was," he said. "I mean, maybe Liam or Tripp—"

"No," Evelyn said. "It's fine. I'm fine."

Rhett looked at her again and leaned forward to put his coffee mug on the table in front of them. "Sweetheart, I know I'm no expert when it comes to women. But anyone can take one look at you and see you're not fine."

"I'm goin' out to the barn," Simone said, and Evelyn turned toward her.

"You are? Why?"

"Callie needs me." Simone had both eyebrows lifted so high—a sure sign of a lie. "Watch that soup, would you?" With that, the back door closed, and her sister was gone.

"Soup in May seems kind of ridiculous," Rhett said with a smile. "But do you think there will be enough to take some home with me?"

"When is there never not enough to take some home with you?" Some of the frustration in Evelyn's system melted away. She also knew what had just happened. Simone had left on purpose so she could be alone with her crush.

Just the fact that she was *still* crushing on this man was embarrassing enough. Simone didn't have to be so obvious about things.

"So." She exhaled, hoping to calm her racing heart. Nope, that had never worked. "Let's see your case one more time."

He grinned at her now, and such an action on such a beautiful face should be illegal. He was tanner this year, with that same rugged jawline, that same long nose, that same black cowboy hat.

She'd learned his wardrobe consisted of blue jeans, cowboy boots, only brown belts, and long-sleeved shirts in a variety of shades. Some solids. Some plaids. Some even striped. The man never left home without a jacket, though Texas could get mighty hot in the summer.

He'd told her that because he worked outside a lot, he needed the long sleeves to avoid bug bites and sunburn. His "forensic veterinarian" tan was a sight to behold, as he sometimes wore short-sleeved T-shirts when he wasn't off the ranch working.

"You sure you don't want to run your things by me first?" he asked. "I feel like you help me so much, and all I do is feed you on Tuesdays."

"Hey," she said. "I need to be fed on Tuesdays. And this week, I want those eggs Benedict you've been promising for weeks now."

He laughed, the sound so wonderful Evelyn almost forgot about her lost client, and got up to get his case files.

She *almost* forgot. Almost.

———

SEVERAL DAYS LATER, Tuesday came, and she was due at Seven Sons Ranch by eight-thirty. Evelyn lingered in her office, her potential client list completely gone now. She'd literally gone through everyone, whereas only a few short months ago, she had so many women wanting her services, she'd been turning them away.

"Oh, you're still here."

She turned at the sound of Callie's voice, a sigh moving

through her whole body. "Yes, I don't want to go sit with Rhett."

"Why not?" Callie came fully into the office. "You've always loved your breakfasts with him." She wore concern on her face, and Evelyn had confided in Callie about her crush on the handsome cowboy long ago. "Simone and I have always been jealous."

"I know." Evelyn picked up a handful of papers and dropped them again. "I have no more clients, Callie. No one wants a matchmaker who can't get and keep a boyfriend." She collapsed into her office chair, feeling hopeless, which was so unlike her.

What should I do? she asked the Lord, but He hadn't been giving her any ideas for the last few months since Patrick had ended things with her.

"I pay for all of our gas and groceries with my matchmaker money," she said, looking up at her sister. "What are we going to do?"

"You just need a boyfriend, right?" Callie asked, easing into the chair Evelyn usually reserved for clients.

"I think that's a step in the right direction," Evelyn said. "The last three men I've tried haven't been interested, and if there's anything worse than not being married, it's going on one or two dates and then not getting a call-back."

It showed other women that she couldn't even match herself with the right man, so how could she possibly find them the right cowboy?

"Then get married," Callie said.

"What?" Evelyn froze, her eyes locking onto her older sister's. "How in the world am I going to do that?"

Callie got up, a look on her face that said trouble. Evelyn knew; she'd seen it before as the girls grew up. Their mother had died when Simone was only two, and they'd been raised by a very busy father and their grandparents.

They'd had plenty of free time to get in trouble, and they'd taken every liberty to do so.

"Callie," Evelyn said, standing up and speaking in her most warning voice.

"I'm just saying that your business would improve if you were married. You just said so. So get married." She stepped toward the exit.

Evelyn's heart beat wildly against her ribcage as she tracked Callie's movement. "To who?"

"To that handsome man you eat breakfast with every Tuesday."

Evelyn opened her mouth to protest, but nothing came out.

Absolutely nothing.

4

Rhett looked west to check on Evelyn's progress toward their breakfast. She'd wanted eggs Benedict, and he'd delivered. But she was late, and now he felt like everything would be cold. If there was something worse than a cold egg, he didn't want to know about it.

Finally, she came around the side of the barn, and his heart flipped and flopped as if it didn't quite know where it was supposed to be in his chest.

He'd long contemplated asking Evelyn to dinner instead of breakfast, showering at the end of the day to be ready for that date and not to get a crime scene off his mind, and showing up at her house with a dozen roses.

He'd never asked.

Number one, she'd had a boyfriend for the first eight months he'd been at Seven Sons. Number two, it had taken at least that long to get the ranch cleaned up and running at full speed again after the tornado. Number three, she'd never seemed that interested in him.

She never wore makeup to their breakfasts, and he'd been the one to suggest them, about six months ago. She'd agreed, but the first time they'd met, she'd asked if it was weird they were eating together when they were just friends.

Just friends.

The words echoed through his mind as she mounted the steps, a beautiful smile on her face. Sure, he called her sweetheart, and he sometimes stole a kiss when he was trying to cheer her up or help her. He always followed such a gesture with laughter, because it kept things casual, and that seemed to be right where Evelyn wanted them.

"There you are," he said. "I was beginning to wonder if you'd forgotten what day it was." He wanted to stand up and hug her, but he never had before, and it felt weird to do so now.

"Sorry," she said, tucking her hands in her back pockets and slowing down. "I was talking to Callie...." Her voice trailed off as she looked back toward her family land. She faced him again, and Rhett could sense the same unrest in her now that had been there last week. And at church on Sunday.

"Come sit down," he said. "And tell me what to do to help you."

Confusion puckered her eyebrows for a moment, but she came and sat in the spot she normally did. Relief moved through Rhett, and he smiled at her. Something about having her there with him made him happy, and he couldn't explain it.

She picked up her fork, but she didn't touch her food. "Rhett, I have a problem."

"A serious problem?" he asked, his heart tap-dancing in his chest. "Or a little problem?"

"It's more of a secret." She ducked her head so Rhett couldn't see her.

He didn't like that, and he reached over and touched her hand. "You have a secret you haven't told me? I thought I knew all about the obsession with toy poodles."

That got her to smile, but she didn't laugh, and Rhett didn't know what to do with this version of Evelyn Foster.

"This is a serious secret, Rhett," she said. "And you can't tell anyone, not even your brothers."

Rhett forgot about the eggs in that moment. He'd throw it all away and order something. Or take her to the pancake house after the secret came out. "All right." He folded his arms and sat back in his chair, watching Evelyn.

She tucked her hair behind her ear, something he'd watched her do when she was nervous. "It's about what I do."

"Ah, of course." The business that wasn't going well that she wouldn't tell him about.

"I'm a matchmaker," she said, her eyes locking onto his. They held absolute fear. "I mean, kind of. I don't really match up men and women. I have female clients, and I...

arrange ways for them to be...to put them in a favorable situation with the man they want to get to know better."

Rhett simply stared. He had no idea what to say. "Is that why you kept trying to get Tripp and Liam to those summer dances?"

"Yes," she said simply. "You have no idea the chaos the four of you have caused by moving here and refusing to date." A flicker of a smile touched her mouth. "Which, by the way, you still haven't told me why. So I'm not the only one with a secret."

He lifted one shoulder, not really willing to tell her about his romantic history. Reason number four he'd never asked Evelyn out on a date.

"My clientele has...lost faith in my abilities," she said. "I'm not married. No boyfriend. People think I can't do my job." She shrugged too, but the pain echoed from her voice, loud and clear.

"You want to go out with me?" he asked, the words coming out easier than he'd ever thought they would.

"No." She shook her head, her eyes flitting all over the place now.

"No." He started nodding, the rejection diving deeper than he thought it would. Wow, his fear of rejection—reason number five he'd never asked Evelyn out—had been very real. No wonder he hadn't asked.

"No, I don't want to just go out," she said. "I want you to marry me."

Rhett sucked in a breath, the air somehow choking him.

He coughed and coughed, a rubber band tightening like a noose around his chest. "Marry you?" he managed to squeak out between trying to stop coughing and trying to breathe.

"It wouldn't be real," she said quickly, her gaze finally settling on his. Her eyes were so bright, and so full of hope. "We don't have to, you know, live together or anything. No one comes out here. Simone does all the grocery shopping. I never really need to go to town. I just need a diamond ring, and I need to be able to tell people I'm your...wife."

She whispered the last word, and her eyes brimmed with tears.

Rhett had no idea what to say or do. How long had she been thinking about this?

Why was he even considering it?

He exploded to his feet. "I need to think for a minute." He grabbed his plate and hers. "I'll go heat these up again."

"Rhett," she said after him.

"It's fine," he said. "Really, I'm fine. I'm just going to throw this stuff in the microwave. I just need a minute to think. Be right back." He hurried into the house and pressed his back against the wall, out of sight.

He couldn't quite breathe properly.

If they got married, he'd get to kiss her.

"Not a real kiss," he muttered to himself.

If they got married, he'd have to tell his brothers something. A story like that couldn't circulate around town and simply be ignored. Jeremiah, Liam, and Tripp would definitely need an explanation.

What would he even say? *Hey, it's just a favor.* He started toward the kitchen and put the plates on the counter.

"Hey." Liam came into the kitchen, his hair still damp. "What's going on? You're not eating with Evelyn?"

"Eggs got cold," he barked, wrenching open the microwave and sliding a plate inside. He couldn't even imagine what a microwave would do to a poached egg and hollandaise sauce, but he was about to find out.

Liam stalled, clearly sensing something was afoot. "Okay, something weird is going on."

"Sure is," Rhett said. He couldn't deny that. He also couldn't stop thinking about marrying Evelyn. It was like she'd taken their relationship from a maybe to full fantasy in two seconds flat.

"I'm headed out," she said from the doorway, and Rhett spun toward her.

"Wait," he said, ignoring Liam as he muttered, "Oh, boy."

Rhett strode toward the sliding glass door where Evelyn stood, glaring at Liam when he muttered, "Ask her out already, Rhett." He touched her elbow and guided her back onto the deck, pulling the door closed behind him.

"Where's Penny?" Evelyn asked, and Rhett took the momentary distraction to look for his cattle dog.

"She's around somewhere," he said. "Maybe Jeremiah took her out on the ranch with him."

"I got her a new ball." Evelyn stepped over to the railing and leaned against it.

"She'll love that." Rhett hated this conversation, and he took a deep breath and faced her. "I'll marry you."

She flinched, a flush creeping up into her face. "You don't need to. Really, it's okay. It was just a stupid idea."

Rhett slipped his hand into hers, feeling like Liam had his nose pressed against the glass and could see everything.

"I want to," he said. "If it'll help."

She leaned into him, and they faced the ranch together. She kept her hand in his, her fingers even tightening in his. "It won't be forever," she said. "Just...for a little while."

He said nothing, because what he wanted to say would reveal too many of the soft feelings he'd had for this woman over the past year. "Just tell me what to do," he said. "And I'll do it."

"Are you sure?"

"If it'll help you." He shrugged. "My big case is over now, and I'm not going to take another case from the state for a while. I'll just be helping around here, so I'll have time." Time for what, he had no idea.

Hopefully more hand-holding. Talking. Kissing....

"Do you want to go to dinner?" he asked, his voice quiet and his soul filled with hope. *Please don't let her say no*, he prayed.

"Yes," she said, pressing closer to him. "Starting with dinner is probably a good idea."

"You're going out with her?" Jeremiah stood in Rhett's doorway, leaning his dirty shoulder against the frame, his arms crossed.

"Why are you so upset about it?" Liam asked. "It's about time one of us went out with someone."

Rhett said nothing as he adjusted the collar on his shirt. A new one he'd bought that afternoon in anticipation of his first real date with Evelyn, the polo felt too slick against his skin, and there was definitely something wrong with this collar.

"We had a pact, man," Jeremiah said. "No women in Three Rivers."

"Did you think we'd stick to that forever?" Tripp asked, stepping over to Rhett and swatting his hands away. "Leave it. It's fine. It's supposed to look like that."

"I don't like this shirt," Rhett said, stripping it off. "I'm just going to wear what I usually do." The woman had already proposed to him. He didn't need to dress up.

Oh, but he knew he did. Evelyn wouldn't be the only one sizing him up that evening, and he could already feel the eyes of every citizen in Three Rivers on him.

He pulled a button-up over his head, a sigh of familiarity moving through him.

"Rhett," Liam prompted.

Rhett turned to face his brothers, particularly the surly Jeremiah. "Look, I know we had a pact, but Tripp's right. We weren't going to stick to it forever, and it's been a year." *A long year*, Rhett thought.

"And I like this woman, and I'm going out with her. You don't have to go out with anyone." Although, Evelyn's business would probably really take off if she could get the icy Walker brothers off their ranch and out to dinner with some women around town.

A sour taste filled Rhett's mouth. Was Evelyn using him?

Of course she is, a tiny voice whispered in his mind. *And you agreed to it.*

And he had. So he brushed his teeth, grabbed his wallet and keys, and walked out the front door to his truck.

He did like Evelyn Foster, and he did want to help her. As he sat in the cab of his truck and made the short drive down to her ranch, he prayed aloud, "Is this okay, Lord? She needs help, and I can give it to her. I want to do this. *Should I do it?*"

He pulled up to the sprawling farmhouse where Evelyn lived with her sisters. The dark-haired beauty he'd been crushing on for much of the last year rose from the rocking chair on the porch.

And Rhett had his answer.

5

Foolishness moved through Evelyn as she went down the steps and Rhett got out of his truck. He wore a clean pair of jeans and a button-up shirt in blue and white checkers. His hat perched deliciously on his head, and there was nothing about him Evelyn didn't like.

The man didn't flaunt his money, but he didn't try to hide it either. "Hey, gorgeous," he said, sweeping one arm around her as if they'd been dating for months. She felt too round in some places, the slacks she'd put on a little too dressy for the dinner-dance he'd booked for them to attend.

He pressed a kiss to her forehead, and asked, "Are you ready for this?"

Something solidified inside her that had been wishy-washy before. "Yeah," she said. "Are you?" She stepped back and looked up at him. "I mean, you don't have to do this. I've been talking myself out of calling you and telling you this whole thing was a joke all day."

"Is it a joke?" he asked, those deep eyes searching hers.

"No," she whispered. "I just...I mean, maybe you'd rather go out with someone else. I mean, not that I've seen you or any of your brothers date much, but I don't know, I just—"

Rhett started laughing, silencing Evelyn. She had been babbling, and her nerves had been bubbling all day long. Since standing with him on his back porch, holding his hand. That had been wonderful. Serene. And in that moment, she'd felt comfort and peace that everything would work out the way it was supposed to.

But since then, every doubt and insecurity in her mind had bloomed and blossomed and bulged until she couldn't contain them anymore.

"Evelyn," he said, one of the rare times he used her name. The Texas man seemed to have an endearment for everything. He'd called her sugar or sweetheart or honeybee —especially when she wore this yellow blouse—every time he saw her. And now, apparently, gorgeous.

She did feel gorgeous with him at her side, his hand resting on her back, the scent of his woodsy cologne in her nose.

She looked up into his eyes, and they were serious while his mouth flirted with a smile. "I want to go out with you." He ducked his head, reclaiming some of his mystery. "I've wanted to ask you out for a long time, actually."

Surprise hit her right in the vocal cords, rendering her mute. "You have?"

"From the moment I met you." He cleared his throat. "Now, come on. They serve dinner right at seven-thirty at this place, and we don't want to be late." He threaded his fingers through hers and led her to the passenger side of the truck.

She still had no idea what to do with his confession. He'd wanted to ask her out and hadn't? Once he got behind the wheel, she twisted toward him to buckle her seatbelt. "Why didn't you ask me out?"

"You were dating Patrick," he said simply.

"We broke up four months ago. Why not then?"

Rhett shrugged, a flush crawling from under his collar, staining his neck and cheeks. "I don't know."

"Yes, you do."

He sighed as he backed out and turned toward the highway that would take them back to Three Rivers. "You said several times that we were just friends. I just figured you'd reject me, and I didn't want to lose our Tuesday breakfasts."

Evelyn had used those words to keep the barrier between them. He'd obviously heard them, loud and clear, and he didn't want to get hurt. Which meant he'd been hurt in the past, and Evelyn really wanted to hear those stories.

"Okay," she said. "But we *are* friends, and I'm glad about that."

"Me too," he said. "And I might have a secret too."

"Oh, a secret. And you said you didn't have any." She giggled, glad the flirting with him was as easy as sitting down to breakfast had been. At least until that morning.

He cut her a look out of the corner of his eye, a smile spreading across his face. "Yeah, I have a secret." He sobered as they bumped along. "I'm afraid you'll be upset by it."

"Please." She scoffed and tucked her hair behind her ear. "I told you all my embarrassing secrets this morning. It can't be worse than that."

"It might." He turned onto the highway, accelerating as they shot toward Three Rivers. When he remained silent, Evelyn didn't press him. They'd been friends for a while now, and Rhett would talk when Rhett was good and ready. After all, he was forty-three-years-old and had never been married. He didn't have to explain himself to very many people.

"Why have you never been married?" she asked.

He choked as the truck jerked to the left a little. After correcting the vehicle, he looked at her again. "So we're going there."

"I know a lot about you," she said. "Your job, your work ethic. How you like your eggs, and that your favorite food is actually that of a ten-year-old boy." She grinned at him.

"Hey, spaghetti is for adults too."

She laughed, because being Rhett's friend was easy. It was being his girlfriend she didn't know how to do.

And you took it all the way to wife, she told herself. She'd texted out *Let's just maybe date a little*, to him about thirty times that day. They didn't need to get married for her business to pick up again.

She simply found herself wanting to see if he'd do it, number one. And number two, maybe she was hoping it would become real at some point.

"But I know basically nothing about your past relationships," she said, watching him.

His fingers tightened on the steering wheel, and his jaw clenched too. "Okay, but this is a ten-minute topic."

"What does that mean?"

"It means I only have to talk about it for ten minutes. Then we can move on to something else."

"Can I get ten more minutes tomorrow?"

"Yes," he said. "That's how it works."

Evelyn marveled at this man, at the things he'd grown up with, the rituals he had. "Is this another of your mother's rules?"

He looked at her, softening inch by inch. "Yes," he said. "She said it was very hard to raise seven boys, because none of us wanted to talk very much. So she'd say things like, 'I get five minutes where you don't stop talking about the prom. Go.' And we'd talk for the five minutes, and she'd stop badgering us."

A pinch started behind Evelyn's heart. "That must've been great," she said.

Rhett chuckled. "I think most of us found it annoying. Except maybe Skyler. He likes to talk a lot."

"I had to tell my dad about prom," Evelyn said. "And

that wasn't fun, let me tell you. He'd ask more questions—where did he put his hands? Did you kiss him? Why would he say that?—than anything else." Still, a fondness for her father moved through her.

"It couldn't have been easy raising three girls by himself," Rhett said.

"No," Evelyn said, shaking her head as memories from her younger years flooded her. "I'm sure it wasn't." She looked at him, feeling vulnerable and like she could share real things with him. "I would give anything to talk to my mom for five minutes."

Rhett reached for her, and if the truck had been older, Evelyn would've quickly undone her seatbelt and moved across the seat to sit right beside him. As it was, she had a bucket seat, and all she could do was try to steal the comfort from his touch by holding his hand.

"I know I've said it before, but I'm sorry about your mom."

"It's okay." Evelyn stared out the windshield as the town of Three Rivers materialized in front of them. "I just miss her extra-hard sometimes."

"I'll bet you do."

She cleared her throat. "So this is a ten-minute topic."

"Right," he said. "Sometimes she'd say, 'I get four questions, and you have to answer them with complete sentences.'"

"Do I get questions?"

"I suppose you can have as many as you want." He

sighed like she wanted to gouge his eyes out with toothpicks instead of learn more about him and his past. "My brothers and I...the four of us moved here for a fresh start. We'd all had something go bad in our lives, and we made a pact when we got to Seven Sons."

He looked at her, his gaze full of nervous energy. "No women. No dating."

Realizations mixed with shock as Evelyn took in what he'd said. "No wonder I couldn't get them to go out with *any*one."

"I figured you might be upset."

"I'm not...upset." She tried to identify the feelings moving through her. "Surprised for sure. You Walker brothers are a hot commodity, in case you didn't know."

Rhett laughed. "I'm sure that's not true. Jeremiah can't hang up a towel to save his life."

Evelyn burst into laughter, the sound of them chuckling together so wonderful. "Well, I'm not sure the women of this town think about that when they see the four of you walk into church."

"What are they thinking?"

"Oh, I'm taking that to the grave," she teased as he skirted around the main part of town toward a ranch that had once been operational. It no longer had cattle or operational barns, but just a few large and spacious outbuildings that served as a mess hall and a dance floor.

The Mendenhall sisters ran the place now, and they served a chuckwagon dinner promptly at seven-thirty, as

Rhett had said. After that, they sang and played guitars, fiddles, and banjos while everyone danced.

Evelyn had been to The Barn Buster several times in her life, and it was always an amazing experience. When Rhett had asked her where they could go that night, she'd suggested it immediately. It was dinner and entertainment all in one, and she'd get to dance with him.

"What are you thinking when you see us?" he asked, joining the line of cars and trucks going onto the Mendenhall property.

"Really?" she asked. "You want to know?"

"Of course I do."

"Well, for the record, your ten minutes about your romantic history hasn't even started yet," she said. "You've said nothing."

"Fine," he said. "Now give me a couple of sentences on what you think when you see us."

"You," she said, about to blow everything wide open. "Just you, Rhett. I mean, your brothers are great men. I like them. I'll smile and say hello to them. But when I see you... well, let's just say you're different."

And he always had been, stemming all the way back to when he'd stumbled down those steps in the storm shelter.

"Have you tried to set me up with other women?" he asked.

"Once," she said. "It was a disaster, and I moved on to try with your brothers."

"Who was it?" he asked.

"A woman named Patricia," she said. "She still likes you, you know."

"Patsy Barney?"

"Yep."

"I helped her move a couch once."

"And a chair," Evelyn said. "And you worked on her gazebo, and ran over when her dog was sick."

He turned and looked at her fully, his eyes wide. "Those...that was you?"

"You were colder than an iceberg. It was like you didn't even realize she was female."

He blinked, his expression darkening. "I knew she was female." He turned back to the windshield, easing forward and rolling down his window to talk to the cowboy there. After getting parking directions, he inched forward again.

"Must have something to do with your history," Evelyn said lightly.

"I was engaged once," he said. "Just before coming here. She still has the ring, and I wasn't interested in repeating that disaster."

Wasn't? Evelyn wanted to ask. Instead, she pressed her lips together and nodded. "What was her name?"

"Angie Lofton. I hadn't had a girlfriend for a few years before her. We dated for a long time, and were engaged for over two years before I finally realized she was never going to marry me."

Evelyn's heart thumped with compassion for Rhett. "I'm so sorry."

"Thank you," he said.

"I can't imagine why someone wouldn't want to marry you," she said, making her tone light. "I mean, I'm leading with that, not waiting for an appropriate time." She giggled, but he only scoffed and shook his head as he pulled into the spot where he'd been told to park. He took the truck out of gear and looked at her.

"What will your brothers say?" she asked. "About you breaking the pact? If we get married right away?"

"They're fine," he said. "I don't have to get permission from them."

"But what do they think?"

"Jeremiah is upset," Rhett admitted, his head dropping a little as he studied his hands. "But Liam and Tripp were supportive."

"What did you tell them?"

"I told them we were going out."

"That's it?"

"Yes." He looked up at her again, clearly waiting for her next question. She supposed she had been firing them off pretty rapidly.

"Okay."

"Okay?"

"Yeah." She reached for the door handle and slid out of his truck. He joined her, claiming her hand in his as they walked toward the counter to check-in for dinner.

"I don't believe you, you know," he said.

"About what?"

"You have more questions."

"I'm sure I do," she said. "But the ten minutes are up, and I just want to eat and dance with you for the next couple of hours." She moved in front of him, so he'd stop walking. She was aware of other people flowing around them, but she didn't care.

As he gazed down at her, it was just the two of them in this moment.

"Thank you for doing this," she said.

"I already told you," he murmured. "I want to." He brushed his lips along the side of her face. "And sweetheart, you're going to have to kiss me before we get married. Is that happening tonight?"

Pure fear and delight moved through her. "Is there a rule for that too?"

"Will your father be questioning you about it tonight?"

She giggled, tucking herself right into Rhett's chest. "No, he won't be. And yes, I think there will be a kiss tonight."

Just thinking about it made her heartbeat accelerate, and she couldn't wait to be alone with him again.

6

Rhett felt like he'd shed his skin and put on a different suit. He still looked like Rhett, but he was doing all kinds of things he hadn't done in a long time. The skin fit perfectly, but it needed to be stretched a little bit. Okay, a lot.

He couldn't remember the last time he'd held a woman's hand, taken someone of the opposite sex to dinner, and fantasized about kissing her.

At the same time, he felt crazy. Was he really going to marry this woman just to help her business improve?

"Hey, Evelyn," a woman said, drawing his attention away from his own thoughts. Rhett looked at her, and he suspected he'd met this woman at least once. "Rhett Walker?" The surprised tone reached all the way into the atmosphere, and a measure of embarrassment trickled through him.

"Beverly," Evelyn said. "Hey." She sounded genuinely interested in this blonde woman, and she stepped away from him to give the other woman a quick hug. "This is Rhett Walker. Rhett, Beverly Willows." She returned to his side but didn't touch him. The nearness of her, though, made a pretty clear statement that they were together. Out together. Not just eating breakfast as friends on his back deck.

"She goes to church where we do," Evelyn said, and Rhett blinked quickly.

"Of course, Beverly. You sing in the choir."

A smile filled her whole face. "That's right. And we need you and your brothers to join us for the summer chorale."

Rhett didn't even know what a chorale was. He looked at Evelyn, whose whole face shone with light. She half-coughed, half-laughed, and turned away.

"Oh, I don't sing, ma'am," he said as another couple joined them. Relief hit Rhett that he knew these people. "Hey, Pastor." He shook Scott Daniels's hand and then his wife's, Crystal.

"He says he doesn't sing," Beverly said, as if such a thing was a town scandal about to start. "I've heard some good things from the row where you Walker men sit."

"That's all Tripp," he said, instantly regretting it. Beverly had hooks in her eyes, and Rhett wanted to shy away from her.

Evelyn seemed to get the message, because she said, "We need to go find our seats. Good to see you all. Pastor."

She nodded and smiled, smiled and nodded, and got them out of there.

Rhett exhaled. "Holy horses. That was terrible."

Evelyn laughed, her head tipping back to reveal her slender neck. He smiled at her and waited for her to quiet. She cuddled into him, and Rhett glanced around to find several people watching them. Some people were there with their families, some were on dates, like him and Evelyn. But it seemed like everyone was watching him as if he were Bigfoot and had finally come out of hiding.

He did his best to ignore them, and thankfully, the chuckwagon dinner started. He chatted easily with Evelyn, as if they were alone at his breakfast table, and before he knew it, a woman stepped up to the mic.

"We're going to be moving over to the dancehall," she said. "There will be more spice cake over there, along with vanilla ice cream, and the Mendenhall Maidens will begin playing in ten minutes. So get your dancing shoes on, go to the restrooms, and don't be late."

The crowd clapped, though Rhett wasn't sure why. Evelyn stood up, straightened her pretty yellow blouse, and looked down at him. "Are you still up for dancing, cowboy?"

"About that," he said, standing too. He collected their tin plates to take to the dishwashing window. "I'm not the best dancer."

"I'm sure you'll be fine," Evelyn said as she went with him. "I mean, I've yet to find something you're not good at."

Rhett shook his head. "That's just not true. I hired out those eggs Benedict. I can barely make toast."

"Who cooks at the homestead, then?" she asked. "I know you guys don't eat out all that much."

"That would be Jeremiah." Rhett put the silverware in the appointed bucket and set the plates on the counter. "Liam is a master at snack preparation, and he can make regular popcorn into something magical."

"Oh-ho," Evelyn said, laughing. "I want to taste that."

"Come on over anytime," he said, realizing that they had so much to talk about. This wasn't just a casual date. This was a public appearance so that when word of their wedding got out, it didn't come out of nowhere. It would be credible.

He sobered as the first strains of a fiddle started up. Scanning the dance floor, he quickly realized he wasn't going to be able to sit on the sidelines. No one else was, and he'd actually stand out if he didn't dance.

So he turned to Evelyn and extended his hand toward her. "I'll try not to break your toes," he said with a smile.

She laughed, and to Rhett, that was the most beautiful sound in the world.

———

AN HOUR LATER, Rhett couldn't believe how much fun he'd had. Pure joy filled him, and he slung his arm around

Evelyn's shoulders as they walked back to his truck. "That was amazing," he said.

"It's fun, right?"

"I had *so* much fun." Rhett held the door for her, taking the opportunity to let his hand slide down her back as she got in. He rounded the truck and got behind the wheel, his heart still dancing in his chest.

He really wanted to kiss her, but he thought they probably needed to get some details out of the way. "So when are you thinking we need to, you know. Do the make-believe marriage thing."

"I don't know."

Rhett wasn't sure, but it sounded like Evelyn didn't want to talk about this. "Can I get five minutes of this topic?" he asked, hoping she'd smile.

She did, and she turned more toward him. "Okay, I'm just feeling like maybe we don't need to do this. Maybe dating is enough."

"Your call," he said as if he didn't care. But if they were just dating, this was numero uno, and he wouldn't kiss her tonight. So he kind of needed to know.

Her phone chimed several times in a row, and he glanced at her as she moved her attention to it instead of him.

Awkwardness descended on them, and Rhett didn't know how to deal with it. Or break it. Or change it.

"I got a few texts from former clients," she said, her voice full of misery.

"That doesn't sound like good news." He glanced at her, but it was hard to see her face in the darkness.

"Jill says, 'Let's see if you can keep this one,' and Dana says, 'I give it two weeks, just like the last guy.'" She sniffled, and Rhett really had no idea what to do now.

His heart beat too fast in his chest as his frustration rose. "Okay, so we prove them wrong," he said, though he couldn't imagine himself ending things with Evelyn in two weeks, even if they were just dating. "Let's get married this weekend."

"This weekend?"

He looked over at the high pitch of her voice. "You tell me, Evelyn. I'm just—I don't want you to be upset."

She swiped at her eyes and said, "I'm not upset."

"Right," he said sarcastically. "I'll find out what it takes to get married in the state of Texas."

"We can't do it here."

"Why not?"

"Did you see how many people were staring at us? And neither Jill nor Dana were at the dinner-dance tonight. Which means people are talking about me. About us. All over town."

"Isn't that what you want?" Rhett's skin crawled just thinking about what she'd said. Everyone was talking about them, and he'd worked hard to stay out of the spotlight in Three Rivers.

"Yes," Evelyn said. "No. I don't know." She slumped in

her seat, and Rhett kept his eyes on the road in front of him, his headlights cutting through the darkness.

"Evelyn," he said gently as the turn for their ranches approached. "It's fine. I already said I'd do this, and I will."

"Yeah, but what happens when we get divorced? Maybe this is just a stupid idea." She looked at him, but Rhett couldn't meet her eye.

Maybe this was a good solution for him, too. He wasn't truly interested in dating, and he liked Evelyn a lot. They were already friends. His thoughts rotated in circles, and he couldn't sort out the rational thoughts from the junk. And his feelings? What a tangled mess.

He pulled up to her house and practically jumped from the truck so Evelyn couldn't run away from him. She tried anyway, and he grabbed her hand, trying to slow her flight. "Wait, wait," he said. "Please, wait."

She stalled, and when she looked up at him, tears shone in her eyes by the light of the moon. "Rhett, this is a dumb idea."

"I don't think it is," he said, walking her up the steps, where someone would have to be pressed right against the windows flanking the front door to be able to see them. His heart thundered in his chest, and he expected lightning to strike at any moment.

Before he got electrocuted, either from his rapid-fire pulse or the sparks between them, he lowered his head and touched his lips to hers. He only meant to see if she'd slap him or kiss him back, but once he'd made contact, he couldn't imagine pulling away and letting her decide what the next step should be.

He'd kissed her, and now he couldn't stop.

And the best part—Evelyn kissed him back, her fingers fisted in the collar of his shirt as if she liked what he was doing.

RHETT EASED into the homestead where he lived with his brothers, hoping everyone had gone to bed a long time ago. Jeremiah for sure would've gone to bed hours ago, as he rose with the sun, and as summer neared, that occurred sooner and sooner each day.

Liam probably had made a valiant effort to stay up to hear how Rhett's date had gone, but Rhett found him snoring softly on the couch. Tripp sat in the armchair, the leg rest up, his reading glasses on as he read the Bible.

"Hey," he said when he heard the creak of the front door. He looked over the top of his glasses as if he were seventy-five-years-old. Tripp took the glasses off and put the leg rest down without disturbing Liam, who could sleep like the dead.

"How was it?"

Rhett could still feel the pressure of Evelyn's mouth against his, and his head felt like it would float right off his body. "It was fine," he said.

"Oh, boy," Tripp said, walking toward him but looking

at Liam. "Let's go into the kitchen. He made ice cream." Tripp led the way and started pulling down bowls. If Rhett had known he'd have to provide a recap for Tripp, he probably wouldn't have done half of the things he'd done tonight.

Scratch that, he totally would have. Tonight had been great.

Tonight had reminded him that he didn't have to be alone.

Tonight had proved to him that he belonged here in Three Rivers.

"So you like this woman," Tripp said, pushing a bowl of chocolate ice cream with chunks of cookies in it.

"I'm going to marry this woman," Rhett said, watching as Tripp's eyes widened. Rhett put a huge bite of Liam's concoction in his mouth so he wouldn't spill about the make-believe marriage, or say that the wedding was in just three days.

7

Evelyn paced in her office, every cell in her body rioting against itself. Wednesday had passed, and Rhett had called to say he'd applied for the marriage license. There was a seventy-two-hour waiting period before they could use it, and that he'd been told he'd have it by Friday.

Thursday was a blur, but she distinctly remembered going to town and buying a new dress. A new white dress, and no one had asked her any questions about it, though she knew the owner of the boutique. Apparently white was in for the summer.

Friday came, and she experimented with her hair until Simone came into her bathroom and demanded to know what she'd been doing in there. Evelyn needed to tell her sisters about her insanity, but she honestly had no idea how to start that conversation.

Callie knew something was up, because she came into

the office while Evelyn was in mid-turn, and she said, "Okay, spill."

"What?"

"Evelyn, you've been acting crazy this week. Something's going on." She stepped further inside and closed the door behind her. "You don't have to tell Simone if you don't want to, but we have no secrets."

Evelyn met her sister's eye, pure panic parading through her. "I did something stupid, and I don't know how to go back."

"Stupid?" Callie's eyebrows went up, her expression alarmed. "Illegal stupid? Or just stupid-stupid?"

"Stupid," Evelyn said. "And it's your fault, because you're the one who said I should get married to save my business."

Callie took a step forward and rocked back, looking down at the coffee mug in her hand. She quickly stepped forward and set the mug down before gripping Evelyn's shoulders. "Are you getting married?"

"Today," Evelyn whispered. "And it's insane, and I don't see how anyone in this town is even going to believe it."

"To who?"

"To who?" Evelyn asked, her voice pitching up. "You don't know?" She moaned and turned away from her sister. "This is never going to work. If I can't even fake out my own sister, no one is going to believe the marriage is real."

"It's not real, is it?" she asked.

"No," Evelyn said. "Of course not." Maybe she'd been

on the best first date of her life just a few days ago. Maybe holding Rhett's hand had been the single best thing that had happened to her in the past couple of years. But she'd still only kissed him one time, and a wave of foolishness poured over her.

"It's Rhett," Callie said, a smile touching her mouth. "Right?"

Evelyn nodded, because she couldn't even vocally confirm.

"And he's okay with it?"

"He seems more excited about it than I do."

"I told you he liked you," Callie said triumphantly.

"Callie," Evelyn whined. "I can't do this. Can I?"

"Are you lying to anyone?" Callie asked, her big-sister look coming into her eyes. "Doing something illegal? Something to be ashamed of?"

Evelyn considered the questions. "No, but—"

"But nothing," Callie said. "No one needs to know why you got married. They'll just know you did—and you are. It's not like you're telling people you and Rhett are married when you're not. That would be a lie."

"This isn't how I envisioned my wedding day," Evelyn said. Out of all the sisters, Evelyn had spent the most time thinking about her wedding. The dress. The flowers. The band. All of it. And she'd never imagined her and her groom at City Hall, no family or friends, flowerless, no reception dinner, nothing.

"There are so many things about our lives we didn't

imagine," Callie said, linking her elbow through Evelyn's. "Now, when is this wedding?"

"One o'clock." The words scraped Evelyn's throat.

"Do you need a witness?"

"Rhett said the court would provide witnesses, but I'd love it if you were there." Evelyn might be able to go through with the ceremony if Callie sat in the front row. She'd always looked to her older sister for advice, approval, and support.

"How were you planning to get out of the house so we wouldn't know?"

"Oh, I don't know. A client meeting."

"Great, and I'll ride along for something, unless you want to tell Simone first." She raised her eyebrows in a silent question.

"Rhett and I already talked about having a sit-down with all of our siblings to tell them," she said. "I don't want to leave him high and dry. Simone won't mind, will she? What do you think?"

"I think I better go see if I have a dress appropriate for my sister's wedding." Callie seemed entirely too enthused about this fake wedding, and Evelyn watched her go, her nerves returning in full force.

She reached for the coffee Callie had brought in, though she certainly didn't need the caffeine. Her phone rang, startling her and causing some of the hot liquid to slop onto the back of her hand.

Rhett's name sat on the screen, and she hurried to swipe

on the call. "Hey," she said, hoping her voice sounded chipper and excited. He deserved to have a wedding he wanted to remember too, and Evelyn suddenly knew why she was so nervous.

"Listen," she said. "I don't know about this."

"Evelyn," he said. "You've said that so much this week. What's the real problem?"

"You," she blurted. "It's you, Rhett. I don't want to take your opportunities from you. There's a lot of great women in this town, and you could really find someone you actually loved and wanted to marry."

"Evvy," he said, a nickname he'd used dozens of times before. "I honestly don't think that would happen."

"It could," she insisted, staring out the window. "If you'd open yourself up to dating."

"Yeah, I don't think so."

"So you didn't like the dinner dance?"

"I loved it," he said. "Because I was with you." His words hung there, and Evelyn felt them sink right into her soul. A feeling of peace came with them, and she drew in a long breath.

"Okay," she said. "As long as you don't feel like I'm taking something from you. I mean, haven't you ever thought about your wedding?"

"No," he said. "I don't think I have."

"Ever?"

"Sweetheart, I'm a man." He laughed, and Evelyn couldn't help smiling too. She'd stood at this window just over a year ago, a dust storm turning into a tornado that had led to her first meeting with Rhett.

"And I'm coming to get you in thirty minutes," he said. "Are you ready?"

"Yes," she said, glancing to the closed door. "I have my stuff in my car, so I can just transfer it over." Her brain screamed at her, and she realized what she'd told her sister and what she'd just committed to Rhett were at odds with one another.

"Uh, I told Callie about the wedding," she said.

"Oh."

"She's actually going to come be a witness, if that's okay."

"So are we not going to lunch first?"

"Yes," Evelyn said. "We are. I just need to tell her she has to drive in separately."

"Did you tell Simone?"

"No," Evelyn said. "So we can still have dinner together tomorrow night. Did you talk to Jeremiah?"

"Yep. He's got a brisket in the smoker already." Rhett didn't sound nervous at all. In fact, he sounded happier than she'd heard him in a while. Maybe he really didn't think he was sacrificing anything to help her.

"Okay," she said, turning away from the window. "I have to go finish getting ready."

"Evvy?" he asked.

"Yeah?"

"I know this probably isn't the wedding you want."

Evelyn couldn't confirm that, though he was right. "Thank you," she said, because what he was doing to help her deserved to be acknowledged, even if he didn't know it.

The call ended, and she sighed. She still had to finish her hair and do her makeup, but she dropped to her knees and just breathed. "Lord," she finally whispered. "Please help me to know if this is wrong or not."

Only silence moved through her, and she wasn't sure what God was trying to tell her.

"So I'm going to do it," she said, pressing her eyes closed, still listening. She didn't get a strong feeling one way or the other, so she stood up and looked at the ceiling. "Okay, here I go."

The Lord still didn't stop her, and she finished her hair and makeup and went out onto the front porch to wait for Rhett. She texted Callie about the new plans, a quick apology that they couldn't ride to the county courthouse together.

It's fine, Callie said. *Go to lunch with your fiancé. I'll see you soon.*

Evelyn's head jerked up and she murmured, "Fiancé." Before she could think too hard about that, Rhett's black luxury truck pulled into her driveway.

It was time.

She got up and picked up the backpack she'd packed with her dress and shoes and went down the steps. Rhett met her, a big smile on his face. "Hey, gorgeous." He swept her right into his arms and held her tight. "Are you okay?"

His soft voice was too much to handle, and Evelyn clung to him as every emotion in the book ran through her. "I'm fine," she said. "I am." She stepped back and gathered herself together.

Rhett stood there and watched her.

"I am," she said, putting a smile on her face.

"We don't have to do this."

"I know."

He reached out and cradled her face, bringing her slowly toward him so he could kiss her. Evelyn appreciated the warmth of his mouth against hers, the gentle yet insistent way he kissed her, and suddenly everything that had been crooked aligned.

His smile broke their kiss, and he chuckled. "I've been dying to do that again," he whispered.

Her first instinct was to ask if he was serious, but she knew Rhett, and he didn't say anything he didn't mean. At least he never had in the past.

"Let's go to our wedding lunch," he said.

Giddiness filled Evelyn, and she let Rhett take her bag and help her into the truck.

"I told Tripp," he said as he settled behind the wheel. "He's coming to witness too."

A surge of adrenaline moved through her. "What did he say?"

"Well, I sort of told him on Tuesday night that I was going to marry you." He chuckled as he backed out of the driveway. "He just didn't realize it would happen so soon."

"But he was okay with it?"

Rhett shrugged like it didn't matter what his brother thought. "He actually had some really good questions we haven't exactly ironed out."

"Oh? Like what?" Evelyn had dozens of questions herself, but she'd been pushing them away for days, because she hadn't been sure until that moment that she'd actually go through with this.

"Yeah, he wanted to know where we were going to live."

Evelyn tried to breathe, but she choked instead. Her heart pounded in her chest, and she stared at Rhett. Oh-so-cool Rhett, who didn't seem frazzled by this conversation at all.

"Well, we—we don't need to live together."

"So we're going to be married on paper only."

"I mean, well...yeah." She stared at him. "Was that part not clear?"

"Sure, yeah," he said, his voice a little strained. "I guess I'm just wondering what that kiss meant if this is just a paper-only, platonic relationship."

8

Rhett learned in the next few moments that he had excellent peripheral vision. He didn't have to look at Evelyn to see the pure confusion and panic on her face. She opened her mouth and closed it a couple of times, finally looking out her window, showing him the curled and pinned up-do.

"I mean, I don't know what you felt just a minute ago, but I kind of liked kissing you." He hadn't hidden how he felt about her—at least not since breakfast on Tuesday.

"We can still kiss."

Rhett didn't think she'd thought through this plan at all. "Evelyn, tell me what you think is going to happen next."

"We're going to lunch."

"And then?"

"Then we're going to get married."

"And then?"

"And then...I haven't thought that far ahead."

"You know what people do when they get married, right?" His face heated just saying the words.

"Of course," she said, an angry undertone in her words now. "But Rhett, our marriage isn't real."

"Oh, it's real," he said. "I have the paper and everything."

"But we're—I thought you knew it wasn't really real."

"I do know that," he said. "But you're trying to convince the town that it is real. Don't you think we should live together?" He glanced at her, though he'd successfully watched her reactions without such direct eye contact. "My place is pretty big," he said. "There's a few rooms on the second floor that we don't even use."

Evelyn remained silent for a few moments. Then she turned toward him and reached for his hand. He let her slip her fingers into his, almost sighing with contentment. It seemed surreal still that their relationship had changed so much in such a short amount of time. But Rhett wasn't complaining. He'd always liked Evelyn, and so what if her desperation had fueled their relationship to move faster than it might have otherwise?

"Okay," she said. "I can move into your house."

"Great," Rhett said. "I think that's probably the best idea."

"Do you think I could keep my office at my house?"

"Sure," he said, easing to a stop as they came to a stop

sign. "So we're going to lunch at the steakhouse. I know you like a good filet mignon."

"I do," she said, and some of the tension between them evaporated. He took her hand on the way in, and the conversation was normal, about his brothers and her sisters, and how things were going on the ranch.

"Do you miss your forensic cases?" she asked.

"A little," he admitted. "I just don't want another one like that monster I just finished."

"Could you take smaller cases?"

"Yeah, probably. But I took my name out of the rotation for a while."

"Evelyn?" a woman asked, and they both looked up at her.

"Hello, Erica," she said, glancing at Rhett. "You know Rhett Walker."

She looked at him, and Rhett thought he should probably know her, because she knew him. "Of course. I'd heard you two were together."

"That's right," Rhett said, beaming up at her. He wanted to tell this nosy woman that they were less than an hour from getting married, but he kept the secret under his tongue. He loved that he had something only him and Evelyn shared, and he couldn't wait to keep getting to know her in different ways.

She started to talk to Erica, and Rhett let his mind wander down paths he never had before. Sure, maybe they were doing things in a strange order, but Rhett didn't mind. It wasn't like he was marrying a complete stranger.

He *knew* Evelyn.

Erica finally left, and Rhett said, "We better get going if we want to have time to change before the ceremony. We're supposed to check in twenty minutes before anyway."

Their eyes met, and Evelyn said, "All right, Rhett. Let's do this."

———

FORTY-FIVE MINUTES LATER, Rhett stood in front of the mirror, looking into his own eyes. He could admit he looked...apprehensive. Fine, he looked scared out of his mind.

"You want to do this," he told himself. "She needs the help, and you can give it." Plus, he liked her. He couldn't forget that. He wasn't getting nothing out of the deal, and he knew it.

"Rhett." Tripp stepped over to him and handed him his dress hat, the one he wore to church each week. "It's time." He put both hands on Rhett's shoulders. "Are you sure you want to do this?"

Looking into his brother's eyes, Rhett once again felt at peace with his decision. "Yes," he said. "This is the right thing to do."

"All right, then," he said. "Let's go do it." They both turned toward the door that would take them out into the room where the weddings were performed. "Have you talked to Callie?"

"Yeah, I saw her," Tripp said.

"And?"

"And you know Jeremiah is going to be livid," Tripp said. "I'm thinking maybe we tell him before the others. Privately."

"I don't know," Rhett said, though he also suspected Jeremiah would take this marriage the hardest. "If I tell him, he might not make dinner."

Tripp snorted. "If you don't tell him, he may never talk to you again."

Rhett paused at the door. "You really think that?"

"I think Jere's had his heart shredded," Tripp said. "He was mad about the pact, bro. He's going to go *nuclear* over a wedding."

"But you're okay, right?" Rhett searched his brother's face, and he found the answer he needed. "Who knows? Maybe you and Callie could have something."

Tripp burst out laughing. "You're really out of touch, aren't you? All those breakfasts with Evelyn. All the pining."

"I have not been pining."

"Oh, you have. Just a little, maybe. But definite pining."

Fine, maybe he had been pining for her a little bit. "What did I miss?"

"It's Liam who likes Callie." Tripp wiggled his eyebrows and pushed into the room. Rhett followed him to find Callie sitting on the front row already, her hands folded in her lap.

She was a pretty woman too, Rhett could admit that. But nothing about her accelerated his pulse. Not the way Evelyn did. The way Evelyn always had.

He took his spot, and the judge looked down at him. "Are you marrying yourself, sir?"

"No," he said, glancing back to Callie. "I mean, I didn't think so."

"She's coming," Callie said, looking to the door opposite of the one Rhett had just come out. The room felt huge, like it could swallow him whole in a single bite. There were so many rows, and he wondered if people actually brought their friends and families here to witness their marriage.

He couldn't imagine that. If this were a real wedding day for Rhett and Evelyn, he knew she'd plan it in a park. Or on her ranch. Pastor Daniels would officiate, and her father and aged grandmother would be sitting on the front row.

Sadness moved through him that she wasn't getting the wedding she wanted. He could've given it to her. Sure, it might have taken longer to plan, but maybe then they would've fallen in love along the way.

The door opened, and his reality set in. This was what she wanted. Evelyn wasn't a weakling. She'd tell him what she wanted, and he'd do his best to give it to her.

"Hey," he said as she joined him, smiling at her softly. Wow, he was already in deep with her, which probably wasn't a bad thing considering where they stood.

"Sorry I'm late," she said, facing the judge. "I'm ready."

Rhett honestly had no idea what the judge said after

Evelyn laced her arm through his. Her touch was enough. The rosy scent of her skin was enough. She was enough.

"I now pronounce you husband and wife," the man behind the counter said, and Rhett faced his new wife.

"I can kiss you, right?" he whispered while she smiled at him.

"No," she murmured. "I'm going to kiss you." And she did. Rhett's head swam with heat and desire, but he kept the kiss chaste. After all, he'd married this woman, but no one needed to know how much he liked her.

At least not yet.

Tripp and Callie clapped, and they came forward and hugged Rhett and Evelyn. For a few precious seconds, Rhett felt the energy of the whole world coursing through him.

"Well," Callie said, blowing out her breath. "What are you guys going to do now?"

———

By the time Rhett pulled into Evelyn's driveway, the sun had gone to bed hours ago. "Thanks for indulging me on a honeymoon," he said, smiling at her.

"It was fun." She grinned and got out of the truck. He joined her under the light of the moon, the air finally starting to cool a little bit. "I've never seen so many windmills in one place."

They'd gone to the American Windmill Museum in Lubbock, and Rhett had enjoyed himself immensely.

"Neither have I," he said. "I love learning about stuff like that."

"We'll have to go back to the Museum of Ranching," she said, reaching up to take a pin out of her hair. He stood transfixed, watching her as she let her hair out.

She shook her head with a sigh. "I should've done that hours ago."

He brushed his hand along her shoulder and up her neck, finally moving his fingers through the curls she's released. Time froze, and Rhett simply let it.

Evelyn looked right back at him, and while she'd been exceptionally good at hiding her feelings for him, he could clearly see them all now. He leaned down and kissed her, maybe a little too hungrily at first.

She kissed him back, slowing the movement of his mouth and pulling away long before he was satisfied. She tucked herself in his arms and said, "Thank you so much for today, Rhett."

"Of course," he said, wondering how he was going to let her walk up the steps and into the house without him. "So I'll come help you move your things over tomorrow. I'm going to talk to Jeremiah too."

"All right," she said. "I can come help with that, if you'd like."

They'd already talked about it on the drive to Lubbock, and he shook his head. "No, I need to do it. Although, if I don't show up for church, you might want to come see where he's buried my body."

She giggled, though Jeremiah's anger was no laughing matter. Rhett liked the sound of it floating into the night air, and he decided he better get out of there before he said or did something he couldn't take back.

He stepped away from her and said, "See you tomorrow." She stayed right where she was while he got in the truck and backed out of her driveway. Only when he was finally going to drive away did she lift her hand in farewell and hurry up the steps.

The door closed, the house swallowing her, stealing her from him. Rhett sighed and faced the dark half-mile back to Seven Sons Ranch.

He'd only taken two steps into the house when Jeremiah said, "There you are. Where in the world have you been all day? I was just about to call the blasted police."

9

Evelyn didn't need a bed. Or her dresser. Or even hangers. She'd been steadily texting with Rhett all day, and he was due to arrive any moment to help take her things over to his ranch.

Her things.

Clothes, mostly. Toiletries—she'd been assured more than once that she'd have her own bathroom. The cleaning service the brothers used would come upstairs now to dust her room, vacuum her carpet, and clean her bathroom.

Evelyn thought it must be nice to be able to afford a cleaning service. With her decline in business, she and her sisters had tightened their belts. They'd cut back on groceries, never ate out, and were making ends meet any way they could.

She didn't need the recliner in the corner of her bedroom, where she read when she couldn't sleep. Sometimes she studied profiles in that chair. Sometimes she simply looked out the window which overlooked the pasture where the horses roamed.

She'd miss that chair, and she picked up her phone to ask Rhett if the room where she'd be living had enough space for it.

Sure, he said. *We can bring over anything you like, sugar.*

She smiled at his endearment, and she suddenly wanted him there with her. Neither of them had gone to church today, both of them thinking it would probably be easier to keep their union a secret just a little bit longer—until they had a chance to tell everyone in their families.

Rhett had talked to Jeremiah last night, and boy, was his brother mad. Ultra-mad. Furious. Evelyn wasn't even sure there was a word strong enough to describe how upset Jeremiah was. Rhett said he'd stormed out in the middle of the night and hadn't come back.

He'd gone out in the morning, and Jeremiah was doing the farm chores, so he was still alive. He'd promptly disappeared again, and Rhett had texted to say they might be eating cold cereal for dinner that night.

Evelyn sighed as she tucked another pair of shoes into her suitcase. She hadn't wanted to cause a rift in the Walker family. The brothers had always seemed particularly loyal to one another, and their strict no-women pact had definitely solidified them. It was the Walkers against Three Rivers—at least until Rhett had broken ranks.

Callie had promised to keep Simone out of the way

while Rhett helped Evelyn move, and they were out on the ranch somewhere. Evelyn began taking her bags downstairs to the entryway, so Rhett could load them easily.

She couldn't carry the chair very far, so she left it, turning away from it as knocking sounded on the door. "Hello?" Rhett called, and Evelyn's blood ran a little hotter in her veins. She practically skipped out of her room and down the hall, peeking around the corner to see him lift a couple of bags and turn to take them outside.

When he returned, she stood in the doorway, watching him. "Hey there," he said, mounting the steps. "Is today a good day?"

"So far," she said, though a skiff of unease moved through her. "Do you think Jeremiah will be there?"

"Yeah," Rhett said. "He came back two seconds before I left. He's not talking to me at the moment." He adjusted his cowboy hat. "But he'll come around. He's just had a rough go of things lately."

"What kind of things?"

"Oh, his last girlfriend really did a number on him," Rhett said. "And she wasn't just his girlfriend. She left him standing at the altar." Rhett met her eye. "He has a right to be upset, but he's got a forgiving heart." He smiled and cupped her face in one hand. "You're beautiful, did you know that?"

She burst out laughing. "It's a good thing we're already married, Mister," she said. "Because that was a terrible pickup line." Still chuckling, she let him kiss her until they were both laughing too hard to continue.

"Come on," she said. "You still need to get my chair."

The move took ten minutes, and Rhett led her upstairs, carrying the recliner all by himself. He certainly had muscles and knew how to use them. "You're right here," he said, opening the door to the last room on the right. "It's the biggest room, and it's connected to the bathroom."

Evelyn followed him inside, taking a few moments to look around her new living space. It certainly didn't feel like the farmhouse where she'd grown up and lived for so long. But it was clean, and it smelled like lilacs thanks to a candle burning on the dresser.

A queen-sized bed sat against one wall, and Rhett put the recliner next to the windows that looked out over his ranch. She moved over to them and pushed the curtains to the side so she could get a sense for the view. "I can see my ranch from here," she said, a measure of delight and comfort filling her.

"It's a great view," he agreed. "Do you need a minute?"

"A minute would be nice," she said.

He nodded, turned, and left the room, closing the door behind him as he went. Evelyn collapsed into the recliner, her heart heavy and full at the same time. She felt like she was on a roller coaster, and she couldn't get off. Up one moment. Happy. Peaceful. And then the doubt and the fear would creep in again, stealthily pulling her down, down, down.

She had dozens of things to think about, but what weighed on her mind was her father and grandmother. She'd take them a jar of Simone's raspberry apricot jam in the morning and tell them. She actually stood as if she'd go get the preserves from the storage room off the kitchen.

Then she remembered she wasn't in her own house anymore. Sitting again, she dialed her father.

"Hey, baby," he drawled. "I didn't see you at church today."

"Yeah, I know," she said, smiling at the sound of his weathered voice. He'd done his best to raise his three girls, and he'd never gotten remarried after Mama had died. "I need to come see you and Gran tomorrow. What are you guys doing?"

"I think we're going to the wildflower festival," he said. "Supposed to be a big bloom right now."

She'd heard about that, and she also knew the wildflower farm didn't open until ten. "I'll bring honey and jam," she said. "Does Gran have any of that homemade bread in the freezer?"

"I'm sure she does." Her dad sounded happy. "Is everything okay, Evelyn?'

"Yes," she said, finally feeling it way down in her toes. "Everything is fine. I'll see you tomorrow."

"All right, baby," he said before hanging up. Evelyn stood and shoved her phone in her back pocket. Her sisters were due to arrive in fifteen minutes, and she supposed there was no better time to go downstairs and face her new brothers-in-law than right now.

She opened her bedroom door to find Rhett sitting on the floor several paces down the hall. He glanced up when he heard her, and she looked down at him. "You're waiting for me?"

"I couldn't go down there without you." He reached up, and she grabbed onto his hand to help him stand. Not that she could really do much. The man was probably twice her size. "I figured we could be a united front."

"Probably a good idea," she said, flashing him a smile. "I'm taking my dad and Gran jam and honey in the morning to tell them."

"I'll call my parents tonight," he said. "If we survive this."

She nudged him, glad she could be strong when he felt weak. Heaven knew he'd been a rock for her these past few days. "We're going to survive. And hey, it smells like brisket."

Sure enough, downstairs in the kitchen, Jeremiah stood in front of the stove, stirring something. He looked up when Evelyn walked in, and they both froze.

"Hey, Jeremiah," she said, her voice a pitch she'd never heard before.

He simply turned back to the stove and said, "The potatoes are almost done."

Rhett squeezed her hand and whispered, "Hey, you got five words. That's more than he's said to me today."

Evelyn tried to smile, but the gesture sort of wobbled around on her face. "What can I do to help?"

"I won't get in someone's way if they wanted to set the table," Jeremiah said gruffly, mostly to the boiling pot of potatoes.

"We can do that," Evelyn said. "Come on, Rhett." She set to work laying out the plates while Rhett followed her with the silverware. Napkins went on next, and Rhett placed glasses on the table too.

Liam and Tripp spilled into the house from the back porch, their voices loud and vibrant, the way Evelyn had heard them many times in the past. She smiled at both of them, glad doing so was getting easier. "My sisters should be here any minute."

"We saw 'em coming," Liam said. "That red truck really sticks out."

"My pops wanted it to," Evelyn said, fondness coming over her. "He said he painted it the brightest red he could find, so when Gran took the truck to town, she'd always be able to find it." She grinned at all four men currently staring at her. She chuckled and shook her head. "You need to meet my gran, and then you'd get it. She was a bit blind, and she shouldn't have been driving at all. The red helped, trust me."

Tripp smiled at her and did a most surprising thing: he stepped right over to her and hugged her. She patted his back awkwardly, realizing everything in the kitchen had frozen. Liam stared openly, and even Rhett wore a look of surprise.

Thankfully, the doorbell rang, and Liam blinked his way out of the stupor that had claimed him. "I'll get it."

"It's just us," Callie said in the next moment, her voice coming down the hall from the front door and piercing Evelyn's heart. She'd never lived away from her sisters for more than a few nights, and she had no idea how she thought she could live here, with four men instead of her two sisters.

"Hey, Callie," Liam said, swiping his hat off his head as if she were the President of the United States. Evelyn couldn't believe the sight before her. How had she missed Liam's giant crush on her sister?

Maybe because her own crush on Rhett had prevented her from seeing it. Seeing anything around her.

"Heya, Liam." Callie gave him a smile, clearly oblivious to what it probably did to his pulse. Evelyn knew, because hers started rioting as Rhett came to her side. Before he could say anything, Jeremiah turned on the electric mixer and shouted over the noise of it. "We'll be ready in five minutes."

But she and Rhett wouldn't be making any announcements over the final dinner preparations, and pure tension filled the air by the time Jeremiah said, "All right, men." He cleared his throat and looked around at Evelyn and her sisters as if he'd just realized they were there. "And ladies. Wash up. It's time to eat."

10

The tension in the house pounded in the back of Rhett's neck. Jeremiah hadn't given an inch, but at least he'd spoken to Evelyn. Okay, maybe talking about potatoes and setting the table didn't count as talking.

Everyone in the room was an adult, but they shuffled their feet and looked at the table as if they'd never eaten together before.

But they had, and Rhett couldn't believe a simple wedding had caused so much unrest. "Okay," he said, taking charge as he often had as kids. Being the oldest of seven boys was no laughing matter, and Rhett was lucky to have survived childhood without more than four scars.

"I'm going to sit here," he said, stepping over to the end of the table and putting his hands on the back of the chair. "Evvy's going to sit by me."

"I'll sit by Evvy," Callie said.

"I'll sit by Callie," Liam said, and Rhett glanced at him.

No one else said anything, but Simone looked at Evelyn. "What's going on? This feels weird."

Jeremiah muscled his way past Tripp and Liam and plunked a plate of softened butter on the table. "She doesn't know?" He glared at Rhett, and everything inside him tensed.

"He's going to tell," Rhett muttered, hoping Evelyn was prepared for what was about to happen.

"Who else doesn't know?" Jeremiah scanned the crowd, pure fire leaping from his eyes.

"I know," Callie said, reaching out to touch Jeremiah's arm. "It's okay, Miah."

"Miah?" Rhett asked at the same time Liam practically yelled it.

"I know, too," Tripp said, and Liam spun toward him. He looked at Rhett, then Jeremiah, and then Callie.

"What's going on?" he asked. "Do you know, Rhett?"

"Oh-ho," Jeremiah chortled. "He knows. *He's* the problem."

"It's not a problem," Rhett said, wishing Jeremiah wasn't quite so hot-headed.

"Oh, it's a problem," Jeremiah said.

"Miah," Callie said while Tripp said, "You're being unreasonable."

"Stop it," Simone yelled above everyone.

Evelyn stepped next to Rhett and slipped her hand into his. "I'm so sorry," she said as everyone quieted.

Simone focused on her. "Someone better start talking."

"They got married," Jeremiah said, pointing at Rhett and Evelyn at the head of the table. "Like, legit, married. They're *married*."

"Are you kidding me?" Liam practically shrieked, but Rhett still heard Simone's shocked gasp.

Jeremiah drew in a deep breath, but it didn't lessen the heaving in his chest.

Callie grabbed his hand and said, "Come with me."

"I'm not going anywhere," he said, trying to pull away. But Callie worked a ranch, and she held fast to his fingers.

"Dinner can wait." She towed him toward the back door.

"I'm starving," Tripp said, pulling out a chair and sitting down, clearly enjoying himself.

"Do you even have a prenuptial agreement?" Jeremiah called over his shoulder. "You're so naïve, Rhett. You have to protect yourself." Callie finally got him out of the house, the glass door slamming behind them after she muscled him onto the deck.

Rhett exhaled. "Okay, so let's just sit down. Callie'll calm him down, and then we can eat."

Liam sat down, the sound thudding through the kitchen. "Are you really married?"

"Yes," Evelyn said, her eyes glued to Simone's.

"For real?"

"It's real," Rhett said quickly, so Evelyn wouldn't explain the situation. No one needed to know he was helping her with her business. Well, Callie probably knew, and the way Simone nodded and went to sit next to Tripp told Rhett she probably knew too.

But his brothers didn't need to know. In fact, he was hoping Evelyn could work her matchmaking magic on the three of them, and then they'd stop badgering him about, well, pretty much everything.

Evelyn shifted closer to him, and he looked around as Simone sat down too. He pulled out his chair and then hers, and they sat too. The silence in the kitchen was almost as bad as all the yelling and confusion from a minute ago, but Rhett knew better than to touch Jeremiah's food.

He looked out the wall of windows to see Callie gesturing wildly, her mouth moving a mile a minute. "How long is that going to take?" he asked Evelyn.

"Oh, she's just getting started."

Simone scoffed—at least Rhett thought it was a scoff. But when he looked at her, she had her hand over her mouth, and she was clearly trying not to laugh. She lost that battle as a giggle slipped through her fingers.

Evelyn started laughing too, and all the ice in Texas broke. Finally.

"I'll get them," Rhett said.

"Maybe you should let me," Liam said.

"Sit down," Tripp said quickly. "I'll go see how long we have to wait." He gave a pointed look to Liam that Rhett didn't quite understand—and which he forgot all about as soon as Evelyn's hand landed on his knee.

He jerked his attention to her, and she nodded toward the windows. Rhett looked out the window to see Callie hugging Jeremiah, and then she gripped his shoulders at arms-length. As Tripp opened the door, the two of them turned toward it, and most of the anger had fled from Jeremiah's face.

The two of them came in, and Tripp closed the door as if he was the butler. There were clearly spots for Jeremiah and Callie between Tripp and Liam, but they didn't sit down.

"Jeremiah's made brisket and mashed potatoes," Callie started, glancing around at everyone. She reached up and brushed her blonde curls out of her face, taking a deep breath. "He's already sliced the rolls, and he even bought a bagged salad, though he doesn't understand green food."

He glanced at her, more unrest melting off his face. She nodded at him, and he sighed.

"Miah," she said in a stern voice.

"Fine," he said. "I'm sorry I caused a scene." He looked around at everyone. "The food should still be hot, and—"

Callie cleared her throat, and Jeremiah looked at her again. She chin-nodded toward where Rhett and Evelyn sat, and he rolled his eyes.

"I'm very happy to have you all here today," he said. "I do like cooking for a crowd." He glared at Callie. "Happy now?"

"Yes," she said, smiling at everyone. "Rhett, you're up."

He was up? Up for what? He looked at her, but he

didn't know Callie nearly as well as Evelyn, and he had no idea what she wanted him to do.

"Call on someone to say grace," Evelyn said, coming to his rescue.

"Oh, sure. Yeah. Right. Uh...Tripp, will you say the prayer so we can eat?"

"Yes." Rhett took off his cowboy hat, and Tripp waited a few seconds while all the Walker brothers did too, and then he said grace.

Jeremiah directed everyone back into the kitchen with their plates, where the food was served buffet-style before sitting back down to eat. The chatter felt normal, lively, the way it had been in the past when the two families had come together for meals. Not that they'd done so too regularly, but they'd shared a few nights together over Jeremiah's food.

His brother still wouldn't look at him or speak directly to him, but Rhett knew he'd come around. Jeremiah was family; he'd forgive Rhett sooner or later.

"So," Simone said once everyone had returned to the table. "Where are you two love birds going to live?"

"Right here," Rhett told her. "At the ranch."

Simone looked at Evelyn, who nodded. Neither of them seemed too happy with the arrangements, and Rhett thought maybe he and Evelyn hadn't discussed every detail as much as they should've.

"Well, I got a new horse yesterday," Liam said, looking directly at Callie. "Want to go see him after dinner?"

"Sure," Callie said, and just like that, the conversation

moved on to something else. Horses, and hay, and Tripp's upcoming summer bucket list.

———

"So she's back at the house," Rhett said to Trooper, the brown and white horse that he liked best. "And I have no idea what to do about it." He glanced toward the homestead, but he could only see the top of the roof above the barns.

After dinner last night, he and Evelyn had sat on the front steps of the house, because the evening sun shone onto the back deck. Her sisters had left. His brothers took naps or went out onto the farm, the way they always did on Sunday afternoon.

He'd sat with his wife, and they'd talked about how awkward that dinner was. He'd assured her things would get better. Then she'd kissed him and retreated up the steps. Thankfully, those were right inside the front door, and she didn't have to see any of his brothers to go to bed. No one else lived on the second floor, so she basically had her own place up there.

He'd gone to his room too, because he didn't want to deal with another family yelling match like the one that had already taken place that day. He'd risen early, dressed, and come out to the ranch.

Jeremiah had come out shortly after that, but he hadn't seen Rhett with the horses in the pasture, and Rhett hadn't had the heart to call to him.

Trooper nudged him, and Rhett pulled out another bite of apple for the horse. "I know," he said. "I should go talk to her. See what she's doing today. Right?" Married couples did that, right? Shared their plans for the day with each other?

His phone rang while Trooper took the apple chunk from his palm, and he saw Barry Forrest's name on the screen. A groan rose up from his very core, but he swiped on the call, hoping the case the animal control officer would offer would be easy.

"Rhett," Barry said, his voice bright. Couldn't be that gruesome of a case. "How are you?"

"Just fine," Rhett said. "You?"

"Good, good." Barry paused, and Rhett simply waited for him to continue. "Listen, I know you just got married, but I'm hoping you'll have time for a small case."

Rhett blinked, the man's words sinking all the way into his ears. Then his brain. Then his soul.

"How did you know I got married?" he asked, fearing his whole world was about to be blown wide open.

11

Jeremiah Walker hated everything about what Rhett and Evelyn had done. Not only that, but the woman was now living in the homestead, and Jeremiah could hear her footsteps upstairs even when she wasn't there.

He should be happy he could feel something, though he was well-acquainted with the fury still coursing through him after last night's dinner.

Sighing, he forced the tension out of his shoulders, his arms. The morning sunshine was too hot, but Jeremiah thought everything was hot these days.

"Including your temper," he muttered to himself. But Rhett really wasn't thinking clearly. Evelyn might seem like a nice woman, but Laura Ann had seemed that way too. In the end, though, Jeremiah knew the marriage wasn't real, and Evelyn could do anything with Rhett's resources before he could even blink.

Callie—the Foster sister Jeremiah was closest to—had insisted that her sister wasn't like that. That Jeremiah didn't get to ruin dinner because he didn't agree with what Rhett and Evelyn had done, and that he should try to make peace with all that ailed him.

She had no idea what she was asking of him. There was no balm for a soul as ragged as his. In the past, he might've tipped his chin heavenward and prayed for help. But God had abandoned him the same day Laura Ann had left him standing at the altar.

No matter how hard Jeremiah tried, no matter how many times he went to church, or how many pans of brownies he took to church picnics, he simply couldn't feel the hand of God in his life anymore.

The only thing Jeremiah needed to do was get through the ranch paperwork. He had cowboys to pay that morning, and then he needed to meet with Orion to see how their mowing schedule was coming along.

Orion was the agricultural specialist on the ranch, and while Jeremiah had his finger in every pie at Seven Sons, he didn't want to be the one to manage the planting, fertilizing, pest-control, or harvesting of the crops on the ranch.

They grew everything from hay to corn to pumpkins, and Jeremiah loved the sprawling vines in the autumn, the ripe corn in the summer, and the waving hay fields that spread across the land.

Everything felt so tense, and he just wanted to get away. But running had never solved any of his problems, and his brothers would simply call and text him until he came back.

That was what the Walker brothers did. They stuck together.

"Help me forgive him," Jeremiah muttered to himself. He really didn't want to talk to Rhett, though he'd been Jeremiah's best friend for most of his life.

Maybe that was why everything felt off now. Rhett had abandoned Jeremiah in what felt like his most dire of needs.

"Hey," a man said, and Jeremiah turned to find Tripp standing there. He approached slowly and leaned against the door of the barn. "You busy?"

"Yes," Jeremiah said, though he could cut a few checks in a matter of minutes.

"Look—"

"I don't want a lecture in Rhett's defense."

"It's not in his defense," Tripp said. "I wanted you to know I was there when they got married. I was a witness, and Rhett, well, he thinks this is the right thing to do."

"I'm sure he does," Jeremiah said sarcastically. "He's had eyes for Evelyn forever."

"So you think he's using her?"

"Absolutely not." Jeremiah looked up from the paperwork. "I think she's...." He didn't know how to finish.

Tripp just watched him, his eyes barely visible from underneath the brim of his cowboy hat. "You wanna ride?"

"Are you going to talk the whole time?"

"Nope."

Jeremiah finally felt like he was relaxing, and he nodded. "All right." They left the barn and walked over to the stables, where Jeremiah's and Tripp's horses were.

"She's not Laura Ann," Tripp said, and Jeremiah simply nodded.

It was hard for him to accept that not all women were as uncaring and unkind as the one he'd known for years. Fallen in love with. Asked to marry him.

He saddled and he tightened and he got in the saddle. The air was suddenly lighter, and Jeremiah wondered if he should get to town more. He liked doing his grocery shopping at the organic grocery store on the southeast side of town, and he liked spending time in the kitchen.

He thought he could be happy with the ranching and the cooking.

"I'm worried," Jeremiah said after only a few minutes with only the sound of horse's hooves hitting the hard-packed dirt.

"About what?" Tripp asked. He and Liam were just slightly younger than Jeremiah, and they'd gotten into plenty of trouble together growing up. They'd also been close, and Jeremiah had snuck out with the twins loads of times. He'd stuck by them in school, and they'd helped him at the wedding-that-wasn't.

They could be loud and obnoxious, but Jeremiah also knew they'd support him in anything. Literally, anything.

"I'm worried everyone will move on...except me." Jeremiah didn't normally express himself so openly and honestly, but this was Tripp. He trusted his horse to keep his secrets, as Stonestepper had been a good companion for several years now.

Through Laura Ann's appearance and disappearance in his life.

"I don't know what to say to that," Tripp said. "Well, maybe one thing. It'll be Liam you'll need to worry about. He's already restless, and word is cowboys do very well at the summer dances here."

The knot inside Jeremiah tightened. "I'm sure you're right."

"We are twins, after all." Tripp chuckled. "And just one more thing. Try to be nice to Evelyn. I really don't think she's going to drain Rhett dry or anything."

"Hm." Jeremiah gazed into the horizon. "I'll try." But he knew there was more a woman could do to a rich man than steal his money.

She could completely steal his heart, his life, his very soul.

———

A DAY PASSED, then two, then three. Jeremiah tried to be nicer to Evelyn, but he only saw her in passing a time or two. Rhett spent time with the brothers still, but it wasn't the same.

He was always checking his phone, and he disappeared without explanation. Jeremiah could hear his footsteps upstairs, and the TV playing, and it annoyed him to no end.

Rhett still slept in his room across the hall from Jeremiah's, and finally one evening, Jeremiah had just put the last container of leftovers in the fridge when he realized that the twins had left.

"What are you doin' tonight?" Jeremiah asked. "Where's Evelyn?"

"I think she's at the Shining Star tonight," Rhett said airily. "Her office is still there."

"Yeah, she's still there," Jeremiah said before he could censor himself.

"What do you mean?"

"I mean, she runs up the steps in the evening and right back down them and out the door first thing in the morning. She doesn't even pour herself a cup of coffee here." Jeremiah lifted his eyebrows at Rhett. "Why'd you marry her?"

Rhett swallowed, and Jeremiah saw it. He saw the panic in his brother's eyes, and he recognized the signs of secret-keeping so well now.

Too bad he hadn't been this savvy while engaged to Laura Ann.

"She's not using me," Rhett said.

"Yeah, I almost believe you," Jeremiah said. "And you like her enough to go along with whatever she needs." He shook his head. "But what I see isn't a marriage. You don't even sleep in the same room."

Jeremiah wasn't stupid. And neither were Liam and

Tripp. Everyone with eyes could tell this marriage was make-believe.

He thinks its the right thing to do.

Tripp's words moved through Jeremiah's mind, and he wondered what he'd do if he thought something was the right thing to do.

Not marry a woman, he thought. That was just insane.

"She's just having a hard time letting go of her ranch," Rhett said.

"Funny, Callie thinks it's her ranch." Jeremiah wiped the counter and tossed the rag in the kitchen sink. He lifted his hand and walked backward for a couple of steps. "Night."

"You're going to bed already?" Rhett asked.

"Yep," Jeremiah said. He had a tablet he could watch a movie on. He used to lounge on the couch with his brothers, eventually falling asleep while they chatted, or Tripp read his Bible, or Liam made a delicious treat.

Things used to be simple, and now everything felt so very complicated—and he wasn't even the one who'd gotten married.

12

Liam Walker didn't have much to do around the ranch. He had a job doing computer-generated imaging, something he was actually very good at.

The work was part-time right now while he looked for another contract, and he liked to go out into the garden in the morning. He didn't like the weeding. He didn't particularly care what grew. That was more of Jeremiah's thing.

But he definitely liked the location of the garden, as it sat right on the fence between Seven Sons Ranch and the Shining Star. He could see Callie Foster when she came outside, and she stood on the front porch and looked around for a few minutes every morning.

He knew she needed help on her ranch, but Liam didn't know how to offer it. So he just lingered in the garden, hoping and praying Callie would come talk to him.

She had several times. Liam's pulse increased as she

came outside wearing a pair of jeans and a bright red T-shirt. Those Fosters did love the color red, and Liam wondered why.

He bent and pulled a weed hiding behind a green pepper plant. Callie's presence came closer, and Liam wished he wasn't so in tune with her.

He really liked her, and that had kept him from talking to her as much as Jeremiah did. They'd grown close, but Liam knew Jeremiah didn't harbor any romantic feelings for Callie.

Liam sure did though.

Hopes and dreams, he told himself. Foolish hopes and dreams.

"Heya, Liam," Callie said, and he straightened as if he hadn't known she was there.

"Oh, hey," he said, his voice way too bright. He told himself to calm down, but there was something about her that didn't allow him to be very calm.

"You're not working today?"

"Uh." He took off his hat and wiped his hand through his hair. "My last contract ended, and I'm working on getting a new one."

"But you don't really need to work, right?" She leaned against the fence post, and if she knew how attractive he found her, she might not pose like that.

She'd also have to be blind not to know. Liam wasn't exactly good at hiding how he felt about a woman, as his previous girlfriend had known his intentions the moment they'd met. Portia had actually teased him with how interested he was for a few weeks before agreeing to go out with him.

And Callie wasn't anything like her. Thankfully. Liam had left his life in Austin because of Portia, and he wasn't looking for a repeat of that.

He understood Jeremiah's reluctance to date, and a blip of fear moved through Liam too.

"I mean, I guess not," Liam said. "But this garden is practically weed-free already, and what would I do all day if I didn't digitally generate some explosions?"

"Is that what you do?"

"That's what I do," he said, leaning against the same fence. He wanted to ask her out. Take her to lunch or dinner or even breakfast. Get her away from the ranch—away from Jeremiah—away from everything. Maybe then he'd know if his feelings were real or not.

"I knew you twins did some techy stuff," Callie said.

"I make delicious treats, too," Liam said, hating the note of pride in his voice.

Callie smiled at him, and she was a glorious angel, with the morning sunshine bathing her face. She said something else, but Liam had no idea what.

Then she was laughing and waving good-bye, and Liam said, "Yeah, okay, 'bye," and watched her walk away.

He sighed and sagged into the fence, because he hadn't felt like this in such a long time. Too long, in his opinion. But Callie Foster felt like she was completely off-limits, and not just because Liam's brother had just married her sister.

His stomach tightened. He wasn't as upset as Jeremiah over the marriage, though he wasn't happy about it either. Number one, it did jeopardize his chances with Callie. Number two, why had Tripp been invited to witness the wedding and Liam hadn't?

He was trustworthy. He would've supported Rhett. He'd always done what he needed to for his brothers.

"Liam!" someone yelled from the direction of the homestead, and he turned back that way. His twin stood on the deck, waving his arm as if Liam wouldn't be able to see him.

He'd been caught staring at the Shining Star again, and he could only imagine the ribbing Tripp would give him. Not that he'd done that much since high school, but still. Liam didn't like having all of his cards so easily read.

"What's goin' on?" he asked as he got closer to Tripp.

"Wondered if you wanted to go to breakfast. I just finished my major project, and I want to celebrate."

"Sure thing." Liam had already had coffee and some of Jeremiah's breakfast casserole, but weeding—and talking to Callie—had worked up enough of an appetite for a second breakfast.

"Great." Tripp grinned at him. "How's Callie?"

"I don't want to talk about her."

"Even for two minutes?"

"Nope." He slid his brother a glare. Their mother might've been able to get away with forcing the boys to talk for specified amounts of time growing up, but Liam didn't have to do that anymore. And not for Tripp.

"I may have seen an email come in," he said.

"What kind of email?" Liam wanted to check his computer now.

"A new, huge, years-long contract for one of the biggest movie franchises in the world."

Liam opened the back door and stared at Tripp. "What? Really?"

"You should check it before we go. It'll give us something to talk about at breakfast."

"We always have something to talk about. I mean, there's this whole Rhett and Evelyn thing, and the Jeremiah freaking out thing."

"And the Marvel universe is looking for a new computer generated imagery artist, and they contacted you." Tripp led him through the kitchen and down the hall to front of the house, where they shared an office. "Check it out."

Liam almost didn't dare click to open his email. Tripp hadn't even tried to hide the fact that he'd opened it, but Liam didn't care.

He scanned the verbiage, and he knew he was qualified for this job. "Holy cow."

"Right?"

Liam straightened. "They're going to need a huge portfolio, and tons of other stuff." He hadn't read all of the bullet points, because he was already overwhelmed.

"I'll help you," Tripp said. "We'll put together the best proposal on the planet. You're going to get this."

Landing such a huge, well-known contract would be amazing for Liam. No, he didn't need to work, but making superhero movies would definitely fill his time. Then he wouldn't have to pine for a woman who seemed to like his brother more than him.

"Let's go," he said. "And I'm going to start making a list on the way."

Tripp drove, and Liam read through the email more carefully. He brainstormed some things with Tripp, and together, the two of them had a decent list of already-completed projects Liam could send to the studio as proof of his skills.

"Excuse me?"

Liam looked up at the sound of the feminine voice. A leggy blonde stood at the head of their table, a smile stuck to her face.

He had no idea what to say, and one glance at Tripp told him his twin didn't either.

"Y'all are new to town, right?"

"No," Liam said at the same time Tripp said, "Maybe."

"Maybe?" Liam asked, swinging his attention to his brother. "We've lived here for over a year." He looked back at the woman. "We're not new."

But being approached by women was.

"My friend and I were wondering if you guys would be at the summer dance next weekend?"

Tripp looked at Liam, and Liam looked at Tripp.

"We have a pact," Tripp said.

"Yeah," Liam responded. But the idea of a summer dance had intrigued him, and he wanted to know more. Did Callie go to the summer dances?

An internal scoff moved through him. Of course she didn't. She wasn't in her mid-twenties—the way this blonde woman seemed to be—and she had a ranch to run.

"No," Tripp said, sliding to the end of the bench and standing up. "We won't be at the dance. C'mon, Liam. We better get back and get started on your portfolio."

Liam stood too, throwing some money on the table for a tip. They'd been at the restaurant for a long time, and he felt a bit bad for tying up the table. He glanced at the woman one last time before following Tripp back out to his truck.

Neither of them said anything until Tripp had navigated through town and had the truck on the highway leading south toward the ranch.

"I might go to the dance next weekend," he said.

"Are you kidding?" Tripp asked. "That woman was way too young for you."

"Maybe there will be someone older there."

"Yeah, and maybe Jeremiah will get over Laura Ann." Tripp scoffed and laughed, and Liam thought he had a fair point.

"I have to do something," Liam said. "I didn't get left at the altar, and Callie's obviously not interested."

"How is that obvious?"

"It just is," Liam said to the passenger window.

"You haven't even asked her out."

"And I'm not going to," Liam said. "Can you imagine if she said no?" And of course she'd say no. "We spend every Sunday afternoon with them."

"I mean, Rhett and Evelyn...they seem to be making things work."

Liam didn't say anything, because he had doubts about the authenticity of Rhett's marriage. But they had the paperwork and Liam supposed he could only go on what his brother said.

"I'm not asking her out," Liam said again.

"All right," Tripp said. "Your funeral."

13

Callie Foster looked around the stables, glad this one area of the ranch was maintained. It took her a long time to keep up the stalls for eight horses, but she loved every one of them, and she couldn't give them up.

Her cattle herd did fine out in the pastures, though it had dwindled to only a thousand head. She didn't know everything she needed to about buying and selling cattle, as they weren't her first love.

She knew she needed food for them, and when she wasn't feeding and watering horses, moving them from the stables to the pastures, or cleaning the stables, she spent the rest of her time and energy on the agricultural part of the ranch.

But her tractors needed work. One didn't even start anymore. She didn't know how to fix it, and she didn't have money to fix it.

Over the years, since her father's retirement, Callie had done the best she could. But things were slowly falling apart, going to seed, and Callie could see the ranch declining more and more as the days passed.

In short, she needed help.

As they'd been doing for the past fourteen months since the Walkers had moved in next door, Callie's thoughts moved in that direction.

Miah ran Seven Sons like a pro, though he claimed to not have any formal ranch training. In fact, he'd mentioned once—very briefly—that he was set to take over his father-in-law's ranch after his wedding.

But he'd never gotten married.

Callie had tried to ask about that, but she'd learned quickly that Miah shut down whenever talk of dating, relationships, or women was brought up.

She'd respected that, because she didn't want to be the nagging friend, trying to get him to go out with everyone. She didn't even know anyone.

She knew that was why they were such good friends. She wouldn't try to get him off the ranch, and he never asked her if she needed help with the Shining Star or why she didn't date.

Their friendship was easy, and she trusted him with everything and anything in her life. If he'd ask, which he normally didn't.

Her mind switched to Liam, where it usually spent the most time. The dashing cowboy had caught her attention the moment he'd shown up on the ranch with his giant personality and quick laugh. Oh, and that big truck. Callie loved Liam's big, black truck.

She'd tried flirting with him a few times, and Simone had laughed and laughed. Evelyn usually played the mediator between the two of them, but even Callie had felt self-conscious about her pitiful attempts at getting Liam's attention.

So she'd given up. He sat by her at dinner most of the time, and he'd invited her out to see his new horse just a couple of days ago. Whenever she saw him working in the Walker family garden, she meandered that way as if she had something to do on the property line between their two ranches.

Maybe she was being too obvious. Maybe she wasn't being obvious enough. Maybe Liam had chosen to remain female-free, like the rest of his brothers.

No matter what, he hadn't asked Callie out, and he was definitely friendly toward her, but he was friendly toward everyone as far as she could see.

She twisted away from the clean stables and hung the broom back on the wall. "Maybe you could just ask him to come work for you."

For free? The thought taunted her, because she couldn't do that. And she couldn't pay Liam.

How humiliating would that conversation be?

No, Callie would figure something out. She always did.

"Maybe Rhett would come," she said. Now that he and

Evelyn were married, maybe it wouldn't be taking charity. He didn't do a lot at the ranch next door, because he worked as a forensic veterinarian. Well, sometimes he did, when there were cases. Evelyn said he'd taken a break from his caseload for a while, because the last one had been such a bear.

And Callie had seen it. Rhett would come over to the house all the time with his notes. He'd lay them all out on the coffee table and go over everything with Evelyn.

Callie had liked his presence in the house, and she wondered if she just needed to set up something like his Tuesday breakfasts with Evelyn with Liam.

He worked too, but maybe they could have a Wednesday lunch or something. Callie liked to cook, and cooking for a cowboy that made her pulse riot? She could definitely do that.

"Hey," Simone said, and Callie turned away from her thoughts as she did the same with the stables in front of her.

"Hey. What's up?"

"Uh, there's a problem in the barn."

"Which one?"

"The hay barn." Simone wore worry on her face, and Callie sighed. The last thing she needed was a problem in the hay barn.

"Okay," she said brightly, though she felt certain she wouldn't know how to fix the problem in the hay barn. "Let's go check it out."

"I was just getting down a bale for the goats," she said. "And I noticed it was wet."

"Oh, no," Callie said. "Is the barn leaking?"

"I think so," Simone said. "And it looks like we lost a lot of hay."

Callie could practically see money draining from her account. If they lost the hay they needed to feed their animals, they had to buy it. And buying it was twice as expensive as growing it themselves.

Her pulse pounded now for a whole new reason, but she wouldn't panic until she had to. She'd learned that much at least.

Simone climbed into the hay loft first, and Callie went up right behind her. She hated ladders and always envisioned herself falling no matter how tightly she gripped the rungs. Plus, she wasn't exactly young or skinny, but she managed to get up the ladder to the loft.

"See?" Simone pulled a bale out, and it was definitely wet and rotting.

Despair clawed its way through Callie. "Yeah, I see." She wished she'd grabbed a pair of gloves before coming up into the loft. "How many?"

"Let's look." Simone tugged on bale after bale, and they all had some mold on at least a third of the edges closest to the wall that had been leaking.

"We can't use the moldy hay as feed," Callie said. "Maybe for the cattle, but it's summer, and they don't need it right now." She wiped her hand across her forehead.

"Let's go through each bale and separate the good hay from the wet stuff. The moldy hay we'll put in our compost pile. We can put it in the garden too."

Her back hurt just thinking of all the work ahead of her. It wasn't easy to pull apart hay bales and move hay from here to the garden or the compost pile, which were much closer to the house.

"And we'll need to fix the barn," she said.

Simone nodded. "I can help, Cal. Evelyn can too, I bet."

"Let's not bother Evvy right now," she said. "But I'd love your help on this for a few days. How are your antiques coming?"

"I'm mostly caught up," Simone said. "A few things here and there, and I'm going to a huge estate sale in Amarillo over the weekend." She smiled, but it was also weary.

Callie loved going into her sister's shed, where she refurbished and breathed new life into old furniture and collectibles she found at yard sales and estate sales.

Simone contributed to the family income with her refurbishing business, and her biggest months were ahead of them as she prepared for the Fall Festival and holiday shows in Three Rivers.

"Okay," Callie said. "Let's take care of this. Let me grab some gloves." She retreated down the ladder and retrieved a pair of leather gloves from a shelf beside the entrance. Back in the loft, she started cutting twine and pulling the hay apart.

"I think we should open the chute," Simone said. "Drop

all the moldy hay down that. It'll be easier to move that way."

Callie sneezed, which also pulled through her back. She nodded, feeling overwhelmed and desperate for help. "Okay," she said. "I'll go open it."

She turned away from Simone before her sister could see her distress. Callie didn't want to stress out Evelyn or Simone. It was her job to run the ranch. Evelyn did her matchmaking, and Simone did the refurbishing. They both helped a little bit, like Simone feeding the goats twice a day.

"It's not like they're blind," she muttered to herself as she left the barn and walked over to the pathetic equipment shed. They had a conveyor belt to get the hay into the loft, and it could get the moldy hay down too.

With great effort, and after she'd bashed her shin against the unforgiving metal, Callie got the conveyor over to the hay barn. Simone had opened the window in the loft, and she piled rotten hay onto the belt before Callie had even turned it on.

Didn't matter. It would all come down eventually.

The sisters worked together, neither of them speaking, and after a few hours of horrible, almost insufferable work in the heat of the barn, Callie could look at a pile of good hay on one side of the loft, and Simone loaded the last of the moldy hay onto the conveyor.

Down it went, taking Callie's spirits with it.

Dear Lord, she thought. *What do I do now?*

She'd always been religious, and her prayers to God

about the ranch had increased to the point where Callie petitioned Him everyday to help her around the Shining Star.

"Maybe I need to call Miah," she said. The thought felt good. It felt right. He wouldn't judge her, and maybe fixing the barn would be free.

"I think that's a good idea," Simone said, moving over to the wall that had been leaking. "I mean, I can patch up a cabinet and sand over it, but I have no idea how to fix this."

"Daddy showed me how to fix fences and a few other minor things," Callie said. "I could probably do some research online and figure it out." She wanted to be self-reliant. She knew it was a very slippery slope once she started asking for help.

"I bet Rhett would do it," Simone said. "Evvy said he finished that new case already, and he's bored. She doesn't know what to do with him."

"She doesn't?"

"I guess he wants them to get their own place." Simone shrugged. "Which, honestly, they should. Who wants to live with newlyweds?" She giggled, and Callie smiled too. They climbed down the ladder, and she wiped the sweat from her brow.

"Okay." She exhaled. "I'll give Miah a call." She nodded like she'd rush right back over to the stables where she'd left her phone and dial him immediately.

But she didn't. And she didn't that evening either, and she didn't when the new day dawned.

She wasn't sure why she didn't want to ask for his help, only that she didn't.

As usual, she went out onto the porch and stretched her arms above her head, the day already sweltering. And yet, Liam worked in the garden. What he could possibly be doing over there, she wasn't sure. Weeds didn't grow that fast.

She walked that way, her heartbeat bumping against her breastbone. "Hey," she said, and he straightened to look at her.

A smile filled that face, and oh, Callie needed to hold onto the fence so she didn't fall down as her knees went weak. "Heya, Cal."

"So my barn is leaking," she said. "I know you have a job and all that, but do you think if I called Miah, he'd come help?"

"Of course," Liam said, joining her at the fence. "You want me to mention it to him?"

"No," she said. "I can call him." She could. She just hadn't. She met Liam's eye, and every worry in her soul went out. How he could do that, she wasn't sure.

The moment between them lengthened until he cleared his throat and dropped his head. "Pizza night tonight. You want to come?"

"At the homestead? Or with you?"

He blinked, a blip of confusion moving through those dark, dreamy, dangerous-to-her-health eyes. "At the homestead."

Of course. It could be pizza night every night if he was asking her on a date. Of course he wasn't doing that.

"Sure," she said. "I'll tell Simone." That way, it wouldn't seem like she'd just asked him if he'd asked her out. Foolishness filled her, and she turned away. "Okay, I better get to work. This ranch doesn't take care of itself."

"Okay," Liam said as she walked away. He said something else, but Callie didn't catch what. She almost turned back to ask him when she realized he'd spoken under his breath. So he didn't want her to hear.

It was true that the ranch didn't take care of itself, but Callie was starting to think she couldn't take care of it either.

14

Evelyn came downstairs, ready to get over to her own house and get to work in the office that had become her sanctuary this past week. She liked spending time with Rhett, but he lived with three of his brothers, and they didn't have any privacy. No living room where they could cuddle and watch a movie without Jeremiah glaring at them every few minutes.

He'd been cordial to Evelyn, but she rarely saw him. She didn't eat breakfast, lunch, or dinner at the Walker's. She worked in her office or met with clients in town, and she did her chores around the Shining Star Ranch. She'd spend a couple of hours with Rhett, kiss him until she was breathless, and then go upstairs to sleep on a state-of-the art mattress. In fact, it might have been that mattress that kept her at the wrong ranch.

She went straight out the front door and practically

steamrolled Rhett. "Oh," she said, stumbling to the right so she didn't crash into him. Grabbing onto the post, she managed to stay on her feet.

"Whoa," Rhett said as if she were a runaway horse. He jumped to his feet and steadied her by the elbow. "Sorry, I didn't mean to startle you."

"I just didn't know you were there."

"Yeah, I can see that."

With both of her feet solidly under her, she looked at him. He clearly had something to say, as she'd seen this look on his face many times over breakfast. "What's going on?"

"There's two things, actually." He stepped back, and Evelyn didn't like that.

"Okay," she said. "Did someone else say something about the marriage?" He'd gotten a call on Monday morning, before either of them had even been to town. He'd been panicked when he'd come knocking on her bedroom door that morning, and she'd explained to him the ins and outs of a small town.

Coupled with the fact that she'd lived there her whole life and ran a secret matchmaking service? Yeah, she should've expected the news to spread across town faster than a wildfire. And it had.

The smoke had mostly died down now, though Evelyn still got a few curious looks whenever she went into town—which was a lot more now that she was booking more clients again.

"No, nothing about that," he said. "But Tripp told me a

woman smashed a bottle of pickles right in front of him at the grocery store yesterday." Rhett cocked an eyebrow, his question very loud though he hadn't spoken.

"Oh, that's too bad," Evelyn said, and she couldn't have convinced anyone with that false, too-high tone. "Did it ruin his boots?"

"No." Rhett drew the word out. "Evvy, we agreed that my brothers were off-limits for your...services."

"Did we, though?" Because Audrey Pitt was perfect for Tripp, even if he didn't know it yet. The pickle-jar-fiasco had even been her idea, and all Evelyn had to do was make sure Audrey knew when Tripp would be at the store.

"Yes," he said. "Yes, we did."

Frustration welled within Evelyn, along with a dose of embarrassment. "Okay, I know. It's just—do you know how many women want to go out with them? They're the hottest commodities in town, and now I'm *in* with you guys."

"*In* with us?" he asked. "You have never eaten a meal here. Jeremiah actually asked me about you last night, and not in a good way."

Evelyn blinked and slowed down for a moment. "What did he say?"

"I don't want to tell you." Rhett reached up and ran his hand along the back of his head, pushing his cowboy hat forward. "Look, can't you just have a piece of toast in the morning?"

"I just drink coffee for breakfast," she said.

"That's so not true," he said. "We eat a full spread every Tuesday."

"And that tides me over on the other days."

Rhett exhaled, and he was clearly not buying her excuse, and he was obviously not happy. Evelyn wasn't exactly riding off into the sunset on a unicorn either, but she didn't know what to do about it. Business was ten times better than it had been before she and Rhett had said "I do," and it had only been a week.

"What's the second thing?" Evelyn asked, because she didn't want to argue with Rhett. She honestly didn't. She just wanted to go back home, get some work done, and make sure she and her sisters had enough to eat.

"You can't just sleep here," he said darkly.

"You wanted us to live together," she said. "We do."

He shook his head. "No, this isn't living together. I think...I think we might need to get our own place."

Evelyn couldn't understand the words. They were clearly English, but her brain couldn't comprehend them. "What?"

"Our own place," he said again. "I've been looking, and there's a—"

"No, no, no," she said with a laugh that wasn't even on the scale of humorous. "No. We're not buying or renting or whatever it is you're thinking a place. No." She started down the steps, her heartbeat thrashing inside her chest.

She'd only ever lived at the Shining Star. That ranch

meant everything to her and had been in the Foster family for generations.

Callie and Simone still live there, her mind whispered as her shoes hit the sidewalk at the bottom of the steps.

"Evelyn," Rhett said, hurrying after her. He grabbed her arm, and she spun back toward him. Everything stilled, because she seriously liked this man. He'd been nothing but generous and kind to her over the course of the past year.

He'd married her just to help her.

"Just think about it," he said.

She nodded a couple of times, because that didn't require the use of her voice, and then she got the heck out of there.

"Okay," she said later that day, a binder open on the table between her and Sami Schwartz. "I have a couple of options for you." She'd had three, but Liam had been tabled that morning. As much as she didn't want to adhere to her agreement with Rhett, she didn't feel right about going behind his back.

"Bennett Lancaster. Blond. Tall. Very strong. He's out at Three Rivers Ranch. Seems like he was a bit of a player a few years ago, but he's grown up a lot recently." Evelyn pointed to a picture of him she'd taken from the town's website. "He loves to dance, loves chocolate chip cookies, and your best bet of running into him is at Heidi's bakery."

Sami looked at Bennett's one-sheet. "I don't know if he'll ever settle down."

"With the right woman, he will," Evelyn said, wondering if she was the right woman for Rhett. He'd been creeping into her thoughts since they got married, which for a normal person, that would be fine.

For her, where their marriage was only real on the certificate Rhett had gotten, thinking quite so much about him didn't seem healthy.

"You've also got Todd Larson," she said, switching the papers. "He owns a large strip of property on Main Street, but his cowboy hat is as big as everyone else's in town."

Sami didn't dwell on Todd. "I think Bennett." She looked up at Evelyn, who reached for her papers. She never left them with her clients, as they took a long time to make, and she could reuse them. "Fair enough. He doesn't get to town much, so we're going to have to be patient and creative with our initial meet."

"How do you know he's the one?"

"Oh, only you can know that," she said. "But based on everything you've said, I think you two will get along really nicely."

There were other matchmakers in town that Sami could try. One who'd lived here a very long time, in fact. But Evelyn operated a little stealthier, and she wasn't really matchmaking. She was simply helping cowboys get out of their own way.

"How did you know Rhett was the one for you?" Sami's

big, blue eyes were so wide, so innocent. But her question had stabbed right through to Evelyn's heart.

It *ska-skipped* every other beat, and the seconds ticking by certainly didn't help her case. She plastered a smile on her face. "When you know, you just know."

Feeling idiotic, she flipped open her folder and put the pages back inside. "I'll start working on the initial meet."

"Okay," Sami chirped. "What do I do?"

"You wait for me to call," Evelyn said. "Hopefully it won't take too long. I have a contact out at Courage Reins I'll call later today." Carly Sanders worked in the reception area there with her husband, Reese, and the two of them had helped Evelyn with two or three cowboys out at the ranch north of town.

In fact, Evelyn thought today was probably a really good day to bake some cookies and go for a drive past all the new housing on the north end of town and out to the biggest ranch in the county.

With three operational businesses on it, Three Rivers Ranch had grown and grown over the years, and Evelyn loved taking a horseback ride there and catching up with the ranch gossip.

You should take Rhett with you, she thought, and she picked up her phone to text him.

We can go horseback riding at Seven Sons, he responded, clearly not getting it. Evelyn smiled at Sami and stood up. "Thanks for meeting with me today."

"Sure." Sami walked her to the door.

"I'll have more for you soon." Back in her car, Evelyn stared at her phone, wondering what to tell Rhett. In the past, she didn't have to run anything by anyone. If she wanted to bake cookies and drive for an hour to ride a horse, she did it.

She pulled out of the driveway and navigated back to Main Street. Dialing Rhett, she joined the line at Pop'n Fizz to get a soda. "Do you want something to drink from Pops?"

"Yeah," he said. "Diet Mountain Dew with mango."

"Okay." Evelyn inched forward as another car moved up. "Listen," she said. "I need to go out to Three Rivers, and I invited you so we could spend some time together." She wanted the fairy tale relationship, where she fell head-over-heels in love with a man as they got to know each other.

Problem was, she'd spent the last year getting to know Rhett. She already knew him. Liked him. Some of the magic and mystery for her had been removed simply because of their friendship.

"Okay," he said. "I didn't get that, but I do now. I'd love to go horseback riding at Courage Reins."

"Okay," she said, looking out the window at the menu, though she already knew what she was going to get. The Summer Lovin' had everything that made Evelyn happy, from the Diet Coke to the raspberry flavoring to the dash of vanilla.

"Also," she said. "I've been thinking about what you said this morning, and you might be right."

"I'm sorry," Rhett said, his voice clearly mocking her. "I didn't quite hear you."

"Yes, you did," she said with a laugh. Maybe the first laugh she'd allowed since the wedding.

"I think you said I was right," he teased.

"I'm hanging up," she said, doing so as he laughed in her ear. She couldn't help shaking her head and giggling— exactly the kind of relationship she wanted to have with her husband someday.

"He *is* your husband," she reminded herself as the girl on the speaker chirped, "Hey, what can I get for you?"

15

"Bang," Rhett said, holding the bit of hot dog high so Penny could see it. She watched it, and he said, "Bang," again, this time using his other hand to push her to the ground. He held his palm flat over her, the sign he'd taught her for stay.

"Good girl," he said, feeding her the hot dog. But she hadn't really done the trick. Rhett couldn't believe this was what his life had come to—training his dog during the day while everyone around him worked.

Sure, he had things to do around Seven Sons, and he did them. But Jeremiah ran the ranch, and they had plenty of hired help. Rhett hadn't been able to help during his stressful forensic case, and he'd never felt this useless. But now, with a very easy case that he'd already finished, he was literally searching for things to fill his time.

He and Evelyn hadn't been able to get out to Three

Rivers Ranch yet, where Courage Reins was, and Rhett was considering going himself just to have something to do. He did have one thing on his agenda that day—look at a house with Evelyn.

It had been a couple of days since he'd suggested they get their own place. He really hated the current situation, but she had tried to make things less awkward around the homestead. She did eat breakfast in the morning, and she'd been joining them for dinner too.

"Let me ask him."

He glanced up as Jeremiah came in, his phone stuck to his ear. "It's Callie. She's wondering if you can help with the barn."

"Yes," Rhett said before his brother had even finished speaking. "I can help." He'd do anything to get out of this house, and the way Penny practically sprinted to the open back door said she would too.

Jeremiah went back to his conversation while Rhett went out on the deck and picked up the big ball Evelyn had bought for his dog. "Ready, Pen?" he called, launching the ball into the air. She booped it with her nose, sending it back up. She barked and chased it around the yard, hitting it to herself and running after it with the speed of lightning.

Rhett laughed at her, because he'd literally never seen a dog play catch with herself before. He turned when Jeremiah came outside too, this time, the phone call over. Rhett hadn't spoken to Jeremiah about Evelyn again, but he'd been warming to both of them as the days went by.

"They're in a tough spot over there," he said. "I feel bad for them."

"I can help," Rhett said. "I literally do nothing." And it was his wife's ranch. He could definitely help them with whatever they needed, from fixing a fence to installing a new gate on their pasture.

Rhett hadn't grown up on a farm, but the past year of rebuilding after the tornado had taught him that he could wield a hammer as easily as he could find evidence in a paw print.

"She's grateful," Jeremiah said, pausing at the railing and watching Penny too. "That dog is somethin' else."

"Yeah." Rhett smiled at her. "So, *Miah*. What's with you and Callie?"

His brother swung his gaze toward Rhett, and he could see everything in those eyes. So much of himself. So much of their father in those deep, brown eyes with a sprinkling of their mother in the freckles across his nose. Only two years younger than him, Rhett had spent almost all of his teenage years getting into trouble with Jeremiah.

"There is nothing between me and Callie," he said, almost coldly. "Number one, I wouldn't do that to Liam. Number two, I am not interested in women. Period."

"Okay," Rhett said, holding up his hands in a show of surrender. "I didn't say you had to date her. I was just asking if there was something there."

"No," Jeremiah said. "Liam holds her in high regard, if you know what I mean."

Tripp had told him that too, and a low laugh started in the back of Rhett's throat. "Well, why doesn't he ask her out?"

"We had a *pact*, bro." Jeremiah shook his head and started down the steps. "I have to get back to work. You can head over to the Shining Star anytime you want. Callie says there will be lunch at twelve-thirty."

Rhett watched his brother walk away. No, they weren't back to where they'd been before he'd married Evelyn. Then, Jeremiah had always been the hot-head, quick to jump to conclusions. But he'd laughed too. He'd sat with the brothers on the couch and fell asleep while they watched their favorite shows.

"At least he's speaking to you," Rhett told himself. He whistled at Penny, and she herded the ball back to the deck. "Good girl," he said. "Now, come on. Let's go see what the women have for us to eat."

He opted to walk the half-mile, mostly to wear Penny out a little bit more. A cattle dog, she could literally run for hours and be happy doing it.

Before he and Evelyn had gotten married, Rhett would've simply knocked on the front or back door and walked right in. So he did the same today, though a bit of awkwardness entered his bloodstream as he called, "Hello? Ladies? It's Rhett."

Footsteps sounded on the wood floor, and then his wife emerged from the mouth of the hallway. "Oh, hey, sugar," he said easily, though the sight of her made everything in him prance and dance and rejoice. "Is Callie around?"

"Callie?" Her surprise was cute, and Rhett drank in the sight of her in those black leggings, that pale pink blouse, her dark hair curled around her shoulders. "Are you seeing another client today?"

"As a matter of fact, yes." Evelyn smiled at him as he drew closer to her.

"I'm glad," he said, keeping track of how many new clients she'd gotten since their wedding. Four. This one today made four. She had to be happy about that, and the sparkle in her eyes testified of it. "So are you saying Callie's not here?"

"She's out on the ranch somewhere."

"Is the house empty?" He trailed his fingers down her arm, watching her shudder right in front of him. Pure heat dove through him, and he pressed his lips to her forehead, about all he could do with his wide-brimmed cowboy hat in the way.

"Behave yourself," she said with a giggle. But he didn't want to behave himself. He wanted to kiss his wife.

"When is your client coming? Or are you going into town again?" He'd been waiting for her on the front steps each morning, and they'd sort of established a new routine. Of course, it had only been two days, but she was sharing more with him, drinking coffee in the kitchen, setting bread in the toaster. Small steps, but important ones too.

"She's coming here," she said, holding onto his shoulders. "So you can't be here." Her words pushed him away, but her hands brought him closer.

"Mm," he said, finally reached up and taking off his cowboy hat so he could kiss Evelyn. She melted right into him, and Rhett felt like the luckiest man in the world. So consumed with the scent of her skin and the touch of her fingertips along the back of his neck, Rhett didn't hear anyone enter the house.

At least until Simone said, "Oh, aren't you two so cute?"

Evelyn ducked her head, a soft sigh coming from her mouth as Rhett kept both arms around her, steadying her. "Hey, Simone," he said as if he'd stopped by to deliver the mail. "Have you seen Callie?"

"I don't think you're going to find her standing there," Simone said with a knowing smile.

But he really had come to talk to Callie. Fine, kissing Evelyn was high on the list too. The doorbell rang, and Evelyn jumped to attention. "Rhett, that's my client." Her warning tone was clear. *Time to clear out.*

"Maybe she'll want to meet me," he said, turning to answer the door.

Evelyn danced in front of him. "You say hello, and go."

"Kiss me again," he whispered. Flirting with her had been oh so much fun. And to think he'd been holding back all these months.

"No," she said through a smile.

"We're still on to look at that house tonight, right?"

"Yes," she said, reaching the door ahead of him and opening it. "Flora, so good to see you. Come on in."

The woman standing on the porch clearly had plenty of money, if the fancy blouse and shiny shoes were any indication. She also carried a purse without a strap, and Rhett knew he hadn't seen one of those around Three Rivers.

"This is my husband, Rhett Walker," Evelyn said, snapping Rhett back to the moment.

"Afternoon, ma'am." He put his hat back on his head and went out the way Flora had come in. "I'll see you later, butternut." He closed the door behind them as Flora giggled, and he may have caught her saying, "Wow, he's handsome," as the door clicked closed.

———

"Okay, I'll admit it," Evelyn said, leaning forward to peer up at the house through the windshield. "This house is really cute."

Rhett had sent her the link to look at it, and he asked, "Did you look at it online?"

"Yes," she said, still drinking it all in. "There's just something about seeing it in person, you know?"

Oh, he knew. The two-story home sat on half an acre on the southern edge of Three Rivers. Just a half a block off the highway they drove to get to their ranches. It wasn't huge, by any stretch of the imagination, but the little white house had three bedrooms and three bathrooms and a great big fenced yard for Penny.

It had been freshly painted, and it gleamed like a shiny, new penny. Their realtor pulled into the driveway behind them, and Rhett said, "Okay. She's here." He got out of the truck and turned toward the petite, blonde woman. "Hi, Betsy." He extended his hand for Evelyn to take, which she did.

"Betsy Palmer?" she asked, and the two women looked at one another. Being new in town, Rhett was used to several seconds of silence while people sized each other up. It meant there was history there he didn't understand, because he hadn't been in Three Rivers as long as some people. As most people, actually.

"Hello, Evelyn," the real estate agent said cordially, though Rhett thought it had probably taken her a great deal of effort to do so. "Of course, I knew you'd married Rhett." She shook his hand and then hers, continuing down the sidewalk as if there were no tension at all.

"What's that about?" Rhett whispered.

"Tell you later," Evelyn muttered back, and for some reason, the thought made him absolutely giddy. He loved spending time with Evelyn, and listening to her talk about her business, her clients, her problems. And the history she had with people in town was one of his favorite things.

"This house is for sale or rent," she said. "Do you know which you'll be doing?" She paused at the top of the steps and started keying in a code on the lockbox.

"Renting," Evelyn said at the same time Rhett said, "I think we'll buy it."

They looked at each other, and he chuckled nervously. "I guess we'll talk about it."

"Hmm," Betsy said, taking the key out of the box and fitting it into the lock. "Well, it has central air conditioning, a brand-new furnace, and has been completely remodeled." She opened the door and stepped inside. "The asking price is a little high, but if you're going to rent, you should be fine." She gave Evelyn a scathing smile—at least Rhett thought she did. It came and went so fast, he couldn't be sure.

The inside of the house was as charming as the outside, and Rhett had only spent five seconds inside before he leaned over and whispered to Evelyn, "I love this place."

She was too busy scanning everything to answer him. She barely said two words for the rest of the tour, and Rhett couldn't decide if that was good or bad. Betsy took them into the backyard, which looked like a tropical paradise to him. Of course, it was the beginning of the summer, and most of this would probably be brown by July.

"I'll leave you two to discuss it," Betsy said, handing Rhett a piece of paper. "Come out front when you're ready." She'd warmed to Evelyn throughout the tour, and Rhett handed her the paper as the real estate agent left.

"Why don't you want to buy?" he asked.

"Because, Rhett." She focused on the paper in her hand.

"Buying means we're permanent, and I don't know." She lifted her gaze to his. "Are we permanent?"

"Maybe not yet," he conceded. "But Evelyn, I feel like we didn't really think this through. You thought your business had tanked because Patrick broke up with you. What will happen to it if we get divorced?"

It was a very valid question, and Evelyn just shrugged. "I don't know. Maybe we made a big mistake." She'd said that before they'd tied the knot, and the idea felt as false now as it had then. "And I thought you bought that ranch, so you'd have something to pass on."

"Oh, Jeremiah will buy it from me," Rhett said. "He's the one who's poured his heart into Seven Sons. Not me." He looked around the backyard. Was this where he was supposed to spend his time and energy?

"You decide," Evelyn said. "I do love this place. It's very...quiet. It's peaceful here."

"Yes," he said. "Peaceful." And he had plenty of money, and he could buy it with cash, no problem. "If you want to rent, that's fine with me."

"There's another thing," she said, tucking her arm through his.

"Yeah? What's that?"

"All of my money goes to support my sisters and the ranch. I can't afford this place."

Rhett kissed her forehead. "I can, sweetheart. I think we should get it."

"Okay," she said. "But I swear I didn't marry you for your money."

"I know that," Rhett said, recalling Jeremiah's words about protecting himself with a prenuptial agreement—which he hadn't done. "I would never think that."

She nodded and turned back to the house. "All right, then, Rhett. You got your way. We'll live together here."

He touched her arm, and she turned back to him. He wanted to ask her if that meant they'd have all the perks of being truly married, but one look at her face, and he knew she wasn't ready for that.

Truth be told, he wasn't either. Sure, he liked this woman a lot, but he wasn't in love with her.

Yet.

"What?" she asked, her voice gentle and filled with concern.

Rhett blinked out of his thoughts. "Nothing." He smiled at her. "Let's go get dinner." As they went through the house to the front yard, Rhett offered a silent prayer that he would know what to do when it came to Evelyn. Because being married to her was turning out to be just as much of a minefield as being her best friend.

16

Another week passed, and Evelyn once again found herself packing up her clothes and toiletries. Rhett had rented the house on Quail Creek Road, and Evelyn was secretly giddy about it. Not that she minded sleeping by herself on the second floor. Just like she hadn't minded living with her sisters.

But this new house signified something else—a new adventure. She'd literally never lived anywhere besides at the Shining Star Ranch. Well, and now at Seven Sons. But she'd never had a place of her own, without Callie and Simone, and it felt exciting.

Not only that, but she'd told her father about the marriage and the new house, and he wanted to meet Rhett. Of course he did. Just because he was seventy-five with a bad back and bad hips didn't mean he didn't want the best for his girls. Since neither her father nor her grandmother could drive, Evelyn had to go into town to pick them up and bring them out to the ranch.

But after she and Rhett moved into their new place, which was happening that morning, she'd only be a skip away from her family, and she'd already invited them to the house for dinner.

After she and Rhett got settled in the house, they had a riding appointment at Courage Reins, where they'd spend their afternoon with the therapy horses—and Evelyn could chat with Carly and Reese.

Things had slowed in her matchmaking business, but she'd signed a total of six new clients since marrying Rhett. "Thank you, Lord," she said as she folded a pair of shorts and put them in her suitcase.

She hadn't done anything wrong. She'd gotten married legally, with a willing participant. She thought of Rhett, and how they'd be living together that evening. "You've already been living with him," she told herself, putting her travel jewelry case in the suitcase too. But this would be different, and she knew it.

They'd be alone. Right next door to each other. No buffer, and no reason for her to go running off to the comfortable office at the Shining Star. She was moving her office too, and she'd work from the little white house in town from now on.

Or at least for now.

She honestly had no idea what the future held, and she'd spent a great deal of time that week beating herself up for not thinking through all the threads of her decision. *Help me*, she prayed. *Guide me. Put my feet on the path they should be on. Don't let me hurt Rhett.*

That man was made of gold, and she wouldn't be able to live with herself if she hurt him. As if summoned by her thoughts, he appeared in the doorway. "Oh, the yellow blouse. Hey, honeybee. We're here for the chair."

He entered the room with Tripp right behind him. "And as soon as you're done packing, we're ready to head over."

"You got the boxes in my office already?" she asked, surprised. She'd only been up for an hour, and the sun not much longer than that.

"Yep." Rhett picked up one side of the chair while Tripp positioned himself on the other. "The desk. The chair. Even the curtains. Callie said those were lucky." He smiled at her and they hauled the chair out of the room.

These Walker brothers were nothing if not efficient. Rhett had been filling his days with work around the Shining Star, and Callie didn't have a single bad thing to say about him. Evelyn got to see his moods, and she knew he wasn't perfect. She got to hear him talk about things that worried him, or something in a case that troubled him. She got to see the vulnerable side of him, as well as the tough cowboy, and she realized as she stood there in that room that had never really been hers, that she could easily fall in love with Rhett Walker.

In fact, she was already sliding in that direction, and she

didn't even need the lucky curtains that had Texas stars on them.

So it was with some measure of excitement that she finished packing, zipped her suitcase, and hauled it down-stairs. Jeremiah took it from her with the words, "Let me, Evelyn," and continued outside.

She watched him go, those broad shoulders and big muscles easy for her to see. It was what Jeremiah kept hidden on the inside she hadn't known about.

"Ready?" Liam asked, pausing with a box in his arms. "This is the last of Rhett's stuff, and I think we're going."

"Yeah." She looked at him, really looked. She'd known all the Walker men for a year now, and she wasn't sure she'd ever really paid that close of attention to anyone but Rhett. Liam had nice strong features, and he hadn't shaved that morning. Anyone with two X-chromosomes who saw him that day would surely swoon, what with those dark eyes and that dimple in his right cheek.

"Why don't you date?" she asked.

Surprise crossed Liam's face. "Rhett hasn't told you?"

"He has not."

"Ah, it's a boring story." Liam flashed her a smile with plenty of pain around the edges. "I'll save it for another time. Today's an exciting day. You and Rhett are moving into a place of your own." He nodded toward the front door. "Go on, I think I hear Jeremiah's disgruntled muttering from in here."

Evelyn giggled, glad some of Rhett's brothers didn't

seem to have a problem with her. He'd called his parents in Grand Cayman, and they'd been surprised and curious about her. The three Walker brothers who didn't live on the ranch didn't seem to have an opinion one way or another.

And none of that mattered anymore anyway. She and Rhett had a place of their own now, and they could do what they wanted.

Problem was, Evelyn didn't know the exact rules on what those things were. She got in Rhett's truck, the engine already idling while he and Tripp strapped everything down.

"We'll see you over there," Jeremiah said, knocking on the door as he went past. He and Liam piled into the big red pickup truck Evelyn had ridden to church in dozens and dozens of times. Hundreds of times.

A pang of sadness hit her as Callie rumbled down the road, the four of them smashed inside the old pickup. Rhett finally got behind the wheel while Tripp went to start his truck too.

"All set?" Rhett asked.

She turned and looked at him, letting the entire future bloom before her. In one single breath, she could see them experiencing life together, making memories, struggling through tough times, and prevailing in the end.

"Yes," she said. "I'm all set."

———

"So this is Three Rivers Ranch," Rhett said a few hours later. They'd left Callie and Simone at their new house to finish unpacking everything. Liam and Tripp had gone into town to buy lunch for everyone, and Jeremiah had taken Tripp's truck back to Seven Sons to do his own ranch chores.

Evelyn was glad she'd escaped the fray, though she was incredibly grateful for all the help. She'd return tonight after a relaxing afternoon of horseback riding to dinner and a house ready to live in. Any furniture they didn't have, Rhett had bought, and it would get delivered that afternoon.

He'd purchased all the beds in the homestead, and Evelyn had asked him for one exactly like the mattress she'd been sleeping on. He'd looked at her for a long moment, and then he'd said, "Of course, sugar. I'm glad you like that bed."

They had not discussed sleeping arrangements, a topic that had been weighing on Evelyn's mind.

"Evvy?"

She turned toward him as if she didn't realize they were in the truck together. "Sorry."

"What are you thinking about?" he asked.

She wanted to tell him, but fear flickered inside her like a flame. It danced and it burned, and she couldn't say it out loud. "Nothing." She put a smile on her face. "Let's go in before we're late for our appointment."

Rhett gave her a dubious look but didn't press the issue. He took her hand in his as they went inside the glass-fronted building of Courage Reins, a place familiar and comfortable for Evelyn. She loved coming to this ranch, which housed this therapy riding facility.

Reese looked up from behind the counter, a whoop coming out of his mouth the very next moment.

"Evelyn," he said, adding, "Carly, they're here," over his shoulder as he braced himself to stand. He used a single crutch to come around the counter, his awkward gait so lovable that Evelyn wanted to squish him.

But she knew Reese didn't want to be squished. He still commanded respect though he wasn't as tall as he once was. "Reese." She laughed as she let go of Rhett's hand and hugged the war veteran. "It's so good to see you."

"You haven't been out forever," he said. "Peony's not going to know what to do with herself."

A blonde woman came out of the hallway, a bright smile on her face and a baby on her hip. "It's Auntie Evvy," she cooed to the little girl. They hugged too, and Evelyn took the dark-haired, dark-skinned girl from Carly.

"This is Rhett Walker," she said, looking from him to her friends. "My husband."

Carly had started to take a step forward, but she froze. "Your what? Evelyn." She searched Evelyn's face, and Evelyn didn't like the scrutiny.

"Wow," Reese said, laughing. "I wasn't expecting that." He shook Rhett's hand and said, "You're a lucky one to get Evelyn, even if she said she'd never get married."

"Is that what she said?" Rhett asked, a perfect smile on

his face. His eyes said something different, but Evelyn hid behind the infant in her arms and dodged his look.

"It's not a big deal," she told Carly. "It was sudden, that's all."

"When you know, you know," Rhett said, and it wasn't the first time she'd heard him say that. Heck, she'd used it too, because it got people off her back.

"And I never said I would never get married," she said, throwing a look at Reese. She probably should've prepped her friends better. "I said it was unlikely that anyone would want to marry me."

She met Rhett's eyes then, the explanation more for him than anyone else. They breathed in together, and then he swept his arm around her and said, "That's just crazy. Who wouldn't want to marry you?" before he kissed her cheek.

"So, we're riding horses today," Reese said, clearly ready to move the conversation to something else. Evelyn had always had a strong bond with Reese Sanders, and she put her hand on his arm as she went by, a silent touch to say *thank you*.

He took them outside to the open pasture, away from the indoor arena. "We've got a couple of new horses for you," he said. "These guys are still trying to earn their way into the program, but they're perfect for riders like you two."

Evelyn knew he meant riders that weren't physically or mentally disabled. "Names?" she asked, handing the baby back to Carly.

"The dark one is Chocolate Licorice," Reese said,

opening the gate and going inside. Evelyn followed him, with Rhett and Carly right behind. "And this tall girl is Black Lace."

"But she's white," Rhett said.

"And so majestic," Reese said, stroking the horse's neck. "All right, Lacey. You do things right. I'm watching you."

"I want her," Evelyn said, moving to stand right in front of the horse. She really was tall—taller than any horse Evelyn had ridden in a while. But something in the horse's soul spoke to hers, and she pressed her nose right against Evelyn's palm.

"Oh, you're ready for this program, aren't you?" She looked at Reese, who just shook his head. "She pulls. Until she stops doing that, she can't be in the rotation."

Evelyn looked back at the horse, noticing someone had braided deep blue ribbons into her mane. "Well, let's show him you don't pull. Okay, girl?" She moved to the horse's side, but there was no way she could swing up into the saddle without a step.

"Clyde'll bring a stool," Reese said, waving behind him. Sure enough, another cowboy brought over a step-stool for her, and she was able to get on the horse easily then.

Everything suddenly became right in the world, and Evelyn tested the weight of the reins in her hands, felt the majestic beast beneath her body. She leaned down and hugged Black Lace. "Oh, you're beautiful."

The horse didn't move a muscle, and Evelyn said, "Look, Reese. She's not pulling."

He rolled his eyes and waited until Rhett had swung into his saddle too. Evelyn simply stared at him. She'd been attracted to him from the moment she laid eyes on him in that storm shelter. But seeing him atop a horse, reins held just-so, and a smile gracing that handsome face?

She couldn't even breathe.

And she couldn't believe he was hers—even if it was only on paper.

17

Rhett let Evelyn lead them out of the pasture, as she'd been out to this ranch before, and he had not. In fact, he hadn't seen much of Three Rivers at all, and he was beginning to realize what a mistake that had been. The town had charm, that was for sure, and everyone who lived here seemed to take care of each other.

Just like Evelyn and her sisters had helped Rhett and his brothers after the tornado. Like he was helping Callie now. He may not be a born and bred cowboy like Jeremiah, but even Rhett could see when a ranch was in trouble. And the Shining Star was a few hay fields away from ruin.

When Rhett had asked Callie why she didn't hire help, she'd said they couldn't afford it. She'd still tried to pay him yesterday, but he'd steadfastly refused.

"You can't work for free," she'd said.

"Yes, I can," he said. "I don't have much of a job anymore, and you need the help."

"Don't tell Evelyn," she'd said, and Rhett had agreed.

He wanted to tell her, but his heart wouldn't let him. She'd signed a few new clients since they'd been married, and he was grateful for that. He'd bought the house on Quail Creek Road, and he hadn't told her that either. It felt like the secrets between them were piling up, and they'd only been married for a couple of weeks.

Out under the clear blue sky and the heavy heat of a near-summer day in Texas, Rhett finally felt like he'd found somewhere he could just be himself. A sigh slipped out of his mouth, drawing Evelyn's attention.

"It's great, isn't it?" she asked.

"I can't believe you can just come here and do this."

"Well, it's not free for everyone," she said. "But if you're a veteran or have a special need, Courage Reins does have a grant that pays for equine therapy."

"It's amazing," Rhett said. "I saw some horses in there kicking balls and stuff."

"Yeah," she said. "That's why these two aren't in the program yet. They have to have the right temperament and abilities to work with people who need the calmest of the calm." She smiled at him, and Rhett thought she was the most beautiful thing in the world.

"I have a confession," he said.

Evelyn watched him. "How many minutes does this conversation get?"

"I only need one," he said with a chuckle. "But I want you to think about it for oh, I don't know. Thirty seconds before you react."

"Wow, thirty seconds. That's a long time if you think about it."

"I'll count for you." He looked away, the waving prairie grasses so beautiful when he'd never found them all that awesome on his own ranch. He'd never felt quite at home at Seven Sons, though he knew God had directed him there.

But Three Rivers Ranch really did possess a wonder and spirit all its own. "I bought the house," he said. "I didn't just rent it. I bought it."

"Rhett."

"Thirty seconds." He cut a look at her, though he'd seen her reaction with his excellent peripheral vision. She didn't seem happy. "Starting now." He didn't really count, but simply let the clomping of Chocolate Licorice's hooves keep the time.

"Okay," he finally said.

"It's fine," she said.

"Oh, boy."

"No, really," she said. "It doesn't make any sense for you to rent it, and since I can't help pay for it, you should just buy it."

He looked at her, fully confident this horse wouldn't get them off-track. He barely held the reins in his hands. "You really think that?"

"Yes," she said. "It's a great house, on a great property. I'm glad you bought it."

He didn't think she was thinking quite as long-term as he was, which was fine. Honestly, it was. Just like he believed this horse wouldn't take him somewhere dangerous, he believed he and Evelyn would find their way toward lasting happiness, despite this strange path they'd stepped onto.

"Maybe you should write a grant for your ranch," he said. "It could be on the National Historic list, and then you ladies would have the funds you need to keep it running."

"We're doing okay," Evelyn said. "But it's an idea."

They rode in silence for a few minutes, until Evelyn said, "Rhett, do you want a family?"

The question nearly unseated him, and his fingers tightened around the reins. He'd never given much thought to having a family, because he'd never had much luck with women. "Yeah," he said slowly. "I think I'd like a family one day."

"Carly and Reese have adopted a couple of kids," she said.

"Do you want kids?" he asked.

"Yes," she said. "I've always wanted one boy and one girl." She threw him a grin. "Silly, I know. You don't get to pick what sex they are."

"No, you don't," he said, feeling his happiness expand and show on his face. She had seemed awfully comfortable with a baby on her hip, and Rhett suddenly wanted that to be *his* baby.

And they were married now, so why couldn't it be?

Maybe because she asked you to order her a separate bed, he thought, turning away from her again. He didn't want to rush Evelyn. He wouldn't pressure her. But one of the reasons he'd wanted to get out of the homestead on the ranch was so they could have some privacy for private things.

The ride ended, and Rhett waited in the truck while Evelyn chatted with her friends about a man named Bennett. When she finally came out, the sun was starting to set, painting the sky with golds and navies and purples.

"It's so pretty here," he said as they started back toward town. The drive seemed to happen in the blink of an eye, though the clock said almost an hour had gone by. But before he knew it, he'd parked and was walking up the back steps into his new house.

His and Evelyn's new house.

And his exhaustion testified that it was time for bed.

The silence in their house was suddenly so loud, and Rhett cringed when he dropped his keys on the built-in desk in the kitchen. "What a day," he said.

Evelyn agreed as she started opening cupboards. "We have everything," she said. "How is it possible that we have everything?" She took out a bowl with a pretty blue line around the rim. "Was this yours?"

"I bought that," he said coolly, hoping she wouldn't ask what else he'd purchased.

But he knew Evelyn better than that, and she pinned him with a look. "Rhett," she said, her voice clearly warning him to start talking, and fast.

"You said to buy what we didn't have. I did. They delivered it today, and our siblings unpacked it for us." He put his arms around her and held her close to him, still a little surprised he could do that whenever he wanted. "It's fine. Don't be mad."

"This must have taken all day."

"I'm sure it did."

"Simone has work on the ranch."

"Jeremiah took care of it." Rhett gazed down at her. "*I* took care of all of it, sugar." He'd wanted moving day to be as easy as possible for Evelyn, and it had been. Mission accomplished.

"You're a little too perfect," she said, frowning at him. "You know that, right?"

He laughed, tipping his head back. "Oh, you need to talk to my brothers more often. I'm definitely not perfect." But she was, and he bent down to kiss her. He moved slowly, so she could stop him if she wanted to. But she didn't, and his blood raced through his body as he explored her mouth and touched his lips to her throat.

"Maybe we should take a tour," she said breathlessly, her head still leaned back. "And you can show me all the stuff you bought."

"Mm." He kept kissing her, sliding his mouth up to her ear. "If you want," he whispered, holding still for a moment.

She didn't move, and Rhett's hopes shot toward the sky. He kissed her again, his hands moving up her back and into her hair. He didn't allow himself to move too fast or get too out of control. He felt her tense up, and he broke their connection.

"A tour," he said, his voice a little bit too low. He stepped back and looked around the kitchen. "I bought the table and chairs. Ours at the ranch belonged to our mother, and I thought my brothers would want to keep those."

Turning toward the living room, he said, "I showed you the couches when I bought them. TV's new, obviously. That recliner." It wasn't like the house had come furnished, and they both lived with family. Why she thought he had a secret storage shed with a house-full of furniture in it, he didn't know.

The hallway went down to the master suite, and he didn't go that way. "I bought the bed down there for you. Shower curtains, all of that kind of stuff." Her office sat right off the front door, and he said, "All of this came from your place."

She moved over to her desk and ran her fingers along the top of it. After a quick touch on the curtains, she turned back to him. "This is great."

"Right?" The steps led up to the second floor, where there were two more bedrooms and a bathroom. He'd furnished those too, with beds in each one for guests—and himself, if he were being honest. They hadn't talked about who would sleep where, but he had just told her he'd put her bed in the master suite.

He wanted it to be his bed too, but he held the words back, buried deep beneath his tongue. "And that's it," he said.

"I like the blue and gray in the bathroom," she said.

"Oh, I didn't pick anything out. I said, make it look like this, and the girl at the department store did it." He chuckled. "Are you hungry?"

She shook her head, her lips pressed together. She wore a look in her eyes that spoke of part exhaustion, part something he couldn't identify. "I think I'm just ready for bed," she whispered.

"All right." He took her hand and led her down the hall to the master suite. "Your stuff is here." Her suitcases sat by the door, and the bed had been put together. "Everything is here for you, sweetheart." He pressed a kiss to her forehead. "I'll see you in the morning."

Before he could go, she grabbed onto him and held him tight, tight. She quivered in his arms, and Rhett wanted to be the one who provided her with everything, so she'd never cry again. He knew that was unrealistic, but his fierce protection of her couldn't be helped.

"Thank you," she whispered, stepping back and brushing at her eyes. She nodded a couple of times. 'Thanks, Rhett."

"Yeah," he said dumbly, and he backed out of the room

before he asked her something stupid—like if he could sleep with her. He didn't even care if he couldn't touch her. He just wanted to be in the same room with her, listening to her breathe as she slept.

"Not happening," he mumbled to himself, walking away from the closed door as quickly as he could without running.

His suitcases had indeed been left in one of the bedrooms upstairs, and he kicked off his boots and sank onto the bed, a hefty exhale coming from his mouth. "What a day," he said. He laid back on the bed and looked up at the ceiling. "Thanks for a good day, Lord."

Maybe he hadn't gotten everything he wanted, but there was still time. And hope. And maybe some healing that needed to happen. He wasn't sure. But he trusted God, and he knew tomorrow would come.

And for now, that was enough.

18

Evelyn lay in bed for a long time, utterly spent but unable to fall asleep. This house felt so big, though it was about half the size of the farmhouse she'd come from. And a third of the size of the homestead.

Everything felt too quiet, which was stupid, as this house actually sat on a street where other people lived.

The bed was comfortable, but Evelyn was not, and she finally sat up and said, "This is ridiculous." She knew why she wasn't comfortable, and it was because Rhett was upstairs and she was down here.

She'd never liked being alone in the farmhouse at night, and right now, she felt absolutely alone. Isolated. Someone could sneak in and kidnap her, and Rhett wouldn't hear a thing.

Her heart pounded in her chest. What could she do?

Was he asleep already? Would he come down if she asked, and if she did, what would he expect from her?

The constant questions had her nerves vibrating and kept her muscles from leaping out of bed and propelling herself upstairs to his bedroom. Finally, the tension across her shoulders was so great, she couldn't hold still anymore.

"I'm just going to go talk to him," she whispered as she pulled a sweatshirt over her pajama top. It wasn't cold enough for that, but she needed the extra layer for some reason. Her door squeaked, and she stilled, almost expecting Rhett to be lying in the hallway.

He wasn't, and a single light in the kitchen illuminated the room enough so she wouldn't kill herself should she need to come in here in the middle of the night for some reason. In the future, once Rhett brought Penny to live with them, she might need to let the dog out in the night.

The stairs creaked as she went up them, and she flinched and cringed with every step. By the time she reached the top, she'd given up trying to be quiet. She was going to wake Rhett up to talk to him anyway.

She knocked on the only closed door upstairs, and said, "Rhett? Are you awake?" The family room spread out in front of her, and it was furnished too. The man must've spent thousands, and Evelyn wondered what the only furniture store in Three Rivers even had left to sell.

"Rhett?" She opened the door this time, and the easy, steady sound of his breathing filled the air. It brought her comfort, and she tiptoed across the room to the other side of the bed. She slipped easily beneath the comforter, every cell in her body relaxing now that they were together.

She didn't know what to make of that. Didn't know why she was so scared to be alone, and yet equally as terrified to ask him to stay with her. This way, she could be near him without him knowing. Then she could sneak back to her room in the—

"Evvy?" he asked, his hand sliding down her arm.

"It's just me," she whispered.

"What are you doin' up here?"

"I couldn't sleep downstairs by myself." She scooted closer to him, glad when he slipped his arm around her and brought her close to his chest. Listening to the steady rhythm of his heartbeat, Evelyn relaxed further. This was nice. This was what she'd dreamed about for so long, and Rhett had always been the man to hold her like this.

She sighed, her exhaustion starting to win now that she was warm and comfortable and right where she should be.

"Love you, Evvy," he whispered, jolting her out of her near-slumber.

"What?" she asked, but Rhett's chest just lifted and fell evenly.

The man was asleep, and he didn't even know what he'd said.

But Evelyn had heard him, and that love he'd just expressed moved through her powerfully. A smile touched her lips, and then finally, sleep claimed her.

———

When she woke, she thought she'd heard the snick of the door closing. She sat up straight, her heart pounding in her chest. She looked to her right, but Rhett wasn't on his side of the bed.

The summer sun lit the room, and she'd clearly slept later than she normally did. Throwing back the covers, she stilled again. A cup of coffee sat on the nightstand, steam still lifting from it. Rhett had been there, and Evelyn smiled at the gesture of warm coffee.

She thought their first conversation of the day would be a bit awkward, what with her climbing into bed with him last night, so she took a moment to just sip her coffee. Stepping over to the window, she opened the blinds, struck with the beauty of the yard this house sat on.

Rhett had said that it would probably all be brown soon enough, and he was right. But today, it sparkled in the morning sun, and a moment later, Penny ran into view, streaking after a ball.

Rhett joined his dog in the yard, finally giving her the big, blue, bouncy ball she could throw to herself. She booped it all over the grass, sprinting after it and making Evelyn laugh. She opened the window and called down, "Good morning."

Rhett turned back to her, holding his cowboy hat on his head as he looked up. "Morning." He waved and started back toward the house while Penny continued to play.

Evelyn's heart beat in her chest with the speed of hummingbird wings, and she took another sip of her coffee—which would only stimulate her further. Rhett didn't knock when he came in, and she didn't need him to. She'd heard his boots out in the hall.

"Hey," he said, his smile wide as he came around the bed to where she stood at the window. "You're awake."

"Yeah," she said, stepping easily into his arms. "What time is it?"

"Eight-thirty or close to that," he said.

"Mm" She breathed in the fresh, cottony scent of his shirt. He carried a hint of coffee with him too, along with his spicy cologne.

"I'm heading over to the ranch for a second this morning," he said. "I couldn't find one of my case files, and I think I left it in the den."

"Okay."

"And are we going to church?"

"Yeah," she said. "I'll shower while you're gone."

He pulled back, brushing her limp hair out of her face. "It was nice to wake up next to you today." He kissed her, and Evelyn tasted the coffee on his lips as she lost herself in his touch.

He ended the kiss sooner than she would've liked, clearing his throat and stepping back. "Okay, I'm going to go." He backed up a step, something afraid and hesitant on his face.

Evelyn didn't want him to go, and she said, "Do you have to go right now?"

"Church starts in a couple of hours."

"Two and a half hours," she said. "Unless it's way past eight-thirty." She'd left her cell phone down in her bedroom, and she had no way of knowing what time it was. And she hated that she'd thought of that bedroom on the first floor as hers.

Rhett pulled his phone from his back pocket and looked at it. "It's eight-twenty-four."

Evelyn's blood heated, and her pulse kicked throughout her body. She wasn't sure why she wanted him to stay, just like she wasn't sure why she hadn't been able to sleep in the master suite alone.

"Then you can stay," she said, stepping toward him and lacing her fingers through his. With both of their palms pressed together and all ten fingers intertwined, she tipped up on her toes to kiss him again.

This kiss held more passion than the previous one, which had been soft and beautiful. But now, Evelyn couldn't seem to get enough of him.

"Evvy," he whispered into her mouth, but she just kissed him again, bringing her hands up to cradle his face.

"Stay," she said again.

And he did.

———

A WEEK PASSED, and then another. One Sunday morning when Evelyn went into her office to check something that had popped into her mind while she'd showered, she found a tall vase holding a single rose.

The sight of the flower made her pause, one hand rising to where her heart beat in her chest. An envelope leaned against the glass, her name written in Rhett's handwriting. That alone made her pulse vibrate faster, and she glanced down the hall toward the kitchen, where she'd left him eating a breakfast of toast and scrambled eggs.

Turning back to her desk, she crossed the room and picked up the card. After opening it, she found a pink heart with the words "For my wife" on the front. She became aware of his footsteps coming closer, and then his arms wrapped around her from behind.

"It's our one-month anniversary," he said, touching his lips to the spot where her shoulder met her neck.

Shivers ran through Evelyn. "Thank you," she said. "It's beautiful."

"Jeremiah just texted you," he said. "I may have peeked at your phone."

"It's about dinner this afternoon," she said. "I told him we'd bring drinks, and he probably sent his request."

"Simmons root beer. He's obsessed with the stuff."

Evelyn flipped open the card and read Rhett's message. *I'm falling more and more in love with you every day.*

She leaned back into his body. "I like the grape soda from Simmons."

"No way," he said with a chuckle.

"Yeah." She turned into him. "Why? You don't?"

"It tastes like cough syrup."

"Yeah," she said with a smile. "It's good." Evelyn stepped out of his arms and over to the other side of the desk. She shuffled her papers until she found the one she wanted, scanning it for the information she hoped would be there.

It was. Jed Thacker did have a black belt in karate, and he'd be perfect for Maddie. Perfect. If she could get him off that orchard and looking her way. Thankfully, it had been Jeremiah who'd given Evelyn the idea she'd needed for that.

Last week at dinner, which the Fosters and the Walkers now ate together every Sunday, Liam had casually mentioned that he would be attending the next summer dance. Jeremiah had nearly upended the table as he'd said, "Another one? I'm going to be the only one left in the pact."

Callie had just laughed at him, and she'd told Liam she thought it was a good idea that he get off the ranch and meet someone. Evelyn had watched Liam glow under her praise and then wilt at the mention of meeting someone else.

She'd been toying with the idea of approaching Liam privately. Telling him she could help him without revealing too much of what she did.

"Rhett," she said, looking up from her paper. "Have you noticed...anything about Liam?"

"Noticed anything?"

"And my sister," she added.

He looked utterly perplexed. "Which one?"

"Well, that answers that question," she said with a smile. "Never mind."

"No, I want to mind," he said, a sparkle entering those dark eyes. "What's going on?"

"Nothing," she said innocently.

"Evvy," he said, coming around the desk too. "You tell me right now." He grabbed onto her waist, which made her squeal, and rubbed his unshaven face against her cheek. "I have ways to make you tell me."

She laughed, trying to get away from him in a half-hearted way. In the end, she fisted her hand in his collar and pulled him close to her for a kiss. That got him to stop, but he didn't get distracted for long.

"So what about Liam?" he asked, swaying with her.

"He has a huge crush on Callie," Evelyn said. "I'm thinking they'd be a cute couple."

"Oh-ho," Rhett said. "I see where this is going. You want to set them up."

"No," Evelyn said quickly, because she'd agreed she wouldn't set up his brothers. "I was just asking you if you'd noticed it, and you obviously have."

"Well, both Tripp and Jeremiah told me."

"You haven't noticed?"

"I mean, when I think back on things, sure. I can see it."

Evelyn considered him. "And Liam's not interested in dating?" Her sister hadn't been out with anyone in so long, and Evelyn wondered if Callie would even go out with one of the brothers next door.

She seemed to have a special friendship with Jeremiah, not Liam, and that probably burned him up inside.

"Let's spy on them at dinner this afternoon," she said, picking up his necktie. "Now, come on. We're going to be late for church, and you don't even have your tie on."

19

Later that day, Rhett carried a case of Simmons root beer as he and Evelyn entered the homestead at Seven Sons Ranch. He was already scanning for Liam, and they hadn't even made it into the kitchen yet.

"We're here," he called, but no one came running. A pinch of annoyance started in his gut, but he ignored it and went into the kitchen to find it empty. Not a single pot or pan sat on the stove, and he put the soda on the counter and turned to Evelyn.

"Where are they?"

"I don't know," she said. "We're even late." She pulled out her phone and swiped, tapped, and lifted it to her ear. A few seconds later, she said, "Cal, where are you guys?" She walked toward the back door. "Oh, it's over there? No, no one told us. Okay, we're coming."

She turned back to him and hung up. "It's at my place today." She wore a sour look, and Rhett knew how she felt.

"Your place?" he didn't mean to ask, but the words just slipped out.

Evelyn stilled, her eyes flitting around the kitchen before landing on his. "I mean...." She obviously didn't know how to finish, and Rhett regretted saying anything.

Of course she'd still think of the Shining Star Ranch as her place. She'd lived there for a long time, and she hadn't wanted to leave. They'd been living in the cute two-story house in town for two weeks, and he had started to think of it as theirs more than his.

Don't be stupid, he told himself. Evelyn had never been as much into *them* and *theirs* as he had, though they'd been sharing a room and a bed for two weeks now. For her, this marriage was still very...something. New, maybe.

No matter what, for him this marriage wasn't make-believe anymore. He hoped and prayed with everything in him that it wasn't for her either.

Maybe you should ask her, he thought, and he took a step toward her to do just that.

"Come on," she said. "We'll be late."

"We're already late," he said, but she was already moving back toward the front door. He looked at the soda, his frustration growing with every breath. "Evvy, do you think you could stay married to me?"

He whispered the words, because he didn't want her to hear them quite yet. The last month of his life since they'd gotten married had been amazing. Sure, there had been some potholes. Some high jumps to make. Some concessions and some sacrifices. But that was what people did when they loved each other.

What he'd written on her anniversary card was true. He was falling more and more in love with her every day, and his heart shriveled at the idea that she wasn't falling for him too. With a sigh, he picked up the case of soda and followed her.

Down the road at the Shining Star, both Liam's and Jeremiah's trucks sat in the driveway, and the scent of something being grilled filled the air. Evelyn went inside the farmhouse first this time, and when Rhett joined her, he got the wall of chatter, activity, and laughter he'd expected at his place.

His place.

No. His brothers' place.

His place was on Quail Creek Road now. He'd bought the house, and he wanted to live there, even if he and Evelyn broke up. *Please don't let her break up with me*, he prayed, thinking he really didn't want to be there that afternoon.

He wanted to be back out at Three Rivers, horseback riding through the countryside so he'd have plenty of privacy to ask Evelyn about how she felt about him. Confess how he felt about her.

"Sorry, we're late," Evelyn said to everyone, and Rhett heaved the soda onto the already full countertop. Callie immediately opened the case, and he didn't even have time to search for Liam before his brother appeared at Callie's side carrying the tub of ice.

She handed him bottle after bottle, and together they got them in the ice and ready to take outside. "Thank you, Liam," she said with a smile, but Rhett couldn't tell if that was normal or not.

"My pleasure." His brother bustled off with the soda, and Rhett had no idea what Evelyn was talking about. She'd picked up a stack of napkins and followed Liam, and Rhett didn't know what to do to help.

"Put me to work, Callie," he said.

"Oh, you do enough work around here," she said, that smile still in place. So she couldn't like Liam the way Evelyn thought she did. Could she? "Go sit down on the deck. Miah's almost done with the burgers."

Rhett did as she said, thinking that if there was someone Callie liked, it was Jeremiah. No one else got a pet name, and no one else called him Miah. In fact, Rhett was surprised he let Callie call him that.

The moment he got outside, Jeremiah turned from the grill. "Burgers are done. Is Rhett here yet?"

"Right here." He raised his hand as if his brother wouldn't be able to see him in such a large crowd. A disgruntled look crossed Jeremiah's face, but he said nothing. Callie crowded behind Rhett, and he stepped out of the way so she could get out of the house.

"All right," she said. "Let's say grace." She gazed around

at everyone as the chatter stopped and hats were removed. "Liam, will you?"

"Sure," he said easily, closing his eyes. He said a nice prayer about having friends and family together, thanking the Lord for the Sabbath day and the opportunity to go to church, and then he said, "And help the mare here at Shining Star get well. Amen."

Everyone chorused amen, and Rhett stood back as the jostle started for plates and drinks and food. Liam didn't go immediately into the fray either, but he watched Callie step over and start talking to Evelyn.

In fact, his brother's eyes tracked Callie until she started toward the line, and then Liam darted over there too.

Rhett smiled at his brother and nodded toward them. Evelyn had been watching too, and she laced her arm through his. "Are you going to eat? You're usually leading the charge."

"What do you think he's saying to her?" he asked.

"Callie, you're the most beautiful woman I've ever met," Evelyn said in a low voice, a terrible impersonation of Rhett's brother.

He chuckled at the same time Callie tipped her head back and laughed at something Liam had said.

"So not that," Evelyn said, giggling too.

"He's practically glowing," Rhett said. "I wonder what he said and how long it took him to come up with it."

Evelyn sighed and leaned her head against his bicep. In moments like these, time froze, and it was just him and her.

The family fray around them didn't exist, and he could feel her love for him way down deep in his soul.

She hadn't said anything about the card. Hadn't returned the gesture. Rhett honestly didn't mind, but it would be nice to know where her mind was at the moment.

"He's working hard," Evelyn said. "Gotta give him credit for that."

"Do you give me credit for the breakfasts?" Rhett asked. Though he and Evelyn saw each other every day now, he missed their Tuesday morning ritual.

She looked at him, surprise written all over her face. "The breakfasts? Those were…."

"I mean, maybe I didn't know what I was doing," Rhett said. "But I knew I'd get to see you every Tuesday, and I never missed a single one."

Evelyn stretched up to kiss him, a quick press of her lips against his. Then she gave him a look that said so much more than that and got in line to get a hamburger. He went with her, because yes, he was hungry, and it was time to eat.

———

THE SUMMER PASSED, and Liam went to every dance. He'd been out with a few women, and by the time the Texas heat became downright brutal, he had himself a girlfriend.

And she wasn't Callie Foster.

Rhett had worked a few small cases over the summer, and he'd managed to get the Shining Star

Ranch more operational than it had been in a long time. He'd doubled their hay harvest that year, and every fence and every outbuilding was as strong as an ox. Their animals were in peak condition, and Rhett mostly worked maintenance on the ranch now, Simone and Callie at his side.

Evelyn's matchmaking business had boomed now that she'd landed herself a cowboy husband, and Rhett hadn't said another word to her about the validity of their marriage. She never brought up anything difficult to talk about, and Rhett wondered how long they'd stay married. She'd never put a date on when they might be able to break up and she'd be able to keep her clients.

He sure liked living with her. Liked waking up next to her and brushing his teeth in the same bathroom she used. He liked holding her hand, and kissing her, and making love to her. She seemed to like all of those things too.

At the end of every month, he bought another rose to signal their time together, and this arrangement he was currently setting out on her desk had a vase with four roses in it. Four months of wedded bliss.

A question had been revolving in his mind for a month now, and he'd never said it out loud. Could they simply stay married?

Okay, two questions: Did she love him?

Because he was pretty sure he was in love with her. He'd been in love before, but that had been so...not right. This love with Evelyn, it definitely felt more like what Rhett imagined love to be. Comfortable. Filled with excitement and sparks. Peaceful.

At the same time, he couldn't even bring himself to talk to her about these important things. Things between them were humming along now, and Rhett didn't want to ruin it, though a sense of quiet unrest lived within him.

His phone rang, and he startled away from the flowers to answer the call from his mother. "Ma," he said loudly as he left Evelyn's office and went out onto the front porch. He'd installed a swing here and he sat down, ready for a long conversation with his mother.

"Rhett," she said, her Texan drawl still heavy though she'd lived in Grand Cayman for a couple of years now. "Daddy and I want all the boys to come to the island for Christmas."

"Christmas?" It was the middle of September.

"You boys will need time to plan," she said simply. "We have plenty of room here, and December is a lovely time to visit."

Right now, Rhett didn't want to go anywhere warm or tropical. "Mom, I'm married now," he reminded her. "Evelyn can come, right?" He didn't think for a minute that she'd want to leave Callie and Simone for the holidays. She'd never spent much time outside of Texas at all, and Rhett couldn't see her journeying to Grand Cayman for an island Christmas.

It had taken him two months to get her to take him to formally meet her father and grandmother. Two *months,* though she'd told them she had married the cowboy down the lane. That was how her father thought of him. He'd even said it when they'd finally met.

Oh, he's the cowboy down the lane.

"Right," Evelyn had said.

Sure, he'd seen her father at church, but they didn't talk much, and her dad acted like she and Rhett weren't married. Didn't live together.

Rhett pushed the memories away, just like he'd been doing for months. Anything troubling or unpleasant, and he pushed it away.

His mother was talking, but Rhett wasn't listening, so he hadn't heard what she'd said about Evelyn coming for Christmas. Maybe Rhett would go by himself. Maybe Evelyn wouldn't need him anymore by Christmas.

Her business was doing so well right now, as it seemed every woman in Three Rivers wanted a boyfriend for the fall festivities and the upcoming holidays. Now that the summer dances were over, the opportunities to meet someone had dried up like the landscape around them.

A car pulled in their driveway, and a lithe, blonde woman got out. She carried a folder, and Rhett recognized it. She was here to meet with Evelyn, and he stood up, so she'd see him there. "Mom," he said while she was in the middle of a sentence. "I'm sorry, but I have to go."

"I'm calling Jeremiah," she said.

"Okay," Rhett said, hanging up in the next moment. He still hadn't quite fixed everything between him and his next oldest brother, but he was working on it. Jeremiah could be unusually stubborn, and he'd been giving Liam the silent treatment too. He was taking this pact super-seriously, though it was already shattered.

"Hello," he said, extending his hand to the woman. "You must be here for my wife." He grinned at her, watching the blonde soften in front of him.

"Yes," she said. "I'm Ivory Osburn."

"Nice to meet you." He pumped her hand and turned to the front door. "C'mon in. I'll go see where Evvy is." He opened the door and almost ran into her. "Oh, she's right here."

"Hey," she said, a measure of panic on her face. "Did you meet Ivory?"

"I sure did." He swept a kiss across her cheek. "I'll leave you ladies to it. I have work to do on a new case."

"Okay." Evelyn gestured for Ivory to follow her into the office. "In here, Ivory."

"Does he have any brothers?" Ivory asked in a stage whisper, and Rhett almost turned back to her to say that yes, he did indeed have *six* brothers, none of whom were currently married. But that Evelyn would not be setting anyone up with them, as per her agreement with him.

After all, Evelyn was very good at making agreements and sticking to them. His heart hurt, and he knew he was being unfair. He hadn't talked to her about anything, choosing to keep the peace instead of getting the answers he wanted.

Maybe it was time to raise a little ruckus. Rhett just wasn't sure if he was capable of doing that. As the older brother, he always kept the peace. Micah, the youngest, blew things up. Jeremiah made snap judgements it took him months to get over.

The twins smiled and laughed and whispered to each other behind closed doors. Wyatt stood to the side and then cleaned up the aftermath. And Skyler stayed away from most family things, because he'd rather dirty his hands under the hood of a car than with family drama.

In that moment, Rhett realized Skyler had probably figured things out the most, but he couldn't go back in time and refuse his best friend when she asked him to marry her as a favor.

Even if he wanted to.

20

Evelyn stared down the hall toward the kitchen after Ivory had left, the numbness she'd been fighting during the meeting finally spreading down her legs. She stumbled into the office and sat down, in complete disbelief.

Ivory Osburn wanted to get to know Tripp Walker, and Evelyn hadn't said no. But she couldn't do it. She'd told Rhett she wouldn't set up his brothers, even if Ivory was perfect for Tripp.

"Even if," she whispered to herself. She'd come up with something for why she couldn't do it. Text Ivory when the power woman wasn't sitting right across from her, those piercing blue eyes almost demanding to know why Tripp Walker was off the table.

So Evelyn had said she'd put a couple of scenarios together, and she'd gotten Ivory out of there. She typically loved her work. Loved the research that went into looking up the cowboys her clients liked. Loved putting facts on paper and seeing if a match could be made. Loved the behind-the-scenes work it took to set up the perfect meet-cute.

She looked up from the pile of folders on her desk when she heard the back door open and then close. How long had she been sitting there? No matter what, Rhett's footsteps came closer, and she couldn't cover up Ivory's folder before he appeared in the doorway.

He'd never paid too close of attention to her business or her clients, always excusing himself as he had earlier if he was home at all.

Home.

Her breath hitched in her throat. When had she started thinking of this house as her home?

"Hey," he said, clearing his throat. "I wanted to talk to you about something. Do you have a minute?" He scanned the desk, but there was no way he'd be able to read her notes from his position across the room, stuck in the doorway. His nerves preceded him into the room, and her own crackled to life.

"Sure," she said. "What's going on?"

He pressed his palms together as he crossed the room and sat in the chair her clients did. "It's about us, Evvy. I'm wondering what your plans are."

"My plans?"

"Yeah." He nodded, those dark eyes burning so bright. "Look, I'll be honest. I was falling for you before we got married. Now that we're living together and doing married things, I'm ninety-nine-percent sure I'm in love with you." He blinked a couple of times as the air left Evelyn's lungs.

"And I need to know where you are. How you feel about me. If this is real, or I've been kidding myself all this time." He closed his mouth and just looked at her.

She had no idea what to say. "I...."

He tilted his head the slightest bit, as if he could catch more sound that way. But her voice had gone on vacation. Completely.

"So you don't know," he said.

"I mean, I guess I do."

"Then what?" he asked. "Tell me what you're thinking."

"I don't know what I'm thinking," she said. "I'm...a little surprised right now. I need a minute."

"You need a minute."

She really didn't like how he was repeating everything she said.

"For what?" he asked. "To decide how to tell me you love me too? Or how to tell me I've fallen for a woman who doesn't love me back?"

"I...don't know?"

Rhett brought one hand to his forehead and wiped it down his face. "Okay, well, it probably shouldn't be this hard to decide. So I guess that's the answer." He stood up. "I'm going to Seven Sons for a while. I won't be back for dinner."

She watched him walk toward the door, and everything

in her told her not to let him leave like this. "Wait," she said. She'd asked him to stay all those months ago, on their first night here in this house. Could she do it again?

If you do, you better mean it, she thought, and she couldn't get herself to ask him. "Don't not come home for dinner."

"Why not? Jeremiah will feed me."

She wrapped her arms around him, glad when he let her and when he put his arms around her. "Because I'm making that pulled pork you love."

"Did you hear what I said?" He looked down at her, and Evelyn saw the desperation there. "I love you, Evvy."

If she hadn't put the words together in that order a moment ago, she couldn't deny them now. "I heard you," she said. "I think I just need more...time to get there."

"So you're not in love with me." He stepped back.

"Rhett," she said. "Does it have to be now or never?"

"I think it's unfair to kiss me and sleep with me and be my wife if it's not now," he said. "We've been playing this game for four months. I'm tired."

"It's not a game," she said, surprised by the power behind those words.

"It isn't?"

"No," she said. "Not at all." She sighed and looked down at his boots. Those sexy cowboy boots he wore everywhere. "I just...I guess I've put off thinking about it, because it scares me."

"I'm terrified," he whispered.

She lifted her eyes to his and asked, "Can I just have some more time to think about it?"

He looked at her for a long, long moment. "I've been waiting for a while," he said. "I suppose a little bit longer won't kill me."

She twined her fingers through his. "Thanks, Rhett."

He swept his lips across her forehead, the touch there and gone in the same breath. Then he turned and went out the front door, never looking back. She moved to the window in her office and watched him back out of their driveway.

Their driveway.

Didn't that thought alone mean she loved him?

She had no idea. But she had a feeling she better figure things out fast.

———

A WEEK PASSED, and she still didn't know. No amount of time on her knees had provided her with the answer.

Two weeks passed, and she could tell Rhett wanted to bring the topic back to life. But he didn't. She prayed harder. Booked three more clients desperate for cowboy candy on their arms that holiday season.

The weather started to cool slightly, and people brought out their Halloween decorations. She'd managed to move Ivory from Tripp to another cowboy who ran the seed and feed, and she felt like she was dodging bullets left and right.

Halfway through October, she had a rare day where she didn't have any client work. Rhett had already gone to the ranch, as he'd been sleeping upstairs since their talk almost a month ago.

She missed him in the bed beside her. Missed his presence and the way he breathed while he was asleep more powerfully than she thought possible. He still showered in the master bath, and she stood at the counter and picked up his toothbrush.

Looking up and into her own eyes in the mirror, she asked, "Are you in love with him?"

She wanted to say yes. But the truth was, the answer was still *I don't know*.

She got behind the wheel of her car and drove out to the Shining Star Ranch. She came out quite often, but as she rumbled along the dirt road, it didn't feel like coming home.

Confused and not wanting to talk to Callie about any of this, she went around the farmhouse to the huge shed on the north side, where Simone would be hard at work on her refurbishing business.

She took a deep breath as she got out of her car, and by the time she walked inside the building, she felt a little bit better. Sure enough, her younger sister sat at a table in the middle of the room, swiping yellow paint onto an old sewing machine.

"Hey," she said without looking up. "What are you doing here?"

"Oh, I had a day off," Evelyn said, scanning the shed. "Wow, Simone. You have a ton of stuff here."

"Yeah, I've been working for months to have the inventory I need for the Fall Festival," she said. "I only have a few more pieces." *Swish, swish* went her brush, and then she looked up, a smile on her face.

Her sister was beautiful, and a tidal wave of love for her rushed Evelyn. See? She knew she loved her sister. Why couldn't the Lord help her figure out how she felt about Rhett?

"You must've been to every garage sale this summer," she said, her words only slightly choked. If Simone noticed, she didn't say anything.

She beamed around at the trinkets and treasures in the shed. "Yeah," she said. "A lot of them, actually."

She had couches she'd obviously reupholstered, dining sets she's repainted, old collectibles she'd framed. And antique or vintage items like the sewing machine she worked on. Simone went to the yard sales and bought items for as cheap as she could. Then she spent hours with her creative vision and her talent, turning the trash into a treasure.

Her contributions to the family income were sporadic, though her Fall Festival money usually provided the sisters with Christmas every year.

A flash of sadness hit Evelyn. Would she be spending Christmas at the ranch this year? With her father and grandmother and sisters?

It didn't feel like she would be.

"Hey."

Evelyn blinked, realizing Simone now stood right in front of her, a concerned look on her face. "I've been talking to you. Are you okay? You look kind of pale."

"I'm okay," Evelyn said through a dry throat. She needed a drink so badly, and she needed to figure out what to do with her life. It felt like everything had shattered the day Rhett had sat down in her office and wanted to know if she loved him.

Why couldn't things between them have just stayed simple?

"How are things with Rhett?" Simone asked, something she literally never did.

"Fine," Evelyn said, her guard up now. "Why?"

"He's here a lot." Simone shrugged. "That's all."

"He's here a lot?"

"He works here," Simone said, peering at Evelyn. "You didn't know?"

"Oh, of course, yeah." She laughed, but it came out too fast and too high-pitched. She quieted and glanced around, ready to leave but not wanting to run out. She didn't want to be alone either, and she realized she had nowhere else to go. She'd always been able to go to her sisters, find comfort in the farmhouse, regain her center when things went badly.

But now, everything in her life was spinning wildly out of control.

"I just came to say hi," she said, turning away from Simone. "I'll go see if I can find Callie."

She'd taken two steps when Simone said, "Are you okay?"

Evelyn wanted to say yes, but she didn't know how. "I don't know," she said.

"What's wrong?" Simone stepped around her again. "Evvy, are you crying?"

"How can I know if I'm in love with Rhett?"

Simone sucked in a breath and held it. "What do you mean? You married Rhett. Of course you love him."

"It was fake," she whispered. "We only got married so my business wouldn't die."

Simone's eyes widened, and she searched Evelyn's face for something. What, she didn't know. Tears spilled out of her eyes. *I asked You*, she thought. *I begged You to make sure I wouldn't hurt him.*

"Didn't Callie ever tell you?" she asked Simone.

"No. I thought you and Rhett were perfect for each other. I mean, you *are* perfect for each other. Aren't you?"

Before Evelyn could answer, the door behind Simone opened again, this time with a crash as it hit the wall behind it. Rhett stormed into the building. "There you are. You set up Tripp and Ivory Osburn?"

"No, I—"

"We had an agreement, Evelyn," he said icily, talking right over her. "My brothers were off-limits in your little game of matchmaker."

21

Tripp Walker studied the crude drawing his twin had done for him. "You need to get to town more," he muttered to himself. Having Liam draw him a map of how to get to the post office was embarrassing.

But Three Rivers had just built a new building for the post office, and it didn't come up on the map app he normally used to navigate his way around this new part of Texas where he'd moved.

So it had been a year. A little over a year. Months past the twelve-month-mark. Didn't mean he knew every in and out of the town's transportation systems. And Liam had gone to all the summer dances by himself, as Tripp didn't want Jeremiah to go nuclear every weekend. Having Rhett married and out of the house had been hard enough on him.

"Dang, I think that was Flower Avenue," he said to

himself. Maybe if he got a dog he wouldn't be caught talking to himself all the time.

He'd considered going to the dances too. Sure, he carried a slight fracture on his heart, but nothing like the deep, bleeding gashes on Jeremiah's.

At the same time, he enjoyed his simple life at Seven Sons. He liked spending time with his brothers, and his part-time animation work kept him connected to the real world. He liked saddling a horse and riding in the early mornings, and he didn't mind offering his hands when there was more work than Jeremiah and the four ranch hands they employed could do.

He fit on the ranch, and he liked it there.

Could there be more though? he wondered. He wasn't sure, and he'd done nothing to find out. Again, keeping Jeremiah somewhat sane was at the top of Tripp's to-do list, so Liam had been the one to shower and douse himself in more cologne than humanly necessary to go dancing on Saturday nights.

And Liam needed that.

He and Tripp shared an office in the homestead, and while Liam certainly didn't share everything, he'd said enough for Tripp to know he liked Callie Foster.

Liked her, like he wanted to take her to dinner and dance with her and kiss her good-night.

He just didn't know how to ask.

The twins had been close their entire lives, and Tripp

had said, "You just ask. Do you want to go to town with me and get dinner?"

"What if she says no? We see them every week. All the time. I feel like she's over here or we're over there every night." Liam had shaken his head. "No, I don't want to make things awkward."

"But what if she says yes?" Tripp had asked.

"And then what?"

"I don't know," Tripp said. The relationship between Liam and Callie certainly seemed complicated, especially when Liam then brought up Jeremiah.

Tripp didn't know how to help any of them. He just did the best he could to be present, and listen, and offer what advice sounded right to him.

But really, he should not be giving advice to anyone. He did need to drop off this signed contract, as the new company he was working with wanted an actual printed, signed in ink, copy.

He'd sent them a PDF as well, and he could afford the twenty-minute drive and the cost of a postage stamp to mail it.

If he could find the dang post office.

He flipped around and made a right onto Flower Avenue, seeing immediately why it was named as such. Blossoms poured out of the boxes along the street. They hung from huge baskets on the street lamps. They brightened everything as far as he could see.

And he could see some amazing restaurants he wanted to try.

"Text Liam," he said, and his truck repeated it to him. "We should go to lunch once a week. Try every restaurant in town."

"Send to Liam?" the truck asked.

"Yes, send," Tripp said, and his vehicle confirmed that the text had been sent.

"Text from Liam," it said a moment later. "Read or wait?"

"Read," Tripp said, still not seeing the post office.

"I'm in," the electronic voice said.

"Call Liam," Tripp said, his truck confirming the command and dialing a moment later.

"Hey, bro," Liam said. "I'm in for lunch anytime. You know that."

"Yeah," Tripp said. "Okay, so I'm on Flower Avenue, and there is no post office here. A bistro, a doughnut shop, a pita place...." Tripp was hungry already, and everything sounded good.

"Yeah, it's down around the corner," Liam said. "You turn right onto Waverly Lane, and then there's a Chinese place, and then the new post office."

"Okay," Tripp said, scanning the right side of the street. "Oh, I think I see Waverly Lane."

"Want to meet at the Chinese place? I heard it's good."

"Oh, you want to lunch today?" Tripp asked. "Right now?"

"Well, yeah," Liam said. "I'm done with my work for the week, and the Fosters are coming over here."

Tripp had noticed that Liam rarely said Callie's name anymore. It was always "the sisters" or "the Fosters."

Tripp turned right, the Chinese restaurant coming into view down the road a bit. "China Isle," he said. "And praise the Lord. There's the post office."

Liam laughed and said, "I'm leaving now. See you in fifteen."

"Okay." Tripp let his brother hang up, and then he turned into the parking lot for the post office.

At least he thought it was the parking lot for the post office. But it wasn't, and unless he wanted to go over the cement barriers, he was parking in the Chinese restaurant parking lot.

Which was fine. He could walk a few extra feet, and Liam would be there for lunch soon.

He pulled in and put the truck in park, collected his large manila envelope, and started for the post office entrance. The driveway for it was way down on the other end, and Tripp was starting to hate everything about this new location.

He made it inside, quickly learning that lunchtime was a very busy time at the post office. He supposed any time was a busy time at the post office, and he could practically hear his momma calling an errand to mail something like descending into the depths where only monsters lived.

He smiled just thinking about his mother, and he sure

wished she was around to go to lunch with. His parents loved their life in Grand Cayman, and Tripp was happy for them.

He loved his new life in Three Rivers too, even if he only got off the ranch for church and the occasional trip to the post office.

With his package finally mailed, he realized he'd be right on time to meet Liam for lunch. He'd taken two steps down the sidewalk outside the post office when he heard an "Oof," and a terrible crashing sound as a box hit the cement.

In front of him, ready-to-be-mailed packages spilled out of the box, and a petite blonde woman knelt, trying to scoop them all back in.

"Let me help you," he said, freezing when she turned her face to him.

Okay, wow. She was beautiful, and frazzled, and Tripp wondered what it would feel like to run his fingers through her hair.

He had no idea where the traitorous thoughts had come from, but Jeremiah could never know.

The woman smiled and tucked her own hair. "It's fine." Her voice unlocked whatever had frozen inside him, and he bent down and picked up one package. Then another.

"I can help," he said. "I'm Tripp Walker."

"Ivory Osburn," she said. "I know about you." She wore a small smile on that pretty face, and Tripp couldn't help grinning back.

"Oh, boy," he said. "What have you heard? I'm sure none of it is true."

The wattage of her smile increased, and Tripp had been out of the dating scene for a while—and his time in it hadn't been great—but he could see something...flirty in her eyes.

"You live out at Seven Sons. Have lots of money. Never come to town." She shrugged as he put her packages back in the box and reached for more. "You know, that kind of thing."

"Hm," he said, because he literally could put a check next to all of those things. "Liam comes to town all the time."

"So I've heard," she said.

"So you didn't go to the summer dances either?" He picked up the last couple of packages and put them in her box, immediately reaching for it.

He was now late for lunch with Liam, but he so did not care.

Ivory shook her head, that coy smile still stuck in place. "I didn't. They're...for a younger crowd, if you know what I mean."

"Liam found lots of dates," Tripp said. He didn't want to argue with her; he was just trying to figure out what she meant by that. She couldn't be older than him, that was for sure.

In fact, she had to be very close to his age. His heart pounded, and he remembered his own advice to Liam.

You just ask, hey, do you want to go to town with me and get dinner?

But somehow, when he wanted his voice to say the words, it wouldn't. It felt like his voice box had taken a vacation, actually.

Ivory had started to laugh as they went into the post office together. "Yes, well, I'm sure you would've too. New cowboy blood in town. Handsome."

He felt every inch of his body as her gaze slid down to his cowboy boots and back to his face. "You know."

He wasn't sure he did, but he did know he wanted to go out with her. He rejoined the monster line he'd just gotten out of, but Ivory said, "Sugar, I don't have to wait in that line. They're pre-stamped and ready to go."

Sugar.

Tripp followed her over to the chute where packages went and held the box while she put hers in. "What are they?" he finally thought to ask.

"Necklaces and bracelets," she said, a hint of pride in her voice. "I'm a jewelry-maker."

"Oh, that's great," he said, noting the plethora of jewelry she wore. He'd been so distracted by those pretty eyes, he hadn't noticed.

"Anyway, thanks." She took the empty box from him, and Tripp sensed his opportunity slipping right away from him.

"Hey," he said, catching up to her. "Are you...uh, do you

have any...would you maybe want to go to dinner with me sometime?"

Wow, that was painful. His throat even hurt.

Ivory paused and looked up at him. "Tripp Walker."

"Yes, ma'am."

She smiled, and Tripp felt like he'd been hooked up to a live wire. "Yeah, I'd like to go to dinner with you sometime."

22

Ivory Osburn could not believe her luck. Only a month ago, Evelyn Foster—who was married to Tripp's brother —had told her she couldn't set her up with Tripp. No amount of texting and begging had changed Evelyn's mind, and Ivory had been forced to move on to someone else.

And now she'd gotten her own date with the man, thank you very much.

She'd done nothing with the man Evelyn had wanted to match her with, thankfully. Otherwise, she might not have as open of a calendar as she currently did.

Oliver ran through her mind, but she didn't need to tell Tripp about her son immediately. In a town like Three Rivers, she'd never even thought she'd be able to keep him a secret.

But the Walker cowboys didn't come to town very often,

and Ivory thanked the Lord above that she'd procrastinated mailing out her orders until that day.

"Great," Tripp said, his handsome smile revealing those straight, white teeth. "Maybe I could get your number? I can call you later, when I'm in front of my calendar."

"Sure," she said, surprised at her own boldness for saying yes. And she never gave her number out to men. Ivory wasn't even sure she wanted to be dating again, after the fiasco that had been her first marriage.

You're not marrying him, she told herself, and she recited her number, waiting as he tapped it into his phone and then repeated it to her.

She nodded and smiled, knowing she needed to make her escape before he realized what a mistake he'd made. But he didn't seem to think so, and he walked her all the way to her car and even opened the door for her.

Maybe she just needed a proper Texas cowboy like Tripp Walker.

"I'll talk to you real soon," he promised, and Ivory smiled again as she closed her door and started her car. She backed out, realizing too late that she'd gone the wrong direction to get out.

Humiliation filled her, as Tripp still stood on the side-walk, watching her. She laughed at herself though she felt her face heating beyond a normal temperature, and pulled back into the spot.

She managed to get her car going toward the only exit, wondering why they couldn't have just connected this parking lot to the one for the Chinese restaurant next door.

When she'd put Tripp in her rear-view mirror completely, she squealed, gripping the wheel a little harder than normal.

A date. She'd just gotten a date with one of the Walker brothers. Some women around town had said such a feat was impossible.

She wondered what they'd say when they learned it was her on Tripp's arm.

As the excitement faded—after all, there wasn't a real date on the calendar yet—the panic set in.

"You'll have to tell him things," she said as she eased to a stop at a red light. He'd have to know about Oliver—he'd have to meet her son. She'd have to tell him about her divorce, and why, and where Daniel lived now, and why she hadn't dated in the three years since the divorce had been finalized.

In truth, she wasn't even sure she was ready to be dating now.

But she wanted to be, so when Tripp called, she'd answer, and she'd do her best to open a door she thought she'd closed a long time ago.

She stood in front of the pickles in the grocery store when her phone buzzed and rang in her purse. She turned away, unable to find the sandwich stackers Oliver loved so much, and fished her phone out.

She didn't recognize the number, but it had a Texas area

code. The call hadn't come to her business number, and her heart started fishtailing in her chest.

"Hello?" she asked, hoping for a deep, sexy cowboy voice on the other end of the line.

Restaurant noise came through the line, and then a chuckle.

"Hello?" she asked again.

"Hello? Can you hear me?" The cowboy tone she wanted to hear made her whole body flush.

"Yeah, I can hear you."

"It's Tripp Walker, ma'am."

"Okay, first, as much as I love the Texas manners, you don't need to call me *ma'am*. Is that how you address your dates?"

That delicious chuckle tickled her eardrums again, and he said, "No...no."

She giggled right there in the grocery store, and if she wasn't careful she'd have rumors circulating about her by evening. "I didn't think so."

"I was wondering when you might be available for dinner."

"It sounds like you're at dinner right now."

"Just lunch with my brother."

Ivory wasn't sure what to make of that. Tripp obviously wasn't going to keep their date a secret. "Do you make it a habit to eat out twice in one day?"

Her mind raced through what she had to do that

evening. Thursday, Thursday... Oliver had nothing on his schedule, but she would need a babysitter.

"What about tomorrow?" Tripp asked.

"Tomorrow's Friday," she said.

"That's right."

Date night. Ivory swallowed. "Tomorrow would be great."

"Perfect," he practically purred. "If you give me your address, I'll come pick you up."

Ivory thought fast, images of her ratty house moving through her mind. And if Kate couldn't take Oliver, Ivory would have to get a babysitter to be with him at the house....

"I'll meet you somewhere," she said. "Name the place and time."

"Oh, you're going to have to do that," he said. "I like food, so anywhere is fine, and honestly, I haven't been to town that much, and I don't even know the good places."

Ivory giggled, unsure of why this man had transported her right back to adolescence, with all the hormones and shy smiles.

"If you like steak, Musgrave's is the best in town."

"Would I be Texan if I didn't like steak?"

"I don't see how." Ivory sure did like flirting with him, the banter back and forth easy and fun.

"Seven?" he asked.

"Seven would be great," she said.

"See you then." He didn't waste words, and the call

ended. Ivory turned around like the shelves of pickles cared about the call that had just transpired.

As if by fate, though, the exact pickles her son wanted caught her eye, and she reached for the jar and put it in her cart.

Then she called Kate. "Please, please, please tell me you can babysit Oliver tomorrow night."

"Uh...well, I have to know why first."

"Which means yes."

"It means Don is out of town, and I was planning a quiet night with pizza, ice cream, and animated movies."

Ivory laughed. "Long week?"

"One of the longest. It's a good thing these kids go to school, or one of them might have been hurt this week." She laughed and then sighed. "Obviously, I wouldn't hurt my kids."

"I know how you feel," Ivory said. Unfortunately, her husband wasn't away on a business trip. Daniel had left to "follow his dreams" one day, and apparently that didn't include his wife of five years, or the son they shared.

Pain lanced through her, and Ivory wondered if it would ever truly be gone.

"I hate complaining to you," Kate said. "I'm so sorry."

Ivory cleared her throat. "No apology needed."

"What do you have going on tomorrow night?" Kate asked. "I mean, I got three please's."

"A date." Ivory hit the T hard on the last word.

"Ooh, a date? Ivory, start talking and don't stop." They

laughed together, and Ivory couldn't remember the last time she felt this happy.

She'd sold forty-seven necklaces that week too, and she hadn't needed Evelyn's help to get the gorgeous Tripp Walker to notice her.

"I ran into Tripp Walker, and he asked me out." Ivory couldn't contain the squeal, though she did regret it when a woman down at the end of the aisle turned her way. "Shoot. Misty McBride heard that."

"Misty McBride? Where are you?"

"The grocery store," Ivory said. "Gotta go. Can I bring Ollie over about six-thirty?"

"Make it six to tell me everything, and you have a deal."

"See you tomorrow at six."

———

The following evening, Ivory chose her sweater with great care. It had definitely started cooling off, and the Fall Festival would be very soon.

Oliver loved the festival, and Ivory could admit that she liked it too. Three Rivers did a great job with having a variety of activities for kids, teens, and adults. Oliver would love the pumpkin carving and Ivory enjoyed the pumpkin spice latte she sipped while she watched him.

She thought of Tripp, wondering if maybe they could go to the country music concert next Friday night that was traditionally part of the Fall Festival.

"Slow down," she coached herself as she put a layer of mascara on her lashes. "Oliver," she called. "Are you putting on your shoes?"

He didn't answer, which meant he wasn't. Ivory finished primping and hurried into the hallway. "Oliver." She found him in his room, shoeless, a truck in one hand. "Put your shoes on, baby. We're goin' down to Kate's. She has pizza and ice cream and movies."

Her son cheered, and Ivory could see so much of the man she'd once loved in him. Maybe she still loved Daniel. She wasn't sure. She hadn't asked him to leave, and the first year he'd been gone had been one of the loneliest of her life.

Thankfully, Oliver didn't give her a problem with putting on his shoes. She walked him down the street and knocked on Kate's door, a little sweatier than she'd have liked.

"Hey, Ollie," Kate said after opening the door. "Dexter's in the playroom. Pizza will be here soon."

Oliver ran into the house, and Ivory stepped in slower. "Do I look okay?"

"Girl, you look like a million bucks." Kate reached out and touched Ivory's blouse, which was a dark blue that she thought brought out her eyes really well. "Tripp Walker is going to get knocked out the moment he lays eyes on you."

Ivory ducked her head and smiled.

"Now, tell me everything."

She accepted a cup of coffee from Kate, though she certainly didn't need the extra stimulant. She recounted the story from the sidewalk in front of the post office, her excitement growing by the moment.

All too soon, it was time for her to go. "Call me later," Kate said, giving her a quick hug. "I can keep Oliver overnight if that's easier for you."

Ivory nodded, but she wasn't going to make Kate keep her son overnight. She wasn't going to invite Tripp back to her place, and she wasn't going home with him. In fact, she was worried the date would be so bad, she'd be back in an hour, still hungry and wondering where she'd gone wrong.

She walked home, got behind the wheel of her car, and drove to Musgrave's. The steakhouse was busy, and fear gripped her right at the top of her lungs. What had she been thinking?

Text him and cancel. The thought appeared in her mind, teasing her and enticing her.

Before she could even move to get her phone out of her purse, someone knocked on the window.

She yelped, a moment passing before she realized Tripp stood there, that sexy smile on his face.

She exhaled as relief streamed through her, a smile adorning her face too. She got out of the car. "Is there ever going to be an encounter with you where I'm *not* embarrassed?"

He tipped his head back and laughed, and Ivory decided right then that this night was already better than any she'd had in the past three years.

23

Rhett did not know he could feel so angry, especially toward Evelyn. But pure fire raged through his bloodstream at the moment, and Evelyn's lack of explanation wasn't helping.

He wasn't going to let her slide again. Not for one more minute.

"Well?" he asked.

"I didn't," she said. "She wanted me to, but I didn't."

"Well, he's going out with her." He forced his fingers to uncurl. "Explain that."

"Maybe you should ask Tripp about that," she said.

"I did," he said. "He said they met at the post office. Evvy. The *post office*? That has *you* written all over it."

"Why? I—"

"Tripp didn't even know where the post office was. Liam had to draw him a map on a paper towel. And he happens to run into one of your clients? Who dropped her boxes all over the parking lot?" He gave a high-pitched, girly laugh that clearly wasn't happy. "I can't *believe* you'd do this."

He turned and stormed out of the shed, leaving himself to wonder when he'd learned how to say her nickname with so much malice. Half of him wanted her to follow him, and the other half wanted her to stay inside the safety of Simone's shed.

Because he felt as unpredictable as that blasted tornado that had brought him face-to-face with the beautiful Evelyn Foster all those months ago.

He didn't like his life much anymore. He hated sleeping upstairs while his wife curled up in the bed they'd shared many times. He hated sneaking out of the house before seeing her so he wouldn't ask her the questions he needed answered. He hated that he wasn't strong enough to confront her and make her talk to him.

But he'd learned one thing over the last month—patience. And more patience. He'd asked God to help him so many times, and every time, his answer had been *Wait a little longer.*

So he'd been waiting. He wasn't sure how much longer he could hang on. He swung up into the truck and slammed the door behind him. He had the truck started and in gear when Evelyn came running up to his window.

"Rhett," she said, her chest heaving. "Wait."

Wait.

He couldn't. Not anymore.

"I'm done waiting for you, Evelyn," he said. "Please move away from my truck." He stared straight out of the windshield, his frustration with her too great for him to focus on her.

"No," she said. "I didn't set up Tripp and Ivory." She paused, as if he'd just accept her at her word and get out of the truck. Maybe kiss her and everything would be magically better.

"You can be mad at me about other stuff, if you want to," she said. "But not this. I did *not* do this."

She sounded firm and genuine. Maybe she hadn't set up Tripp and Ivory, but he couldn't ask Tripp, and he didn't have Ivory's number.

He just needed Evelyn to leave him alone. Sadness filled him, as he'd never wanted to be with anyone but Evelyn. "I need some space to think." His fingers curled and uncurled around the wheel. "Please, can you back up?"

She sighed and stepped back. "You're coming home tonight, aren't you?"

He looked right at her, her light brown eyes filled with tears. Had she been praying as much as he had? Had the Lord been telling her anything at all?

"I don't know, Evelyn," he said. "I guess we'll see tonight." He eased away from her when he wanted to spray dirt and gravel behind his wheels as he got as far from her as he could get, as quickly as he could.

He looked in the rear-view mirror when he reached the

turn, and Evelyn still stood in the path in front of the shed where her sister worked. Rhett had been inside several times, as he often brought lunch out to Simone for Callie.

All of the Foster sisters were extremely talented, and they would do anything to make ends meet. He'd seen that first-hand, and he admired all of them on many levels.

"Evelyn," he said, shaking his head angrily. Could Ivory had spilled her boxes on her own? At the exact moment Tripp happened to be there? "No. That was Evelyn." It had to be. There was *no way* that meeting had been by chance.

He reached the lane that led down to Seven Sons. Looking that direction, he didn't feel like that was where he should be. No, the white house on Quail Creek Road was his home now. His heart hurt, but it continued to beat steadily.

He wanted to go home.

So he did.

―――――

Evelyn didn't return to the house until almost dark, and by then Rhett was already upstairs in his bedroom. He'd ordered dinner, hoping she'd be the one who came home to eat it, but she hadn't.

He heard the door close, and he looked up from his case notes. He usually spread them across the kitchen table and asked Evelyn for her help in seeing things he couldn't while they ate or talked or sipped their morning coffee.

Since he'd marched into her office a month ago, things between them had been strained. But they'd been civil. They'd spoken, and he'd even kissed her lots of times. But he'd moved out of the bedroom, and the one up here on the second floor felt so small.

She did not come upstairs to talk to him, and Rhett laid there, his mind churning.

"Lord?" he asked, and this time, there was no prompting to wait. He got up and headed for the door. He could be brave again.

Sixty seconds, he told himself. In sixty seconds, he'd be downstairs, and the conversation would be started. After that, he'd deal with what he had to. Say what needed to be said.

He made his footsteps loud on the stairs, so she'd know he was coming. She sat at the kitchen counter, the salad he'd ordered for her in front of her. "Thank you," she said, looking at him.

He nodded, because he hadn't expected to be met with appreciation. "You didn't come home for dinner."

She gave half a shrug. "I don't know what to do, Rhett."

"I do," he said. "This clearly isn't working. You don't love me, and I don't trust you." As he spoke, he realized how true the words were. "I'll take care of everything."

He wanted her to contradict him, but she asked, "Everything?" instead.

"The divorce," he said. "It's not free to file."

"Have you researched this already?"

"No," he said. "I just—I just know it's not free." How he knew, he wasn't sure. But he knew people didn't just waltz into City Hall and get divorced the way they did to get married. They probably should have to do more to tie the knot, as it had been entirely too easy for Rhett and Evelyn to get to this point.

His heart hurt. No, it ached. Why couldn't she love him the way he loved her? They'd been such great friends.

Evelyn pushed her salad away. "I'll go get packed."

"So that's it?" he asked, watching her stand up.

"This is your house," she said. A tear slipped down her face. She swiped at it angrily, and everything inside Rhett collapsed. How could he be mad at her when she was crying?

"This is *our* house," he said, his voice creaking a little bit on the words. "When I thought about where I wanted to go this afternoon after talking to you, it was here. To this house. This place feels like home to me now, and it has nothing to do with the house." Rhett's throat burned, but he forged forward. "It has to do with *you*. And even if I'm sleeping up in that stupid bedroom by myself, I'm okay, because you're still here."

Evelyn cried openly now, and Rhett had no idea what to do. He'd said everything. Made it through the hard sixty seconds.

"What do you want from me?" she finally asked.

"I want to know you love me as fiercely as I love you," he said. "I know I said I didn't need a big wedding or anything fancy. And I don't. I've never thought I'd ever fall in love, but I have."

He drew in a big breath, searching for the last bit of courage he had. "And I deserve to be loved by my wife. So if you don't love me, just say it."

She had to say something, one way or the other. Rhett couldn't wait any longer, and he'd once again spoken true. He did deserve to be loved. She had to learn to talk to him about hard things.

Maybe he had to learn more patience. He didn't know. Standing there in the kitchen he loved, facing off with his wife who still wouldn't say anything, Rhett felt like he'd gotten his answer.

"You don't have to move out," he said. "The house is yours. Stay here. I know you love those big trees out back." He did too, but he turned away before he said something he'd regret.

"Rhett," she said after him, but he didn't stop, and he didn't go back.

He also couldn't stay in the house with her there, so he swiped his keys from the dresser upstairs and headed right back down to his truck.

His brothers would ask tons of questions, and Rhett would have to admit to all of them that his marriage had been a farce. Fake. Make-believe.

His breath hitched in his chest as he backed out of the driveway and headed down the road. But this was the right thing to do. He couldn't keep living in a loveless marriage.

He'd told Evelyn that months ago, when they'd talked about a platonic relationship. That wasn't what he wanted with her, and he didn't believe she wanted that either.

Instead of turning right to go back to the ranch road, he went left and continued into town. He pulled up to the first hotel he came to, hoping they'd have a room on this lonely Wednesday night.

————

THE NEXT DAY, he filed for divorce, signing his name to the petition that would open the case with a heavy heart. Evelyn would get notified legally, so he didn't pull out his phone and text her. He wanted to hear her voice. Wanted to taste her lips as he kissed her goodnight. Wanted to have her be his soft place to fall when he had a bad day or just needed someone who loved him no matter what.

"She doesn't love you at all," he told himself as he left the courthouse. He wasn't sure where to go or what to do that day. He'd always been welcome at the Shining Star, but he was sure that would change, if it hadn't already.

His phone chimed several times at once, almost like he hadn't had service inside the courthouse.

He'd gotten a couple of messages from Tripp, one from Callie, and three from Evelyn.

He tapped on Tripp's first. News is out, bro. Callie just told Liam that your marriage to Evelyn was fake.

True or not true?

Rhett's heart seized, and then started hammering. Of course, Tripp had asked if it was true or not. He was a good brother, and Rhett didn't want to lie to him.

True, he typed out and sent before navigating to the next text.

Callie had asked if he'd be at the ranch that day. Do I need to be? he sent back to her. I think I'd like the day off. I'm going through some stuff right now.

No sooner had he sent the message did his phone ring, and Callie's name sat on the screen. Feeling guilty, he didn't answer it. If she was telling Liam things about Rhett's marriage, then Evelyn had to be at the ranch.

Which meant Rhett would not be going there today.

He opened Evelyn's messages next. The first said, *You stayed at a hotel?*

The second: *You might as well have announced to the whole town that we're splitting up.*

The third: *Where are you right now? Why won't my calls go through?*

With every word he read, his anger grew. By the end, it foamed into great peaks of fury. She didn't care about him. Not even a little bit. No *How are you? Are you okay? Where did you go last night?*

No, those texts showed that all Evelyn cared about—all she'd *ever* cared about—was her matchmaking business.

I filed for divorce, he sent back to her, intending to get behind the wheel of his truck and just drive until he ran out of gas. Throw his phone out the window and buy a new one when he could.

Before he could even make it to his truck, his phone rang.

It was Tripp.

Sighing, Rhett swiped on the call and waited for his brother to start demanding what in the world Rhett had been thinking.

Instead, Tripp said, "Come back to the ranch, Rhett. We're here for you."

24

Evelyn sat in her car outside the church, the October wind trying to get through the glass. One day had passed since her argument with Rhett. Well, it really hadn't been an argument. He'd done most of the talking, and he'd said really awesome things.

"Why can't I be like him?" she asked the building. Of course, it didn't answer. No one had been talking to Evelyn much. Callie was angry with her for letting Rhett walk out. Simone didn't know what to say. Rhett had never looked so hurt nor sounded so angry via texting as he had the last twenty-four hours.

"And he has every right to be upset with you," she told herself. What she didn't know how to do was fix what she'd broken.

She hadn't lost any clients—yet. But she'd heard from Nancy Stopper that Rhett had stayed at the Roadside Inn last night, which meant all the gossip mills in town were running. After all, Nancy Stopper didn't care about Evelyn. She may have been her mother's friend decades ago, and sure, she brought a fruitcake every Christmas.

But she didn't know Evelyn. She worked at the flower shop in town, and she'd heard about Rhett from her daughter.

Evelyn could practically trace the conversation back through Tracie to probably Bethany, who'd probably heard it from Heather, who worked at the gas station across the street from the hotel. She'd probably gotten the news from Dylan, who worked the lobby at the hotel overnight and always stopped across the street for doughnuts before she went home.

The fact that Evelyn knew all of that only added fuel to the simmering fire in her stomach.

Just because she hadn't lost clients yet didn't mean she wouldn't. Once they all heard the truth, she'd be ruined. She wouldn't be able to get a single woman in Three Rivers to hire her.

She hadn't been able to stay in the house last night either, but she'd had enough sense to stay out of the public eye. Her old room at the Shining Star felt claustrophobic, and she'd ended up on the couch for most of the night.

She'd slept little, and when her eyes closed, they burned. She kept them closed anyway, relishing the tears that came to soothe them. A horseback ride would help her feel better, but it wouldn't cure this pain spiraling inside her.

Nothing would.

Rhett might.

The thought suddenly sprang to her mind, and she had no idea where it had come from. But in the past, when she'd had a problem she couldn't solve, Rhett had been there. Asking her questions. Making her think. Feeding her buttermilk pancakes and freshly squeezed orange juice.

Though it was Thursday, she really wanted to eat breakfast with him and find out where things had gone so wrong between them.

Her phone buzzed, and she looked numbly down at it. *He's not coming to the ranch today.* Callie had been a huge support to her for years, always playing the motherly role since they'd lost their mom so early in life.

And she suddenly knew where she needed to go. She put the car in gear and eased away from the church building, intending to drive just down the road and around the corner to the cemetery. It bordered the church along the back fence, but the entrance was down here. And after she visited her mother, she needed to go see her dad.

She hadn't brought a jacket, and the weather didn't truly require one. Not really, though the wind seemed to be whipping around town today. Evelyn walked down the rows of headstones, searching for a reason to be happy.

She came to her mother's grave, and she knelt down to trace her fingers along the letters in the granite. She'd only been five years old when her mother had died. Evelyn only knew her through pictures and stories, but somehow, she felt a very real connection to her mother.

She didn't talk to her. Burden her with the things she'd done wrong. Ask for help. She simply stayed with her mom until it felt like she was alone again. That moment came quickly this time, and Evelyn bowed her head and said a silent prayer of gratitude that she'd gotten any time with her mother at all.

"Now," she said, standing up and facing the rest of the graveyard. "Tell me what to do to make things right with Rhett Walker."

No immediate answer came, but she knew where she needed to go next.

When she arrived at her grandmother's home, her father's truck wasn't there. She glanced up and down the street, as if a neighbor had borrowed it or something. Thursday morning...she didn't think he or her grandmother had anything that took them out of the house on Thursday mornings.

Gran's hair appointments were always on Tuesdays. She went to the senior citizens center on Mondays and Wednesdays, and on Fridays, she and Evelyn's father did their grocery shopping.

A born and bred cowboy, her father liked doing things by a schedule. She'd never known him to be step out of the house one minute earlier or later than six-thirty in the morning, and his internal alarm was forever set an hour before that.

That hour gave him time to make his girls breakfast, pack their lunches, and sip his coffee. Gran drove the girls to school, and in the winter months, he sometimes didn't see them before he went to work on the ranch.

Evelyn used to love to set her alarm for six-twenty-five just so she could see him for five minutes. As she made her way up the front sidewalk to the door, she really hoped they were home. Maybe her dad's truck was in the shop or something.

She couldn't stand to be by herself anymore, and she had nowhere else to go. "Dad?" she asked as she opened the front door. "Gran?"

They weren't home, and she sighed as she turned around and sat on the top step. Maybe they wouldn't be gone for too much longer, and honestly, it wouldn't matter if they were. She didn't have anything to do today.

She flipped her phone over, realizing she'd missed some messages when she saw the flashing blue light. Simone had texted to ask if Evelyn could help with the Fall Festival set-up tomorrow night.

Of course, she typed in, dread filling her entire body cavity. *I'll be there.*

But the last thing she wanted to do was show her face in town. The Fall Festival was very popular in Three Rivers, as it brought men and women off their ranches and into town. It was part celebration of the harvest, which the farmers and ranchers participated in, and part family fun for Halloween.

It ran for eight straight days, and Simone was hoping to

sell out of everything she'd been working on for months. Evelyn was hoping for that too, and she couldn't refuse her sister her help.

But Evelyn didn't want to be seen around the festival. There would be dozens of women there, setting up their own tables. And they'd have plenty of questions for her. She could hear them all now, and the imagined noise of them made her cringe.

Several minutes later, her father's old truck sputtered into the driveway. For one horrible moment, Evelyn thought he might hit her car, but he managed to park beside it with a foot or two to spare.

She went down the sidewalk again, her heart thrashing against her ribcage. "Hey, bugaboo," he said in his raspy farmer's voice. "What brings you here?"

"Hey, Daddy." She grabbed onto him a moment before the sobs shook her shoulders.

"Oh, hey." He held her tight, and though she was forty years old, she really needed the love of her father right now. "What's wrong? Hey, it's okay. Whatever it is, we'll fix it."

If only that were true. "It's me and Rhett. We split up."

"The cowboy down the lane?"

"He was my husband, Dad," Evelyn said, trying to breathe through her tears. Her husband. In some ways, she'd certainly treated him like her husband. In many others, though, she'd held him at arm's length, never allowing him to truly take part in her life. And by refusing to talk to him and share her troubles with him, she'd kept herself out of his life too.

"I've made some mistakes," she said. "Did you and Mom always get along?"

"No, they did not," Gran said, hobbling around the truck. "I remember this one fight they had. Your mother threw eggs at his truck."

"Oh, Mom," Evelyn's father said, shaking his head. "But she's not wrong. Come on, bug. Come tell us all about it over coffee. We ran out, so we had to go get some more."

"Dad, there's no way you ran out of coffee," she said, following him at a snail's pace down the sidewalk. "You get two containers every week."

"Well, I couldn't find it," he said.

The moment they were in the kitchen, Evelyn started opening cupboards. Most of them were overflowing with dishes or bags of pretzels. Sure enough, in the fourth one she opened, she spied the coffee, right next to the sugar and the flavorings her grandmother had discovered. "Right here, Dad."

"That's empty," he said.

Evelyn opened it, and sure enough, it was empty. "Then why do you still have it?" She threw it in the trash, noticing how full that was too. Looking around, Evelyn quickly became overwhelmed with the state of things inside this house.

"When's the last time you threw *anything* away?"

Neither her father nor her grandmother answered, and

Evelyn started cleaning up the trash. Empty grocery sacks and bread twist ties, empty bottles of water, and old mail. It all went in the garbage, and she emptied it into the big black container by the carport.

The house didn't smell, but the amount of stuff her father and her grandmother owned could make anyone stop and stare. Literally every surface held something, whether it be a knickknack or a picture frame or a stack of books.

Each item held a memory, though, and Evelyn did like that. She picked up a picture of her mother and father, obviously taken on their wedding day. Her mother looked so much like Callie, it was almost freaky. Evelyn had gotten the rounder face, the lighter eyes, more of her father's jaw. Simone was an equal mix of the two of them, and Evelyn could pick out the parts from each parent for each sibling.

"Coffee, bug?" her dad asked, and Evelyn replaced the picture on the side table.

"Yes, please."

"Tell us what happened with Rhett," Gran said. "You two always looked so happy at church."

With a jolt, Evelyn realized she'd spent so much of her time with Rhett pretending. First, she'd pretended not to like him at all. Then she'd pretended they were just friends.

Then, they'd had an entire pretend marriage. And she pretended to be so joyously happy whenever they went out in public together.

It was time to stop hiding and face the truth. Time to stop pretending.

"I'm bad at communicating," she said. "So that's made things hard."

"That would be your dad's fault," Gran said. "He was never good at telling you girls how he felt."

"They know how I feel," her dad shot back at his mother. "But I will take some of the blame for that." He gave Evelyn a kind smile.

"You just need to channel some of me, dear." Gran patted her hand. "There's nothing you've done that you can't undo."

Evelyn thought of the fake I-do. Pretty sure that could be undone, and in fact, Rhett had told her he'd filed for divorce that morning. So Gran was wrong about that.

"Can you go back to not being in love?" she asked. She wasn't even sure she had fallen in love with Rhett, but with the way her misery pulsed around her, she was starting to think she had.

Love was like a thief in the night. It could sneak up on a person when they weren't even awake, making them say and do irrational things. Or, in her case, keep everything bottled up tight.

"Oh, sure," her grandmother said, waving her hand. "That's the easy part." She continued talking, but Evelyn watched her dad shake his head.

He waited until his mother stopped speaking, and then he said, "No, Evelyn. Once you fall in love with someone, there's no going back. You'll always love them, at least on some level. That's why married couples can forgive each other."

"What if I've done something Rhett can't forgive?"

"Apologize," he said. "Make it right."

"Make it right," she echoed, wondering if she could really just say *I'm sorry* and everything would magically be okay.

She didn't think so, and she knew she needed to look inward before she could go to Rhett.

Please help him wait for me a little longer, she prayed. And please help me figure out what's wrong with me so I can make that right first.

Praying was the only recourse she had left, and she figured God had never given up on her yet. He surely wouldn't now.

25

Callie hefted another box out of the back of the bright red pickup truck, her back aching. But Simone couldn't set up her table for the Fall Festival alone, and Callie had always gone to help.

She wished she'd called Liam, because surely the man could schlep boxes and still look like a western wear super-model. She'd managed to become friendlier with the man, though he still showed zero interest in spending time with her outside of his garden or off their respective ranches.

But she sure would like to see him lifting boxes…. Her thoughts went down a road where he wasn't wearing a shirt while he flexed, and embarrassment heated her face.

Banishing all fantasies of the handsome Liam Walker from her mind, Callie managed to get all the boxes in from the truck. She and Evelyn had already carried in all the bigger items—a couple of antique desks, a cabinet that had taken all three of them to maneuver into the festival, and various lamps, end tables, a recliner, and two formal dish cabinets.

Everything was beautifully painted and embellished, and Callie stood back and admired her sister's work.

"Did we bring the sign?" Simone asked, opening a box. "Oh, yes, here it is." She pulled out a long banner. "Evvy, help me with this. Cal, you can start putting the price tags on everything."

Simone looked around, but she wasn't the only one setting up. In fact, today was only for set-up, and everyone had selling space in various arrays of disorganization.

Callie stepped over to a box down on the farthest end of the table, which bore a blue sticker. She knew that meant everything on this table was the same price, and she better make sure she got the right items in the right spot.

She'd helped Simone set up for enough events to have a slight clue about how to position the handprinted coasters or the antique radio Simone had tinkered with for half a day before finding the faulty wire and fixing it.

"This doesn't look like blue-tag stuff," she said, drawing Simone's attention.

"No, that's red," Simone said. "Was that in the blue box?"

"Yes." Callie watched panic roll across her youngest sister's face. "The coasters, maybe. The radio, no."

"If I have to go through this stuff item by item...."

Simone sounded one breath away from exploding, and her face reddened.

She yanked a set of tea towels out of the box. "These are blue." Another item, this one a vase Callie had watched Simone throw on the spinning wheel in her shop. "This is a green item."

A sigh leaked out of her mouth. "Okay, Callie." She put the vase down and stepped back.

"Hey, it's okay," Callie said. "We have all day, and we're all here to help." She wished she could burden her sisters with how badly the ranch was doing, but she hadn't said anything before. Now wasn't the time either.

"So I'll label the tables with the colors," Callie said, reaching for the stickers her sister had already given her. "And you pull items out and tell us what color. We'll put it on the right table."

"Okay," Simone said, blowing out her breath. "Okay." She got to work, and they made short work of the boxes.

"I'll go get some coffee," Evelyn said, exhaling too. "Phew, Simone. You've been working too hard in that shed." She smiled, but it wobbled quite a bit.

Callie glanced at Simone, who'd obviously noted their sister's distress.

"Coffee would be great," Simone said. "And get some lunch too, and then we'll talk about you and Rhett."

"I'm not talking about him," Evvy said.

"Yep," Callie said. "You are. Because that's what we do."

She put her arm around Evelyn. If the tables were turned on her though, Callie would clam right up.

Her phone chimed, and Callie pulled it out of her pocket to distract herself from spilling everything about the ranch and how they'd be in the red within six months if something didn't change. And something drastic.

Rhett had texted, and Callie's stomach dropped to her feet. *Do you know where your sister is?*

She's here with me and Simone, helping to set up the Fall Festival, she typed out. *We're at the downtown park and will be for a while still.*

Thank you, Callie.

Callie felt like crying, and she wasn't even the one married to Rhett. She couldn't imagine how Evelyn was feeling, and she rolled her neck out, trying to ease some of the tension there.

If you could just text me what you need done around the ranch, I'll make sure I do it.

Callie shook her head, wanting to call Rhett and argue with him. She liked his presence on the ranch, and for the first time in her life, Callie was thinking she could use a good cowboy like him. And not just to help around the Shining Star.

But a good man in her life that would do more than help her around the ranch.

She both liked and hated that her mind went right to Liam Walker.

I'll text you, she said to Rhett, because there was no use arguing with him. Evelyn returned several minutes later, a brown bag of food clutched in one hand and a drink carrier with plenty of coffee.

She looked like she'd been crying, and the moment Callie took the coffee and set it on Simone's red table so she could gather Evelyn into a hug, the tears started falling again.

"Honey, it's okay," Callie said, echoing something her mother had said to her years and years and years ago. She missed her momma powerfully in that moment, and sadness moved through her slowly that Evelyn and Simone couldn't remember that their mother used to say such things, that she used to crawl into bed with the girls and sing to them.

"It's not okay," Evelyn said. "I just got served with divorce papers."

Callie had no idea what to say. To say she was surprised was an understatement.

"You sure seem to like him, Evvy," Simone said. "What's keeping you from being with him?"

"Me," Evelyn said. "I am. *I'm* the problem."

Callie identified with this more than she'd like to admit, and she didn't know what to do to help Evelyn—or Rhett. She knew him well enough to know he'd be hurting too.

"Okay." Evelyn stepped back and wiped her face, sniffling. "I'm okay. And I'm starving. Let's eat."

"What did you get?" Simone asked.

"All the carbs," Evelyn said. "Soup and bread bowls. And everything pumpkin at the coffee shop that they had."

"Bless you," Simone said, opening the bag and pulling out a pumpkin muffin with maple frosting on top. "I hope I survive this festival."

"You will," Callie said. "And Evelyn will fix things with Rhett, and everything will go back to normal." She smiled around at her sisters and nodded, as if what she said would certainly come to pass just because she wanted it to.

But she knew that hardly ever happened, and she also knew the next best thing to do was to pray. So she did that.

———

Hours later, Simone's booth was beautiful and labeled properly, and she headed toward the pickup truck she loved so much. The wind gusted, and Callie wished she'd thought to grab a sweatshirt before she'd left the ranch that morning.

She still had chores to do to get her horses and the three goats fed, and she needed to get out to the cattle and make sure they had water.

Behind the wheel, Callie found she didn't want to make the drive alone. Do the chores alone. Pull something frozen out of the freezer and eat it alone.

Feeling slightly crazed and definitely exhausted and overwhelmed, she pulled out her phone and called Liam.

His line rang a couple of times before he said, "Heya, Cal," as if he didn't have a care in the world.

"Liam," she said. Her courage failed her completely, and she stared out the windshield.

"Callie?"

"I'm starving," she said. "And I have a ton of chores to do, and I was wondering if you could come help me get those done and if you'd like to stay for dinner."

She pressed her eyes closed and held her breath. She was much too old to feel this nervous about talking to a man. But the fact remained that she was nervous. So, so nervous.

"Depends," he said, his voice full of a tease.

"On what?"

"On what I can buy you for dinner."

Everything tight inside Callie released. "You choose," she said. "I'm in town and can pick something up."

"Okay, I'm calling for pizza right now, and Slice of Pie is fast. Like, lightning fast."

"I'll head over there now," Callie said.

"I'll go start with the goats."

"You don't—"

"I'll see you in a bit," Liam said over her, ending the call a moment later.

Callie felt lighter than she had in months, and she made the quick drive to the pizza parlor. Liam had ordered three pizzas—"Really?" she wondered aloud as she took the food back to the truck—and she made the drive back to the ranch.

She pulled into the driveway and parked beside Liam's beautiful truck, smiling at it as if she'd be kissing the man before he left there that night.

But that wouldn't happen, and she knew it.

Her stomach growled, and she carried the pizzas up the

front steps and into the house. She'd just set the food on the counter, and she'd just reached for her phone when Liam walked in the back door.

"Hey," he said.

"Liam." Callie dropped her phone and leaned into the countertop. She didn't want to cry in front of him, but the tears were brimming in her eyes, and she wasn't sure she could control them.

He said nothing as he strode toward her and gathered her into his arms. "Hey, it's okay, sweetheart," he said, and Callie melted into his embrace. "What's goin' on?"

"Just glad you're here," she said, sniffling. And she was—so, so glad to not be alone in this huge house, with loads of work to do before she could go to bed.

26

Liam had dreamt of this moment, when he could hold Callie Foster in his arms. Of course, she wasn't crying, and he didn't smell like horses, but the fantasy was almost complete.

She was beautiful, and soft, and she smelled exactly the way he'd imagined she would. Like oranges and roses and everything sweet Liam liked.

Several moments later, she stepped back. "Sorry," she said quietly, tucking her hair behind her ear. "Three pizzas, Liam? How many people did you think you were feeding?" She gave him a look that made him think maybe she liked him.

Could she like him?

Liam's heart filled with hope, and the only thing keeping him from floating right off the face of the planet was a woman named Lori Jennings.

His girlfriend.

He'd text her and break things off right now if he had any chance of being with Callie. Any chance. Any at all.

"Well, I'm *famished*," he said, coming back to the moment. "And Simone will be at the Fall Festival all week, and you'll need something to eat."

"I can't eat the same thing for every meal."

"Then I'll come help you finish it," he said. "And I can bring you something different any time you want."

Too obvious, he told himself, pulling back on his thoughts and emotions.

"And if you need help around the ranch—"

"I don't," Callie said. "Rhett is already helping, and I—"

"You need help here, Callie," he said, knowing he was stepping over the line. It was an invisible one, but he somehow knew right where it was. He and Callie had become better friends since Rhett had married Evelyn.

"And you have a job," she said, flipping open the pizza box. "As soon as Rhett comes back, I'll be fine."

"Okay," Liam said, closing the door on the argument. He didn't want to fight with her. He didn't want to put himself in her life where she didn't want him.

He picked up a piece of the wild mushroom pizza and put it on one of the plates she'd gotten out. "I got the horses fed and watered. Goats too. I can go out to the pastures with you after we eat."

"Thank you, Liam." She opened another box, and this one was the Margherita pizza he loved.

"Oh, that one's going to be my breakfast," he said, putting a lighter note in his voice that would make things between them less awkward.

"What's this last one?" she asked.

"Your favorite," he said, which was also probably too obvious.

She glanced at him, and he nodded toward it. "Go on. You know you want to find out."

"It better have meat on it, cowboy," she said. "Because neither of these do, and that's just wrong."

Liam chuckled as she opened the last box, which was an all-meat pizza with pan crust. Callie's face lit up, and she turned back to Liam.

She threw herself into his arms again and said, "Thank you, Liam."

"Anytime, sweetheart," he said, wondering if she knew he wanted her to be his real sweetheart when he said that. But he'd been calling her—and everyone in Three Rivers—that since the day he arrived. So she probably hadn't read anything into it.

"How does Simone's booth look?" he asked, and Callie started talking.

Every so often, he'd ask her something else. "How many cattle do you have?"

Or "What do you want for lunch tomorrow?" Or "If you could get a pet, what would it be?"

Callie talked, and Callie laughed, and Liam enjoyed every last second of his hours with her. They did get the cattle fed, and he'd ignored every text from his brothers, though they'd agreed to a game night to keep Rhett occupied and hopefully smiling.

When he finally made the half-mile drive from the Shining Star back to Seven Sons, he knew he'd have to explain to everyone why he'd disappeared for the evening. He hadn't even told Tripp before grabbing his keys and running out of the homestead.

He sat in the dark cab of his truck and texted Lori, because he couldn't keep seeing her when he had feelings for Callie. He'd been hoping someone in town, someone at one of the summer dances, would make his heart thump the way she did.

Then maybe he could stop looking next-door and start living a more normal life.

But he didn't like Lori half as much as he liked Callie, and it wasn't fair to her to keep going out with her when he wasn't very interested.

Okay, Lori said. That was all.

Liam's heart flopped, though he was glad he hadn't hurt Lori. That wasn't his goal.

The front door opened, and Tripp came out onto the porch. "Hey," he yelled, and Liam got out of the truck. "What are you doing out here?" He came down the front steps. "Where have you been? Jeremiah is losing his mind."

"I'm fine," Liam said. "Why does Jeremiah care? I'm a grown man."

"And Rhett may or may not have tracked your phone."

Tripp grinned at Liam. "We knew you were next-door. How's Callie?"

"Wipe that stupid smile off your face," Liam said, walking past his twin. "Nothing happened."

"Right," Tripp said, falling into step beside Liam.

"No, really," Liam said. "But I did break up with Lori."

"Of course," Tripp said.

Liam paused at the bottom of the steps. "Look, I didn't tell everyone when Ivory broke up with you, and I'd appreciate some discretion here."

Tripp nodded, his eyes turning serious. "Yeah, sure, bro. But maybe you should answer your texts and calls if you want that."

"Just...nothing happened, and I wouldn't lie to you."

"Okay," Tripp said, not a hint of sarcasm in his voice. "We couldn't even sweeten up Jeremiah, because no one has the skills with sugar that you do, and we couldn't get in touch with you."

"I shouldn't have ignored my phone," Liam said. "I'll own that." He climbed the steps. "Is it too late to make caramel corn?"

"Not for me," Tripp said. "But Jeremiah has already gone to bed."

"Great. So he can stew over my absence all night?"

"Go get him up then," he said.

"You go put the bacon on and babysit it while I go talk to him."

"Bacon caramel corn? This night just got so much

better." Tripp practically danced into the house, and Liam chuckled as he followed him.

Rhett sat in the living room, and Liam went straight to him. "Hey," he said, accepting a hug from his oldest brother as he rose to his feet.

"How's Callie?"

"She's overwhelmed, honestly," Liam said. "You work that ranch. How much time does she have?"

"Truthfully?" Rhett sighed as he sat back down. "Not long. Eight months. A year."

Liam exhaled loudly. "Sorry I wasn't here tonight. I had to choose, and she seemed like she needed me more than you." Liam looked at his brother. "But you don't look great either."

"I'm not great," Rhett said. "But get this. I explained everything to Jeremiah, and he said it sounded like I'd done the right thing." He smiled, and it was as joyful as Liam had ever seen.

"Wow." He laughed, filling the house with sound. Jeremiah appeared at the end of the hall, a stormy look on his face.

Liam leapt to his feet. "Hey, Tripp is starting the bacon for the bacon and caramel corn."

"I can smell it," Jeremiah said. "How's Callie?"

"She's okay," Liam said. "You would know. She talks to you."

"She does," Jeremiah said. "But tonight, she called you."

"And I chose to go."

"You shouldn't ignore your phone," Jeremiah said. "No one knew where you were. We live out in the country."

"I'm sorry," Liam said. "It won't happen again." He turned back to Rhett. "And I heard Rhett told the whole story."

"He did."

"Don't you feel stupid for being such a jerk?" Liam asked, a laugh exploding out of his mouth a moment later.

"Yeah, yeah," Jeremiah said. "I already apologized."

"He did," Rhett said, chuckling. "We're good."

"And I'm making Jeremiah's favorite treat," Liam said. "So it's a good night all around." He looked at the brothers he'd come to this ranch with, and a sense of gratitude overcame him.

"I love you guys," he said.

"Love you too," Rhett said, and Tripp yelled it from the kitchen. Liam looked at Jeremiah, where a smile twitched against his lips.

"I love you, which is why I almost called the cops." Jeremiah nodded toward the kitchen. "I want that with extra caramel."

"Deal," Liam said. "Now." He took a big breath. "What did we decide to do about Rhett's situation?"

"*Rhett* has no situation," Rhett said. "He's going to eat some of this delicious popcorn and go to bed."

"Nothing from Evelyn?" Liam looked between Rhett and Jeremiah. "I just don't get it. You guys have always been so perfect for each other."

Of course, Liam thought he and Callie were perfect for each other too.

"He doesn't want to hear that," Jeremiah said. "And I don't blame him." He nudged Liam toward the kitchen. "Go on now."

"All right, all right." Liam glanced around the room. "So, let's talk about Christmas. I know we're going to Grand Cayman, but I still want to decorate here. Who else is in?"

"Me," Tripp said, and Jeremiah just shook his head.

"Rhett?" Liam asked.

"I'm up in the air," he said. "And I haven't even told Momma I'm coming to Grand Cayman."

"Are you?" Tripp asked.

"I don't know," he said, and Liam could practically hear the wheels in his brother's head turning. If he had any chance of spending the holidays with Evelyn, he'd choose that over the tropical vacation to Grand Cayman to see their parents.

Liam would do the same for Callie, and he had no idea if that made him pathetic or romantic. So he just went into the kitchen and put a bag of popcorn in the microwave.

27

A week passed, and then two. Evelyn didn't contest the divorce, and Rhett only went back to the house on Quail Creek Road after he'd texted Callie to find out where Evelyn was. She'd been helping Simone set up tables at the Fall Festival, and he'd run to their house to pack his essentials.

Everything else he left in the house. He didn't need more couches or a bed at Seven Sons. Just his clothes. Somewhere to stay without tension and awkwardness.

His brothers had welcomed him with open arms, and he'd confessed everything to them about the marriage. In the end, it had shockingly been Jeremiah who'd said, "Wow, Rhett. It sounds like you did the right thing."

"Yeah," Liam had agreed. "Don't you feel stupid now for being such a jerk?"

"Yeah, actually." Jeremiah had given Rhett a big hug and then cleared his throat. "I'm sorry, Rhett."

And those words had fixed things between him and his brother. He'd typed them out a dozen times for Evelyn, but he couldn't get himself to send the message. He knew she was back on her family's ranch too, and he was dying to know how things were going for her.

Had her clients all bailed on her? What would she and her sisters do without her income?

He'd visited the idea of giving them a bunch of money, but he knew he'd be doing it just to ease his conscience. Callie wouldn't take it anyway. She might be willing to let him work for her for free, but she wasn't going to take his money outright.

He'd never committed to his mother about going to Grand Cayman for the holidays, and she was hounding him daily now. He finally relented and said, *Yes, Mom. I'll be there.*

With Evelyn?

Evelyn and I broke up. He stared at those words for a long time before sending them, hurrying to add, *I don't want to talk about it. I'm fine.*

His mother didn't call, but she did send message after message until Rhett had to silence his phone and leave it face-down on the desk so he wouldn't go insane.

Fall finally arrived in Three Rivers, and Rhett found himself starting a new routine. He'd been through a fresh start half a dozen times since coming to this new town and Seven Sons Ranch.

When he'd first come, he'd started each day with damage assessment, and he spent the day working through task after task. He had so much to do, he sometimes forgot to eat. His brothers had arrived, and with the extra muscles and manpower, they'd gotten their ranch back to operational within a decent amount of time.

His routine had shifted then, as each of the brothers settled into their role on the ranch. Jeremiah shouldered the bulk of ranch management, dealing with their permanent hired help and day-to-day operations on the ranch. Tripp and Liam did chores around the ranch, but they both still worked in the tech industry part-time.

Rhett had taken to making sure everything around the property was in good repair and putting up new gates and decorations. He'd helped the Foster sisters next door the most. He'd had his breakfasts with Evelyn. He was basically the public relations director for the Walker family.

Then he'd married Evelyn, and everything in his life had changed. A sigh came from his mouth as he made his new morning drive into town for his breakfast and coffee. This new routine got him up and out of the homestead. Away from Tripp's glances and Jeremiah's whisperings with Liam.

He wasn't satisfied with replacing seeing Evelyn in their kitchen with breakfast at the pancake house, but honestly, he didn't have anything else.

"Morning, Sandy," he said when it was his turn at the

hostess booth. She owned the pancake house, but she still worked right out front with the customers.

"Rhett." She smiled. "Back again?"

"It's my new thing," he said, following her to a booth in the corner. He'd specifically requested somewhere he could stay out of the way and stay as long as he wanted. The pancake house seemed busy no matter what day of the week it was, which was fine by Rhett. But he wanted to nurse his coffee and maybe order another pastry while he psyched himself up to go back to the ranch.

He was still working at the Shining Star, and he liked to go over later in the day. That way, he had less of a chance of running into any of the Foster sisters. Callie had been kind, and she texted him the things she wanted him to look at or work on each week. He texted her back when he finished.

He didn't go into the farmhouse for lunch anymore, and he hadn't seen Simone in days and days.

"Well, I know a lot of women have started making it their thing too." Sandy smiled as she handed him the menu he didn't need.

"What?"

She leaned down as she poured his coffee, the delicious steam rising up to meet his nose. "Come on, Rhett. You Walker men are like the lottery. No one quite knows how to win you, but everyone wants to try." She looked right and left while Rhett tried to figure out what was going on. "Since you started coming in every morning, I'm serving at least a dozen more women too."

She straightened, that smile still stuck in place. "You're good for business. Now, if you could get that Jeremiah off the ranch, you'd be a rockstar." She left then, and Rhett glanced around too.

There were definitely groups of women in the pancake house. His divorce wasn't even final, and he felt sick to his stomach. He wasn't interested in anyone else, and he ducked his head and started doctoring up his coffee with cream and sugar.

A waitress came over, and said, "Same thing, hon?"

"Yes, ma'am." He handed her the menu, and she smiled before walking away.

He stayed as long as he wanted, eating the Western omelet he loved with salsa and a hefty side of bacon. He didn't glance around again, and as he prepared to leave, a text came in from his brother Wyatt.

"He's retiring?" He picked up the phone and swiped to get the full message from his middle brother. Well, technically, Liam was the middle brother, as he was born seven minutes behind Tripp. But as far as brothers went, Wyatt started the younger ones. He'd been riding the rodeo circuit for almost two decades, and his text said he was hanging up his spurs in December.

Wondering if you have room at Seven Sons, the end of his text said.

Of course. Rhett sent the message without checking with anyone else. The brothers all got along decently well, and Wyatt had never caused a problem for anyone. And there was plenty of room at the homestead. *Have you told anyone else?*

Been talking to Jeremiah, Wyatt said. *He said to ask you. It's your ranch.*

Rhett scoffed at his phone. He may have put down the money for the ranch, but it was as much Jeremiah's as his at this point. He probably should talk to the brothers about that, so everyone knew he wasn't the king of Seven Sons. They could make decisions together.

We'd love to have you, Rhett sent. He pulled out his wallet and threw some money on the table before getting up and leaving the pancake house with a tip of his hat to Sandy.

Heard about you and Evelyn, Wyatt said next, and Rhett almost tripped over his own feet. *Sorry about that.*

Rhett paused and looked up into the stormy sky. He was sorry about it too, but he'd said everything he needed to. He'd thrown the ball into Evelyn's court a dozen times. She had to decide what to do with it, and he knew that could take months, if she ever did anything with it at all.

A sense of peace came over him, and he closed his eyes as he tilted his face toward the sky. It began to rain, and he normally didn't like the feel of the raindrops on his skin. But today, he let them wash him clean, and he thanked the Lord for the peace and comfort, even if it only lasted for that moment.

———

"Family meeting," he said later that night. His thumb throbbed from where he'd sliced it on a piece of fencing. It had bled like a stuck pig, and he had gone into the farmhouse to get some help. He wasn't squeamish when it came to blood, but Seven Sons had been too far for him to reasonably go.

Callie had been in the kitchen, and she'd taken one look at him and scampered off to get salve and band-aids. She'd fixed him right up, and it sure had been nice to have a female presence in his life again.

She'd asked about Evelyn too, and Rhett had simply shaken his head. He didn't want to talk about her with anyone, least of all one of her sisters.

"What's this about?" Jeremiah asked, finally sitting down on the couch. He looked exhausted, and Rhett reminded himself to tell Jeremiah what a good job he did around the ranch.

"It's about the ranch," Rhett said. "We all work here—you the most, Jeremiah. And just because I bought it doesn't make it mine."

Tripp looked at Liam and back at Rhett. "Uh, that's exactly what it means."

"Well, I don't want it to be mine." He exhaled, not sure how to explain his feelings to his brothers. It was the same feeling he had about the white house on Quail Creek Road. "This is *our* ranch," he said. "We live here and work it together. Everyone has their part. In fact, I do the least around this ranch."

"Yeah," Liam said. "If we went on how much work someone does, you'd own the Shining Star."

Rhett sucked in a breath, his heart suddenly racing. Something must've shown on his face, because Jeremiah leaned over and smacked Liam's chest. "Shut up, bro." He looked back at Rhett. "So what do you want to do?"

"I don't know. I just don't think Wyatt should have to ask for my permission to come live here after he retires. It's Seven Sons Ranch. It's for all of us." He wanted it to be a safe place for him, for his brothers.

"What happens when one of us gets married for real?" Tripp asked.

"Are you going to do that?" Jeremiah's eyebrows shot sky-high. "You and Ivory? Already?"

"He broke up with Ivory," Liam said.

"Already?" Rhett asked at the same time Tripp said, "Hey, we lasted longer than you and whoever you were with last time. That was so short, I can't even remember her name."

"Lori," Liam said coolly as Jeremiah started laughing.

The family meeting had degraded quickly, but Rhett couldn't help smiling. He sat down on the hearth and listened to his brothers bicker, feeling like maybe he did belong here with them.

"Guys," he finally said, and they quieted down. "Since none of us are even close to being married for real, I think that question can be tabled for now. It's something we can discuss when and if the time comes."

"There's plenty of land here," Tripp said. "Whoever it is can just build another house if that's what he wants."

"Or he can live in the one on Quail Creek Road," Jeremiah said, cocking one eyebrow at Rhett.

"I might live there," Rhett said. "When I feel...." He didn't know how to finish the sentence. Each brother across from him wore a look of sympathy on his face, and Rhett actually appreciated it.

"You'll go back," Jeremiah said. "You love that house, and you and Evelyn will raise your family there."

Rhett shook his head. "Yeah, I don't think so."

"You don't think you'll get back together?" Jeremiah seemed genuinely surprised.

"No," Rhett said. "I don't think so." He took a deep breath and surveyed his brothers again. "Okay, let's talk about Thanksgiving. We've celebrated in the past with the Foster sisters, but I think it's obvious I don't want to do that this year. Thoughts? Ideas? Will they be hurt if we don't invite them?"

"I talked to Callie about it already," Jeremiah said. "They're going into Three Rivers to their grandmother's house."

"So we're in the clear." Relief spread through Rhett at the same time disappointment fluttered in his heart. "You're making a turkey?"

"Sure thing," Jeremiah said.

"We should order those mashed potatoes from Big Ray's," Tripp said. "They're so good."

"And the mac and cheese," Liam said.

"Is mac and cheese a Thanksgiving food?" Jeremiah asked, and the conversation was off the rails again as the brothers argued about what was appropriate to serve for Thanksgiving dinner.

Rhett didn't care. The meeting was over, and he dove into the discussion too, saying, "Maybe I'll get some of that sweet and sour pork I like," to which Jeremiah actually booed.

Evelyn sat in the back row at church, Pastor Daniels behind the mic way down in front of her. The congregation seemed unusually large that day, but she supposed the Christmas season was almost upon them, and a lot of people came to church during the holidays.

Thursday would be Thanksgiving, and it had been six weeks since Rhett had stood in their kitchen, asking her if she loved him or not.

Her chest shook as she breathed in, because she did love Rhett Walker, at least on a base level. He'd been her best friend before she'd ruined everything with her insane proposal.

The hearing for their divorce had been last week, and she hadn't gone. As the filer, he'd had to attend, but she didn't. So she didn't. She couldn't contest the marriage, because if she was going to make things right with Rhett, she'd want to marry him the way she'd been dreaming about since she was a little girl.

With flowers everywhere, and all of their family there, and her father walking her down the aisle.

She'd been spending more and more time with her father and grandmother. It got her out of the farmhouse, which gave Rhett clearance to come work on the ranch the way Callie needed him to.

She had two clients left, but everyone else had either moved on or given up on her. She didn't blame them, and once she was finished with Fiona and Eliza, Evelyn was going to get a regular job.

One where she didn't have to make phone calls to the pancake house or get texts from the butcher as to which cowboy was where. She wouldn't have to make one-sheets and match women to the cowboy they wanted.

She could sell shoes or help people deposit their paychecks or restock the oranges when they got low at the grocery store. Something.

Their ranch had been operating better than ever since Rhett had been working for them, and Simone's sales at the Fall Festival would keep the sisters afloat for several more months. If she'd known improving things around the Shining Star would help, she might have done that instead of her matchmaking.

But she certainly wasn't going to now, not with Rhett's presence everywhere outside the walls of the farmhouse.

You need to talk to him. It wasn't the first time she'd had the thought, and Evelyn knew she needed to follow the prompting. She wasn't really broken. She just didn't like contention, and she certainly didn't like talking about her feelings.

Instead of doing that, she'd kept Rhett at arm's length when he wanted to be closer.

"There's nothing wrong with you that the Lord can't fix."

She looked up at Pastor Daniels's words. "In fact, there's nothing wrong with you at all. God made us all the way we are. Does that mean we can't or shouldn't change? Of course not." He smiled out at the worshippers, and Evelyn felt a keen sense of love for him in that moment. He'd always been good at saying the right things, but this felt like a particular message just for her, straight from the Lord.

"This is the perfect time of year to look inward," he continued. "If you find something you don't like, make a change. Now, some of you will say, 'But Pastor. Change is hard!' And it is. But as someone who's done exactly what I'm telling you to do, it's usually worth it. Changing can help you become the person God wants you to be. The type of person He *intended* you to be."

The type of person He intended you to be.

Evelyn didn't believe that God wanted her to be unhappy, and she'd been absolutely miserable without Rhett.

Go talk to him.

That thought plagued her, and she flipped her phone over on her leg. Could she just text him?

No, came instantly to her mind. He'd been brave enough to come down to the kitchen and talk to her. Look into her eyes while he said the things of his heart.

She'd have to do the same.

Fear trembled through her, and she glanced to her right, where Rhett sat with his brothers. She'd been arriving later and later to church so she could sit somewhere behind him. She didn't want him to see her, so she bolted out the back door as the choir sang the last number, and she'd been driving around town for a while before returning to the ranch. Then she didn't accidentally run into him or his brothers on their way home from church.

Basically, she'd been avoiding him as much physically as she'd been doing emotionally and mentally for months.

The preacher finished his sermon, and the choir got up. That was usually her cue to leave too, but Evelyn stayed in her seat. Her fingers started to shake, and her teeth chattered, though it wasn't cold in the chapel at all. She was just horribly scared of talking to Rhett. Of having a difficult conversation. Of any confrontation at all.

He did it, she told herself again and then again. He'd fought for them. It had been her who'd ruined everything. Who'd been unable to say what needed to be said. Who'd asked him for so much and not provided anything in return.

The song ended, and the closing prayer did too, and still Evelyn sat in the back row. Rhett would walk right past her to leave, and she stood up. She didn't move into the aisle though, and people began to move past her as they went out into the lobby.

The weight of their eyes landed on her, almost crushing the air from her lungs. She held her head high, because in that moment, she realized she didn't care what anyone thought of her—except for two people.

God, and Rhett.

He came into view, and Tripp's eyes met hers. Surprise filled his whole face, and he elbowed Rhett, who had his head ducked. He looked at Tripp, who nodded toward her.

Rhett looked in her direction, his eyes locking onto hers as if they were opposite ends of a magnet.

Fear competed with love as they rose through her, and Evelyn had another Earth-shattering realization.

She was in love with Rhett Walker. Full-blown love.

She wished it could calm the trembling in every muscle in her body or make her voice work, but all that blasted love did was cause tears to prick her eyes.

Rhett paused and let her step into the aisle in front of him, and Evelyn took that as a very good sign. She couldn't breathe inside the church, with all those people, and she made her way to the door, hoping Rhett was still behind her.

She burst into the sunshine, glad the air was a little cooler now that it was almost December. She pulled in a big breath through her nose and turned around. Rhett hung back several steps, and their eyes met again.

Stepping out of the stream of people, she lifted her hand

in a wave and took a couple of steps closer to him. "Hey," she said.

"Evelyn," he said, his voice professional and guarded. Everything about him, from the way he stood with his hands in his jacket pockets to the way he kept his head partially down, screamed of the defenses he'd put between them. That she'd *caused* him to put between them.

"Can we have breakfast on Tuesday?" she asked, hoping with everything in her that he would forgive her, the way her father said married couples did.

"I'm busy this week," Rhett said.

Her heart wailed, but she nodded so he couldn't see how much those four words had hurt her. Maybe it was just too late for them.

"Well, the invitation is open," she said. "Every Tuesday at the house." She shrugged, assuming he'd know which house. He just looked at her, and Evelyn took one last moment to memorize the handsome lines of his face, those deep brown eyes, that strong jaw. Then she turned and walked away.

She couldn't make him come back to her. But she had talked to him, and though her feet wobbled in her heels, she felt like she was walking more confidently than she had in a while.

––––––––

Lunchtime on Tuesday found Evelyn cleaning up the breakfast she'd made for her and Rhett. He had not come, true to his excuse of being too busy. She hadn't been back to the white house on Quail Creek Road in a while either, and she'd missed the most beautiful part of autumn.

Sighing so she wouldn't break down into sobs, she stepped out the sliding glass door and onto the deck, hugging her arms around herself. "I'm sorry," she said to the yard. "I'm sure you were spectacular."

In the distance, a dog barked, and she thought of Penny and how much she missed that silly dog. This country lane was so peaceful and so beautiful, and Evelyn moved over to the outdoor couch where she'd worked several times when she'd lived here.

She didn't mean to begin crying, but the tears tracked down her face anyway. "What else can I do?" she asked the landscape before her.

She'd invited Rhett to breakfast, and he'd once boasted that he'd never missed a single Tuesday breakfast. Maybe he hadn't planned to start a relationship with her through those breakfasts, but he had. He was the only person she wanted to be with, and everything radiated with pain now that she was alone.

Life wasn't easy, and she didn't want to live it alone anymore. She'd always had her sisters, and she did now too. But she also now knew that while sisters were important and amazing, they could not replace the tender touch of a man. They couldn't replicate the way Rhett had looked at her just before kissing her. They didn't possess his strength or laugh with her the way he did.

She wasn't sure if Rhett ever came to this house, but she didn't think he did. It has an unused feeling to it, and she hated that. He'd said she could live in it, and she wanted it to vibrate with life again.

Of course, she didn't have much to offer the house, but as she quieted and her tears subsided, she decided she could at least decorate it for Christmas.

Over the course of the next week, she spent money she didn't really have and several hours browsing the shops and stores in Three Rivers for the perfect holiday decorations. A star for the front door, of course. A tree that would stand in the window in her office, shining its light out to the street and anyone who would pass by.

Stockings over the fireplace—one for her, one for Rhett, one for Penny. She kept everything in the boxes and bags in her car, wanting to have everything ready before she began.

Another Tuesday came, and Evelyn sat in her car in the driveway at the house, waiting for Rhett. She didn't go inside, and she hadn't cooked anything at home. If he showed up, she'd take him to the pancake house and buy him breakfast.

Her heart skipped a beat and it felt like the Lord Himself had flipped on a light switch.

"The pancake house...."

Hadn't she gotten a text about Rhett eating breakfast at the pancake house? Weeks ago, from one of her former clients. Gillian or maybe Trixie. She couldn't remember who, because she hadn't answered the group text. But she'd definitely read that her soon-to-be-ex-husband now ate breakfast every morning at the pancake house. She'd been disgusted to see the women of this town making groups to go on certain days so they could see him, maybe catch his eye.

They really did need her help, and she was sure they'd included her on the text by accident.

It still burned, and she couldn't stomach the thought of Rhett eating breakfast with anyone but her. Ever.

So go eat with him.

She flipped the car into reverse and backed out of the driveway. She didn't want to cause a scene, but she'd spoken to him at church. She could try again.

In fact, she'd keep trying until he forgave her. He loved her, and hadn't her father said a person didn't fall out of love? *Once you fall in love with someone, there's no going back. You'll always love them, at least on some level.*

The parking lot didn't seem terribly full by the time Evelyn pulled into the pancake house. She scanned for Rhett's giant truck, but she didn't see it.

But she was going to see this through, so she marched over to the front door and went inside. Sandy Jorgenson stood at the hostess stand, but her hand stilled in reaching for a menu when she met Evelyn's eyes.

"Evelyn," she said.

"Hey." Evelyn tried to smile, but it felt a little stretched and didn't last long. She scanned the part of the pancake house she could see. "Have you seen Rhett this morning?"

"Of course," Sandy said, blinking rapidly. "He left about twenty minutes ago, muttering to himself."

"Muttering?" Evelyn focused on Sandy again. She was a nice woman, and she'd made all of her dreams come true by marrying a handsome helicopter pilot and buying the pancake house, pretty much simultaneously.

"I have to say, that was a new development. He usually just sits in his booth for a couple of hours, reading on his phone and sipping his coffee." Sandy hooked her thumb over her shoulder. "Do you want to sit in his booth?"

Evelyn's heart bumped harder, and she nodded. "Yes," she said. "I would like that." She had no idea what sitting in a booth in a noisy pancake house would do for her, but she followed Sandy anyway, praying for God to send her an idea for what she could do next to get Rhett back into her life.

Talking to him hadn't worked as well as she'd hoped. What else could she try?

29

R hett swiped on the call from Barry, ready for a new case. "Go for Rhett," he said.

Barry burst out laughing, and Rhett smiled too. He currently stood near a fence on the Shining Star Ranch, watching the horses graze. He loved everything about horses, and he'd been thinking of making the drive out to Three Rivers and Courage Reins and going riding again. Problem was, he couldn't imagine doing that without Evelyn, and he'd stood her up for two Tuesdays in a row now.

For some reason, he couldn't bring himself to just excuse everything she'd done—or hadn't done—because she invited him to breakfast. She hadn't even apologized, and there was so much more that needed to be said before he sat down to a meal with her.

"Maybe you'd get that apology and all the answers you

want if you'd *go*," Tripp had said. He'd been badgering Rhett a lot since Thanksgiving, and Rhett was tired of it.

Barry finally stopped laughing, and he said, "Hey, I'm calling for a weird reason."

"All right," Rhett said. "Shoot."

"One of my co-workers lives on Quail Creek Road, and she noticed a package show up at the white house there. She thinks you bought it?"

"Yeah," Rhett said, trying to think of what he would've ordered that would've come two months later. Nothing. In fact, Rhett didn't order anything and have it mailed to him. Online shopping was more of Liam's or Tripp's specialty.

"She didn't know how to get in touch with you, and I said I'd call. So there's a package on your front porch. Amelia says it's been there for a few days."

"Okay," Rhett said, suddenly glad to have something to do that afternoon. "Thanks, Barry." He hung up and stepped over to the shaggy horse that had come closer during the conversation.

"I have to go, Rider," he said. "But I'll be back." He ran his hand down the horse's neck and smiled. "Maybe Santa's brought me something special for Christmas." He chuckled to himself, because he'd get the same thing he always did. Jeremiah would give him a chocolate orange on Christmas Eve. As Rhett greatly enjoyed the chocolate orange, he didn't mind this tradition.

Liam and Tripp always did twin gifts, and they'd give Rhett something that came in a pair. He'd gotten salt and pepper shakers in the past. His favorite coffee and a mug. A pair of shoes.

Of course, this year, they'd all be in Grand Cayman, so he didn't actually know if they'd all haul presents across the Gulf of Mexico or not. Wyatt would be on the ranch right after Christmas, and he usually had the best gifts. Little things he'd picked up in the cities where he traveled for the rodeo.

One year, Micah, a carpenter by trade, had built them all birdhouses, and Skylar had brought them all vintage bikes he'd used his mechanic skills to fix up.

Rhett felt warmer just thinking about Christmas with his brothers. They'd had so many good years together, and though they bickered and argued from time to time, they were family.

"C'mon, Penny," he said to his dog, and she trotted alongside him, her tongue lolling out, until they got to the truck. She jumped in the back and put her front paws up on the rim, making him smile some more.

As he drove down the highway toward Quail Creek Road, his thoughts turned to Evelyn. She had been his family for a brief time. His fingers clenched as if they had a mind of their own, and he almost missed the turn onto the road where the cute white house stood.

He inched down the road, the tall trees on either side of it almost barren of leaves now. He'd missed seeing them change colors and fall, though he had paid a lawn service to come clean up the aftermath. He wanted to keep the house in livable conditions, because he was seriously thinking about returning to it in the New Year.

Or just as soon as his heart healed. Maybe after the divorce, which was set to go through sometime before Christmas. Evelyn hadn't come to the hearing, not that he'd expected her to. She'd signed the papers, and he told the judge that neither of them wanted anything from the other. They just wanted to go their separate ways.

The judge had said he didn't see why that wouldn't happen as soon as the mandatory sixty-day waiting period ended, but sometimes things took longer, depending on what was on the docket.

He'd get notified either way. Not that he cared. He wasn't looking to start dating again anytime soon. After all, he'd given his heart to Evelyn, and she hadn't given it back yet.

The thought that he should've come out here for breakfast that morning rang through his mind. Had she come? Would the house smell like bacon or sausage, dunking him further into the pool of regret he was already swimming in?

"You're not going inside," he told himself as he turned into the driveway. It certainly didn't look like anyone lived here, and he got out of the truck to collect the package. The box wasn't that big, but it weighed quite a bit. The address label had Evelyn Foster on it, and the words burned his retinas.

She hadn't even changed her name when they'd gotten married. He should've seen all these red flags from the beginning. Planted those in his heart so he wouldn't have fallen for her. He'd done so much wrong in this relationship, but most of all, he missed his best friend. Normally, he'd still have Evelyn to talk to, run things by, solve problems with.

Not anymore.

His eyes caught on the words *Knife of the Month Club*, and the next thing he knew, he was opening her package. Sure, it might be a federal crime to open mail that wasn't his, but he didn't care.

Inside, he found a box with four pocketknives in it, thus the weight, as well as a welcome letter with his name on it. He'd be getting a new box every month, with a new tactical or pocketknife in it.

She'd bought him pocketknives, probably for Christmas. His chest squeezed, and then squeezed tighter. He'd told her one time—exactly one time—how much he loved his pocketknife. How useful it was out on the ranch. How he wished he had a whole collection of them.

She'd giggled in his arms before admitting she loved the Internet more than anything. That had been their conversation that night—one thing they absolutely loved and couldn't live without. He'd said pocketknives. She'd said the Internet.

Then he'd kissed her and made love to her, and that might've been the night she replaced the pocketknife as the one thing he absolutely loved and couldn't live without.

"You idiot," he said to himself, looking up and across the yard. Evelyn hadn't used the words "I'm sorry," last week when she'd asked him to breakfast. But her coming to him—

waiting for him after church—and inviting him to eat with her had been the apology.

She just didn't communicate the same way as normal people. When she said, "Stay," or "Wait," she meant "I love you." When she said, "I don't know," she meant "I need more time to be sure."

Rhett walked slowly back to his truck, wondering what he could do now that he knew the ball was in his court. How had she passed it to him, and he hadn't even known it?

"Stupid cowboy," he muttered. "Always standing in your own way." He needed Evelyn to create a situation so he'd be able to see her, standing right there in front of him all this time.

Maybe he could text her and say he'd be at next week's breakfast. Maybe he should go to the Shining Star and ask for her right now.

Maybe you should slow down, he thought only seconds before a siren blared and red lights flashed behind him. Yeah, he definitely should've slowed down—and not just his spiraling thoughts.

———

The next morning, Rhett sat in the same booth, looking out over the diners at the pancake house, his phone flat on the table in front of him. He'd started making a list yesterday after he'd gotten home from the Quail Creek house, pocketknives and a speeding ticket with him.

He was currently up to five things he could do to try to get Evelyn to move breakfast up a few days.

He'd finished his omelet a while ago, but his waitress kept topping off his coffee, for which he was grateful. The extra caffeine really got his mind working, and he tapped out another idea.

Send her a candy-gram.

Okay, it was a stupid idea. The top two were Find her and talk to her or Text her and ask her to meet you at the pancake house.

They were probably his best options, and yet he couldn't bring himself to do them. Part of him still harbored hurt feelings, and he couldn't just look past those. He'd tried, but they were stubbornly holding on, despite the pocketknives and the gesture behind them.

A cinnamon roll appeared in front of him, the plate making a loud clang as it got set down. He looked up to tell Lucy he didn't want a pastry today.

But it wasn't Lucy standing there.

"Evelyn," he said, his voice turning hoarse by the third syllable. He tried to stand and get out of the booth at the same time and ended up banging his knees against the bottom of the table.

"She said you sometimes like these," Evelyn said. "Can I sit down?"

"Yeah," he said, swiping his phone off the table. He didn't need her to see that lame list. "Yes. Please, sit down."

She eyed him warily, but she slid into the booth. "What were you doing on that phone?"

"Nothing," he said a little too quickly.

Evelyn brought the cinnamon roll toward her and picked up a clean fork. "We might not have talked for a while, but I still know you, Rhett Walker. You were doing *some*thing."

He didn't know what to say or what to do. She'd shown up at the pancake house, and he glanced around to see if anyone was watching them.

Entire tables were, and they didn't even look away when he made eye contact.

"You didn't come to breakfast at the house," she said, her voice small and seemingly far away. "So I came to you. Is now a good time to talk?"

30

Rhett looked like Evelyn had shown up with a two-by-four and hit him with it before she sat down. Of course, he looked like a cowboy male model still, with that sexy hat perched on his head and his trademarked T-shirts that seemed tailored for his shoulders and biceps. No wonder the man had legions of women here, stalking him as he sipped coffee each morning.

Today, he wore a dark purple T, with a brown leather jacket over that, and he was dark, dreamy, dangerous, and delicious.

"I'll start, so that if you're busy doing something super important on that phone, I can just say this, and you can get back to it." Her heart flailed in her chest, but she kept talking anyway. "I'm sorry, Rhett. I ruined things between us when I had no right to do that. You're my best friend, and I miss you so much." She reached up and wiped the silly tears from her eyes. Everyone was watching them, and she wouldn't be surprised if someone was recording this.

She forged on, reminding herself that she didn't care what anyone else thought. No one but him.

"I'm in love with you," she said. "And I want us to live together in that white house again. I bought all these stupid Christmas decorations, and I can't even get them out of the car. We should be there, doing that together."

She sniffed. "And I know you've already filed for divorce, and I don't blame you. Honest, I don't. But I don't want to get divorced."

Searching his face, she found surprise, of course. And that love he'd harbored for her before. She'd seen that look before he kissed her, while they made love.

Her heart took courage, and she said, "My business is done. I have two clients left, and I'm not even trying to get more. I don't care about that anymore. I just want to be with you."

She breathed, glad she hadn't eaten any of that sugary cinnamon roll yet. Evelyn felt certain it wouldn't have played nice with her nervous stomach. "That's all. I love you. I want to be with you. I get it if you don't love me anymore and don't want to be with me. I hope you can find a way to forgive me, though."

He just had to forgive her. She'd never thought of him as an unforgiving person, but he hadn't come to breakfast for two weeks in a row, and that fact stung like a razor burn.

He just looked at her, and she needed something to do

with her hands. Something else to look at. "That's all. That's the whole speech. I'm not as good at this as you are." She focused on the cinnamon roll and poked it with the fork in her hand. She hadn't even remembered picking the utensil up.

"You think that wasn't good?" he asked, drawing her attention back to his face.

"I don't know," she said.

"Evvy, that was perfect." A smile spread across his face one slow centimeter at a time, until his whole being shone with it. "Do you have the Christmas decorations with you right now?"

She nodded, somehow a little stung that he'd chosen that to focus on.

"Great, let's go." He slid out of the booth and stood up, extending his hand toward her.

"Right now?" she asked, glancing around.

"Yes. Come on."

She put her hand in his, and he pulled her to her feet and right into his arms. He held her close, and she was aware that all activity in the restaurant had stalled. Rhett looked right into her eyes and said, "I'm still hopelessly in love with you. If you want me, I'm yours."

Joy tap danced through Evelyn's heart, and she reached up and slid her hands along the sides of his face, as if she needed additional proof that he was here. That this was happening. That he'd just spoken the exact words she wanted to hear.

"I want you," she whispered, and Rhett swept his hat off his head and held it against her back as he lowered his head to kiss her.

The pancake house erupted with applause and cheers, making Evelyn want to laugh and cry at the same time. But she did neither, because she was kissing Rhett Walker—and he was kissing her back.

———

RHETT PULLED up to the house where he and Evelyn had started their lives together, but neither of them got out. She liked him driving her car, and she liked holding his hand while he did. She liked that they hadn't had to talk during the whole drive from the diner, and she liked that he wanted to be here with her, doing this.

"I got the pocketknives," he said, still staring at the green door. "A neighbor called and said there was a package here. I came yesterday afternoon." He turned his attention to her, and Evelyn wanted to sigh at the beauty of his face. The depth of emotion in those eyes. "I didn't know how to get in touch with you. I was going to come to breakfast next Tuesday."

"Sorry to ruin your surprise," she said, not sorry at all.

Rhett laughed, and Evelyn smiled. She'd forgotten how wonderful the man's laugh was. "Okay," she said. "Let's take everything in and get started." She got out of her car, and he popped the trunk.

"Whoa," he said. "How much did you buy?"

She looked down at the bags full of decorations. "I may have gone a little crazy. I don't shop very often, but when I do, it's almost like therapy."

"Okay, well, that's been noted," he said, reaching for the first bag. "There's no Christmas tree."

"I managed to put that in the carport," she said. "Otherwise, I wouldn't have had enough room for all of this."

He chuckled, and together they got everything inside. He hauled the tree in through the front door, and she asked, "Can we put it right there, in front of that window?"

"In your office? What about over here?" He looked to the right, where another window sat in the foyer.

"Sure," she said. "I don't care. I just want to see it through the front window."

"There's more room in the office," he said. "But it might be kind of fun here, because we'll be able to see it when we go up and down the steps, in and out of the house...."

Evelyn honestly didn't care. "Let's put it here." They started unboxing it, and Evelyn couldn't believe the love and peace she felt in that moment. "Thank you for forgiving me," she said quietly.

"Evvy." He stopped working, and she did too. "There's blame on both sides."

"Maybe," she said. "But I know I'm not good at expressing myself. I'm working on it, and I'll keep working on it."

"I won't give up on you," he said with a smile. "In other

news, my brother Wyatt is retiring from the rodeo circuit. He'll be living at the ranch after Christmas."

"That's great," Evelyn said, her first thought how she'd have another potential cowboy for her clients. Then she remembered she didn't have any clients. "I'm going to be getting a job after Christmas."

"Business is bad?" he asked, cutting her a nervous look out of the corner of his eye as he untangled the cord to plug in two sections of the tree.

"It died," she said. "And I'm okay with it."

"Are you?" He looked fully at her then. "I'm surprised by that."

"Yeah, well, I'm not the same person you married, Rhett Walker."

He laughed, sobering quickly. "I can see that, Evvy. I don't think either of us are the same as we were when we got married."

"About that," she said, her heart starting to beat wildly in her chest. She focused on helping him slide the top part of the tree into the bottom, and then she bent to plug the two cords together so the whole thing would light up. Plus, the action hid her face. "What are we going to do about the marriage?"

"The divorce will be final before Christmas," he said. "I don't know if I can stop it."

"I don't want you to stop it," she said, employing every ounce of bravery she had to straighten and look him in the face. "I want to marry you in front of the whole town. I want there to be a lot of flowers, and I want my father to walk me down the aisle. I want your parents there, and all of your brothers, and then I want to come back to this house and start my life with you. My *real* life."

Rhett smiled at her, his eyes a little bit glassy. He stepped over the Christmas tree box and the uppermost section of the tree and took her into his arms. "I want all of that too, Evelyn."

"Okay, so we'll get divorced."

"Yes," he said. "We'll get divorced. And then I'll find a clever way to ask you to marry me, and you can have the dream wedding you want."

Evelyn held onto him, because he was her anchor in a loud and tumultuous world.

They finished setting up the tree, and Evelyn moved on to the stockings, then the window clings, then the kitchen towels. When they'd gone through everything she'd bought, she collapsed onto the couch, her stomach grumbling for food. She hadn't eaten breakfast today, because she wasn't sure she'd be able to stomach talking to Rhett.

"Wow," he said, looking around at the silver, the green, the red. "This is beautiful."

"Will you be here on Christmas?" she asked.

"I was going to go to Grand Cayman with my brothers," he said. "But I don't have to go."

"Oh, I think you do," she said. "Your mom wants everyone there, doesn't she?"

"Yeah, but I think you're more important."

"She won't see it that way," Evelyn said.

"Come with me, then."

"I can't do that."

"Why not?" Rhett looked at her, his hand tightening on hers. "Why can't you?"

"I don't know. I don't...travel?"

He laughed and bumped her, nearly knocking her onto her side. He hovered above her, a dangerous glint in his eyes. "Evelyn, it's time you started traveling. It's fun." He kissed her, and she detected the passion he'd had for her previously.

"My sisters," she said, her voice little more than a rasp as he moved his mouth to her throat.

"They can celebrate Christmas without you for one year," he said, his lips lighting a fire along her skin. The holiday was still a couple of weeks away.

"I don't have a passport."

"Oh, now that is a problem." Rhett sat up and pulled her up too, though she sure had been enjoying the kissing. "I'll talk to my mother. See how important it is that I go."

"Fair enough," she said. "We'll have lots of Christmases together."

"I hope so, sweetheart," he said, gazing at her. "I sure do love you."

"And I love you." Evelyn's smile radiated through her whole body, and she honestly felt loved by the cowboy down the lane. And it was the best feeling in the world.

31

Callie entered the house through the back door, glad Evelyn had called and said she and Rhett would bring dinner to the ranch. As winter had set in, the work around the ranch had become more tedious. She couldn't even imagine working a ranch somewhere where it snowed, though sometimes Mother Nature did drop the white stuff in Three Rivers.

"Hey," Evelyn said from her spot in the kitchen. "We brought that cheddar biscuit chicken pot pie you love."

"Oh, thank you," Callie said, stepping to the sink to wash her hands.

"And I want to call a Foster family meeting," Evelyn said.

Callie's stomach dropped to the soles of her feet. "Why?"

"We'll talk about it when Simone gets here." Evelyn wouldn't look at her, and that didn't settle Callie's nerves.

She and Liam had been getting along great, though she still hadn't been brave enough to establish something as regular as a Wednesday lunch.

Simone walked in a moment later, and the tension in the room escalated. "I'm so hungry," Simone said. "What is that I can smell?"

"Chicken pot pie," Rhett said.

"Oh, it's a good thing you're already married to my sister," Simone said. "Or I'd snatch you up myself."

Everyone laughed, and Callie managed to join in. For some reason, she felt like she was about to be ambushed, and she wasn't sure about what. Her feelings for Liam? What would Evelyn say? Had Liam said anything to Rhett?

More thoughts flew through her head. She hadn't paid Rhett for months for the work around the ranch. He didn't need the money—and she didn't have it to give him. Could he possibly ask her for it?

That makes no sense, she told herself. Not much did at the moment. Rhett getting plates out of her cabinets. Evelyn laughing as she stirred the sweet tea. Simone leaning over the aluminum foil container as if she were smelling the roses.

"Can we do the meeting before we eat?" Callie asked. She may have yelled it, because Rhett, Evelyn, and Simone all froze.

Callie leaned against the counter behind her and looked at them.

"Callie," Rhett said in his rolling, smooth voice. "I've been working here at your ranch for a few months now, and I sure do like it. I'm doing the best I can."

"I appreciate your help," Callie said, lifting her chin. Where was he going with this?

He exchanged a glance with Evelyn, who nodded. "I can't help but notice...certain...things that need improvement. And I'd like to offer to help with those things."

Callie blinked at him. "You're already working for free."

"Yes," he said slowly. "Which I'm happy to do, honestly. I love you girls." He reached for Evelyn's hand and squeezed it. "I'm proposing a grant, of sorts."

Callie held up her hand, suddenly everything becoming crystal clear. "You want to give me money."

"It's not—"

"That's exactly what it is." Callie started laughing, but it wasn't a very happy sound. "I'm not taking anything from you, Rhett."

"He works for us for free," Simone said, almost under her breath.

Callie's gaze shot to her, her heart pounding in her chest. "We're doing fine here. Simone had a killer Fall Festival, and she sold every piece at the holiday art show. With Rhett's help, we're ready to plant more crops this year than every before. We're going to be fine. The ranch is *fine*."

She looked around at everyone in the kitchen, desperate for them to understand.

No one said anything, and finally Evelyn took a step forward. "Callie, it's not charity. He's my husband."

She shook her head. "No, it's charity. And he won't be your husband for much longer."

"We're going to get married again," Evelyn said, her eyes hardening.

"We all love the ranch," Simone said.

"I know that," Callie said. "And we're doing fine. Even without Evelyn's matchmaking money. We're doing fine."

"Okay," Rhett said, lifting both hands in surrender. "Okay. I was just offering."

Callie nodded, her appetite completely gone.

"All right," Evelyn said brightly. "Let's eat."

Callie wanted to run, but she didn't. She picked up a plate, and she listened to the buzzing of her thoughts as Rhett said grace, and she sat at the table with everyone else.

She was glad she wasn't alone, but she honestly wanted to be. She just needed space to think. The ranch was fine. Things were tight, sure. But Callie was a master of squeezing a stone and getting water.

She didn't need Rhett Walker's money.

She absolutely did not.

"This makes no sense," Liam said, holding up a package of Christmas balls. "We're leaving for Grand Cayman in a few days."

Tripp grinned at him, pure glee running through him. "You're the one who said you wanted to decorate the ranch."

Liam studied his brother, and Tripp sure didn't like that. His twin would see right through Tripp's good mood, and he really didn't want to talk about Ivory.

"Oh, this isn't about Christmas decorations at all." Liam took a step closer, not even trying to take out the Christmas balls Tripp had tossed to him.

"Of course it is."

"No," Liam said. "This is about Ivory. Did you kiss her last night?"

"Not talking about this," Tripp said, though he'd totally

kissed Ivory last night. They'd been seeing each other for a couple of months now, and Tripp sure did like the woman.

"Which means yes," Liam said, laughing. "About time, too."

Tripp said nothing. He didn't mind going slow, as Ivory had revealed to him that she had a seven-year-old son. He'd never gone to her house to pick her up, and he hadn't met the boy yet.

Tripp could be patient, and he'd let Ivory set the pace between them.

"Can we just decorate this tree?"

"You do the tree," Liam said. "I'm going to tackle the front fence and gate."

"Deal," Tripp said. He set up the ladder and started climbing up and down, hanging the oversized ornaments he'd bought online. It didn't matter that the tree was an oak and not a pine. It didn't matter that they wouldn't be here on Christmas Day to enjoy the magic of the holiday. Tripp loved Christmas, and he was secretly hoping they could leave the decorations up well into the New Year.

Jeremiah would probably go nuts about that, and Tripp was actually looking forward to seeing that. He enjoyed Jeremiah's temper a little too much, as long as the negative energy was directed at someone other than him.

And Liam was the perfect target for the Christmas decorations, as he'd been the one to bring them up in the first place.

Tripp chuckled to himself and kept tying ribbons and

metallic strings to the ornaments. Soon enough, the whole tree was filled with them, and he walked down the driveway toward the gate.

He turned and looked at the tree, and his breath caught in his lungs. "Wow."

"Lookin' good," Liam said. "I actually really like it."

"Right?" Tripp took in the ornaments and garland on the fence. "Nicely done, bro." Happiness pulled through him. This was definitely a better Christmas than last year, though he'd been glad and grateful to be in Three Rivers, at this ranch, with his brothers.

And the Christmas before that? Yeah, he never wanted another holiday like that one. He'd gotten back all of the gifts he'd given his girlfriend that Christmas, and he'd left Austin a few months later.

He was so much better here in Three Rivers, and he liked that he got off the ranch a bit more now. He and Liam had been frequenting a different restaurant every time they went to town. And he'd seen more of town, learned about the history of the statue near the downtown park, and held Ivory's hand as they spent more time together.

Ah, yes, this Christmas was going to be amazing. And he hoped the New Year would be too.

33

Rhett stood in the kitchen at Seven Sons Ranch, the mail spread out before him. His brothers had left for the airport a couple of hours ago, and everything felt too quiet without them here.

His mother had said he should stay in Three Rivers with Evelyn for the holidays, so that was what he'd decided to do. She'd moved back into the house on Quail Creek Road, but Rhett hadn't dared to do so too.

Number one, he'd want to do married things with her, and their divorce should be final any day now. He shuffled another envelope, looking for the one from the county courthouse. Christmas was in four days, and it had been sixty-seven days since he'd filed. Without any assets, children, or anything to contest, it should be done.

Number two, he liked going to visit her there. Get to

know more about her. See her run a house and talk about what she wanted to do with the front yard in the spring. They'd talked about children, and they were on the same page there. Evelyn would be forty years old in March, and she wanted to get pregnant as soon as possible.

All of her beloved wildflowers would be on display in May, and she'd already set a date for their real wedding.

He did need to find a ring and ask her to marry him.

He moved another envelope, and there it was. The one he'd been looking for and waiting for. With slightly shaking hands, he ripped open the envelope and pulled the single sheet of paper out.

Their divorce was final. The marriage was no more. Over. Done.

Relief poured through him, along with a measure of disappointment. It made no sense, but Rhett knew most feelings didn't.

He picked up his phone and texted Evelyn. *It's done.*

He wasn't sure how she would respond, and he watched to see when she'd read his message. A few seconds passed, and then it marked the text as read. A moment later, her response came in.

Okay.

When are you going to propose?

He laughed, though there was no one around to hear it. Joy filled him, and he started tapping again. *When are you free to go ring shopping?*

Right now, cowboy. I just finished with my last client.

I'll be there in fifteen minutes. Rhett looked up and out the glass doors that led outside. He walked out there, pausing at the table on the deck where he and Evelyn had eaten so many Tuesday breakfasts together.

They'd been eating breakfast together every morning at the pancake house, and the only one not happy about it was Sandy. The hordes of women that had been coming to watch Rhett eat pancakes and sip coffee had dwindled, and she teased Evelyn about being bad for business.

When he pulled into the driveway, Evelyn rose from the porch swing and walked toward him. "I feel kind of stupid," she said as she got in.

"Why's that, love?"

"Making you buy me a ring. Do a fancy proposal." She seemed a little grumpy, and Rhett took a long look at her.

"Sweetheart," he said. "What else am I supposed to do with my time and money?"

She looked at him, startled. "You're not joking."

"Of course I'm joking." He laughed as he put the truck in reverse and backed out. "But Evvy, I don't think God led me to Three Rivers—right next door to your ranch—for no reason. He knew I needed to be there. He knew you needed me there."

"Callie won't take your money," she said.

"I know," he said. "But we'll be married in five months, and then what? She'll refuse a gift from a family member?"

"I don't know what she'll do."

"And you don't have to work until May either," he said. "I don't care about the money."

"I know," she said, looking out the window.

"God blessed me with the money so I could use it for good things," he said. "And you're a good thing. The Shining Star Ranch is a good thing." He reached over and took her hand in his. "Could we maybe try talking to Callie again?"

"If you want to repeat that nightmare, go ahead." Evelyn shook her head. "I'm afraid she's more stubborn than I am."

Rhett chuckled and brought her knuckles to his lips. "I don't think that's possible, baby."

"Ha ha," she said. "Very funny."

Rhett grinned and put both hands on the wheel. "Okay, is there a ring store in Three Rivers?"

"They're called jewelry stores, and yes, there are three."

Rhett tried not to laugh. He really did. But the fact that she knew there were exactly three tickled his funny bone. Thankfully, she laughed with him, and then she directed him to the one she wanted to try first.

As she peered down into cases and tried on different settings, he couldn't help but stew over the Shining Star Ranch. He and Evelyn had called a Foster family meeting, and he'd proposed the idea of giving them "a grant."

Callie had seen right through that, and the meeting had not gone well. She would not take a dime from him, and she hadn't given him any work to do for a week afterward either.

Not very many people knew about the zeroes in Rhett's bank account, and he wanted to keep it that way. But the Fosters knew, and he wanted to help them.

He didn't want Evelyn to work if she didn't want to. She'd gotten a job at a boutique in town, and she said she wanted to do it. Which was fine with him. But he didn't want money to be a concern for any of them. Not anymore.

He firmly believed God had blessed him with the money to take care of people he loved, and he loved Callie and Simone as sisters.

"What do you think?" Evelyn asked, and Rhett focused on this shopping trip.

"I think it's great," he said. The band was yellow gold, which the traditionalist in him liked more than the white gold. It looked too much like silver to him, and that didn't spell out forever and always to Rhett.

"It's expensive," she said, and Rhett almost rolled his eyes.

"If that's the one you like, let's get it," he said. The diamond was huge, and actually looked like a diamond. Several other clusters clung to it, and Rhett could see the beauty of it.

"It's too much," she said. "I need something simpler."

"You do? Why?"

"I'm kind of simple."

"Evvy," he said. "You're the least simple person I know."

"I don't think that's a compliment." She handed the ring back to the jeweler. "I like that cut, but maybe something a little smaller? And with less going on." They moved down the counter, and Rhett trailed behind, wanting her to be happy and wishing there were no price tags on the bands.

In the end, Evelyn didn't find a ring she liked until the third store—and the sixth hour of shopping. Rhett dropped into bed that night, exhausted though he had little to show for the hours he'd been awake.

"Thank you, Lord," he prayed. "It was a good day."

Evelyn's ring would be ready just after Christmas, and he sat up and started texting. Maybe Liam or Jeremiah would have an idea for a fancy proposal.

CHRISTMAS MORNING DAWNED to find Rhett already on the back deck, his hot coffee steaming slightly as the sun rose. Evelyn slept later than him, but he felt like a little boy unable to sleep because Santa had come.

He was going to propose today, and he'd been up for most of the night getting everything ready. At six-thirty, he got in his truck and drove down the highway to the house he'd bought months ago.

Evelyn's car sat in the driveway, and everything seemed peaceful. If she'd been up already, she'd have seen everything he'd done the night before. He walked quietly to the door leading into the house from the carport and fitted his key in the lock.

Inside, the furnace hummed, and the scent of Evelyn's

rosy perfume hung subtly in the air. The poinsettia petals he'd scattered all over the floor were still intact. The ring box still sat on the counter. His propped-up card still waited behind it.

A smile touched his face, and in the next moment, he heard something bump in the house. Several more seconds passed, and then the door creaked open. Footsteps came down the hall. Evelyn appeared, rumpled from bed and oh-so-beautiful.

"Merry Christmas, gorgeous," he said, and she gasped.

Her hand went to her throat as she drank in what he'd done last night. He'd put flowers all over the floor, leaving a path that led right to the kitchen counter. To the ring box. To him.

"I'm in love with you," he said as she started walking toward him again. "And I want to share every Christmas right here with you, in our house."

He picked up the ring box. "I made a sign in case you woke up before I got here." He smiled at it, his heart beating crazy-fast in his chest. He wasn't sure why he was nervous. He'd married this woman before.

But there had been no ring. No engagement. No preparations.

"Evelyn Foster, will you marry me?" He cracked the lid on the ring box to show her the ring she'd picked out, every second like torture.

"This is great," she said, her voice choked. Her eyes met his, and they were filled with tears. "I love you, Rhett. Of course I'll marry you." She cupped his face in her hands, ignoring the ring completely, and kissed him.

She pulled away and pressed her cheek to his. "For real," she whispered.

"For always," Rhett promised.

34

Evelyn turned in a slow circle, looking at the back of her wedding dress. "I should've lost ten more pounds," she said, to which Callie scoffed.

"Evelyn," she said. "It's your wedding day. You're beautiful."

And she was forty, and frankly, losing weight had been terribly difficult. About March, she'd given up. Rhett didn't care what size her wedding dress was. The only people who did care didn't matter, and Evelyn had re-centered her focus on where it should be: her relationship with Rhett, and her relationship with God.

She looked into her sister's eyes. "I'm getting married." Hot tears sprang to her eyes as Callie engulfed her in a hug.

"You sure are, sweetie."

"Guys," Simone said, hurrying into the room as quickly as her bridesmaid dress would allow her to. "It's time to go.

No more hugging." She tugged on Callie's arm, and her sister fell back.

"Okay, we're going to go take our seats," Callie said. "You're about to become Mrs. Rhett Walker." She squealed and followed Simone out of the room.

Evelyn stood in front of the mirror for another moment. She'd never changed her name the last time she and Rhett got married, but she couldn't wait to do it this time. "Thank you, Lord," she whispered. "For everything. For the ability to change and learn and grow. For a good man like Rhett."

She paused at the door, and then opened it to find her father standing several feet down. He turned and hurried over to her. "Wow, you look beautiful." He hugged her, and Evelyn held him tight, tight.

"I wish Mama was here," she whispered.

"She is, baby," her dad said, stepping back and linking his arm through hers. "She is."

Evelyn beamed at him and moved down the hallway. The kitchen where Rhett had proposed came into view, but her goal was the backyard. She'd worked all winter on the yard, and while it wouldn't bloom until next year, she'd found a wildflower farm that would come set up everything exactly how she wanted it.

So she had Texas bluebonnets and Indian paintbrush in pots, on the ground, along the deck railings, everywhere. Callie met them at the back door and handed Evelyn her bouquet, which also had bluebonnets in it, along with white roses and Rhett's favorite flower, the calla lily.

She smiled at his brothers as she went by. His parents that she'd met over the weekend. Her grandmother.

This was how a wedding was supposed to be. A huge celebration, where only love prevailed. Rhett waited for her in his fancy, black tuxedo, a cowboy hat perched on his head, and a smile on his face.

When her father reached him, he passed Evelyn to Rhett and said, "Be true to one another."

"Thank you," Rhett said, because they had experienced a bit of a rocky road with her father. Apparently, he'd been quite hurt that he'd been left out of the first ceremony, and Evelyn had taken Callie and Simone over to the house to explain the make-believe marriage —twice. He'd finally understood what had happened, and he'd forgiven Evelyn and come around to liking Rhett.

"Don't you look amazing?" Rhett asked, sweeping his lips along her cheek before they faced Pastor Daniels. A slight breeze shook the treetops, but other than that, the weather was perfect. The altar stood between them, their wedding bands on it. Rhett had shown up. Everything was going according to plan.

"Welcome," Pastor Daniels said. "It's my pleasure to be here with two good friends, who are taking their lives from one path and merging them into another." He continued with wise words about finding joy and happiness even in the tough times.

Nothing was said about the previous marriage, and

when it was Evelyn's turn to say, "I do," she did so with great gusto.

"I now pronounce you husband and wife," the pastor said, and Rhett turned toward her, a child-like light in his eyes.

"Don't you dare dip me," she warned, recognizing that mischievous grin. "Rhett, we talked about this."

"I know, honeybee." He kissed her, and the crowd cheered. The last time that had happened, Evelyn had gotten all the pieces of her heart back. This time, she could see her whole future with Rhett in front of her, and it was glorious and grand.

Until Rhett dipped her, whispering, "I'm sorry. I couldn't resist," and then pressing a sloppy kiss to her lips as he laughed.

———

Keep reading for a sneak peek at the next book in the Seven Sons Ranch in Three Rivers Romance™ series, **Tripp!**

Sneak Peek! Tripp, Chapter One

Tripp Walker rolled his shoulder, the ache there bothering him and it wasn't even lunchtime yet. He needed to get up from this computer, take a walk, and breathe in some of the summer air, even if it did have the consistency of soup.

Right after he finished this last animated sequence. Then he'd be done with this project for at least a week while the on-site animators in California went through his work and pieced it together. They'd send him notes, and he'd fix whatever they wanted him to fix.

But not today.

Right now, he wanted to spend a few minutes with Penny, Rhett's dog, and then he wanted lunch.

His chair scraped the wood floor as he stood, and he exhaled heavily as he stretched.

"Done?" Liam asked from his desk.

"Yes," Tripp said. "I'm heading outside for a few minutes. Then we should get lunch."

"I'm in," Liam said. "I have maybe twenty minutes of work left before I can go."

"Take your time," Tripp said, but his stomach wasn't happy with the words. "I'm going to go teach Penny how to roll over."

His twin laughed, and Tripp knew enough to laugh at himself too. Penny was a great dog, but she did not want to roll over, especially in the dirt. Tripp wasn't going to give up on her though. He was simply going to take advantage of Penny living at Seven Sons for the next few weeks while Rhett and Evelyn were on their honeymoon.

He missed his older brother, though Rhett had been living in the house he'd bought on Quail Creek Road for a few months now.

After stopping at the fridge for a piece of cheese, Tripp stepped onto the back deck and let the summer sunshine beat down on his shoulders. He whistled, hoping Penny would hear him and come running. He heard a bark, and he whistled again.

The dog came running, and when she reached him, he laughed at her and bent down to give her a healthy scratch. "You ready to roll over?"

Penny barked as if saying, No thank you, Tripp. Where's the treats?

He took the cheese out of his pocket, and Penny sat down,

her front paws twitching as she kept her eyes right on that treat in his hand. "Good sit," he said, smiling at the dog. "Shake." He put his hand out for Penny, and she put her paw in his fingers.

He gave her a bit of cheese. "Lay down."

She did. Treat. He worked through all of the things she could do really well, and then he said, "Roll over."

Penny went onto her side, but she would not roll all the way over. She whined, and Tripp tilted his head at her. "Just roll over, girl," he said. "You've done it before. Go on. Roll over." With a little more coaxing, Penny did what he wanted.

He cheered and gave her the rest of the cheese, scrubbed her ears and said, "Good girl. Rhett is going to be so proud of you."

He straightened, realizing what his life had become. The best part of his day was getting a cattle dog to roll over. Standing in the brutal June sun was enjoyable.

Tripp really needed to get out more. And not to lunch with his twin. But with a woman.

A specific woman who hadn't answered his last text. "Ivory Osburn," he whispered. He'd been out with her a dozen times over the last nine months, but she was hot and cold with him. She'd go out with him three or four times and then say she needed some space.

He'd given it to her when he really wanted to keep seeing her. Meet her son. Ivory hadn't allowed him to meet Oliver, and Tripp didn't want to push her on that. A mother should get to decide when to bring people into her children's life.

The thought to text her and ask her to dinner crossed his mind, but he crossed it off his list just as quickly. She'd just ignore him again, driving the pin further into his heart.

He wished he could let her go, but for some reason, he couldn't. Hadn't, at least. Maybe with some effort, he could.

"Ready?" Liam asked, and Tripp spun toward him. His mind cleared, and he'd made it a personal rule not to eat out twice in one day. Besides, Jeremiah would make dinner, and Tripp loved his brother's food.

"Yes," he said, following Liam back into the house. "I'll drive."

"You and that fancy truck." Liam chuckled, but Tripp just took his keys off the hook in the kitchen and went into the garage.

He'd bought a new truck a couple of months ago, true. It was dark blue and full of all the bells and whistles. The truck made the twenty-minute drive to the town of Three Rivers almost fun, and Tripp adjusted the radio and the air conditioning when he got behind the wheel.

"Okay, where are we going?" he asked once they got off the lane where the ranch sat, the truck's wheels rolling well over the asphalt.

"I'm feeling like Chinese," he said.

"The one by the post office?" Tripp asked. "That's the one I like."

"China Isle," Liam confirmed. "That's the one. I'm feeling like the chicken noodle bowl."

"You and your love of noodles." Tripp shook his head as he smiled.

A mile or two passed before Liam asked, "Do you think we should've invited Wyatt?"

"Oh," Tripp said, surprise moving through him. "I mean, maybe. He wasn't in the house, though." He glanced at Liam. "And we didn't invite Jeremiah."

"I'm just saying I forget about Wyatt sometimes," Liam said. "He's so quiet."

Tripp laughed then, and that definitely wasn't quiet. His mother had always told him he had the best laugh out of any of the boys, and Tripp liked his laugh.

"Yeah, well, compared to us, anyone would be quiet." Tripp caught sight of the outskirts of town, and his stomach grumbled as if he needed a reminder that he was hungry. "Wyatt seems happy enough, though."

"Yeah, he has a way with the horses," Liam said. "And he doesn't want to train them for the rodeo, which I don't get."

"Well, he's working at Bowman Breeds, and that's what they do. Maybe he feels like this town is too small for two rodeo training operations."

The truth was, Tripp didn't really know how Wyatt felt. His brother had said he needed some time to figure out his life without the rodeo in it, and everyone had left him alone to do that.

"It's fun having him here," Tripp said as he turned to go down the right street.

"Yeah, totally," Liam said. "I just don't want him to feel like we've left him out."

"Fair point," Tripp said. "We should be more careful of that." Sometimes the two of them got in their twin space and didn't realize that the other brothers might feel like they weren't welcome.

He turned into the parking lot and started looking for a spot. "Wow, this place is popular during lunchtime." He swiveled his head left and right, searching. "Anything over there?"

"No, and I had no idea this many people liked Chinese —watch out!"

Tripp slammed on the brake pedal, having just saw the woman bent over in the middle of the parking lot. She'd dropped a bunch of packages, and a very keen sense of déjà vu hit him right in the chest.

So hard that he unbuckled his seatbelt and slid from the truck. "Ivory?" he asked. The first time they'd met, she'd dropped an armful of packages right in front of him at the post office.

She sniffled and snatched the last package before he could help her. His pulse sang and skipped through his veins. At the same time, he realized that there was something wrong with Ivory.

"Are you okay?" He actually glanced at the front bumper of his truck just to make sure he hadn't touched her.

"Tripp." She balanced the packages in one arm and used her free hand to swipe that dirty blonde hair out of her face. "I'm fine."

But she wasn't fine. She'd been crying, and while Tripp wasn't well-versed with crying women, he sensed an opportunity here.

"Let me help you," he said, taking some of the packages before she could protest. With three or four in his hands, she only had a couple left to carry. "You're taking these to the post office?"

"Yes," she said, walking now. He met his brother's eyes through the windshield, and even without their freaky twin communications, Liam would've gotten the message to slide over and get the truck parked.

This is Ivory Osburn, Tripp thought, suddenly so glad he'd waited for Liam to finish his work before coming to lunch.

"Why'd you park over here?" he asked.

Ivory just glared at him, then she picked her way across the decorative rocks that separated the restaurant parking lot from the post office one. "No reason."

"Ivory, wait," he said, frustrated she was already pushing him away again. "There's something wrong. A blind man could see it. Let me help you."

"You want to help me?"

"Yes," he said, though her voice bordered on dangerous.

She stepped onto the sidewalk and faced him, her face filled with irritation and anger. Her eyes brimmed with tears. "I don't need help. They're just necklaces." She started taking the packages from him and ended up bobbling all of them, dropping them to the ground again.

A frustrated moan came from her mouth, and she bent to collect the packages again.

"Ivory," he said, feeling helpless with a hint of humiliation.

"I'm fine, Tripp," she said. "I mean, if you can get more people to buy my jewelry, I might be better. Or if you could get my addled mind to remember where to turn to park at this blasted post office, that might be good too. Or you know what?" She straightened, all of the packages securely in her arms again.

"Maybe you could get my ex to drop the custody challenge he started. Can you do that?" She cocked her eyebrows at him, and Tripp had no idea what to say.

"I didn't think so." She turned and marched away from him. "Don't offer to help if you can't actually do it," she said over her shoulder.

Tripp turned to look behind him, sure some help would be standing there. No one stood there, and Tripp watched Ivory walk into the post office and right out of his life.

Again.

Sneak Peek! Tripp, Chapter Two

Ivory leaned against the counter, her breaths coming in huge gulps. She was seconds away from having a panic attack in the Three Rivers post office, where everyone would see her.

She could not believe Daniel was suing her for full custody. And the worst part? His claims were true. She had no money. She could barely afford to feed herself and Oliver. The cable had been turned off. Their Internet. Anything Ivory didn't have to have to survive, she'd gotten rid of. They needed air conditioning and heat. Electricity. And her phone, which she used for Internet service too.

But she was months behind on the mortgage, and it was only a matter of time before she didn't have a house either.

And that meant Oliver wouldn't have a place to sleep.

So Daniel's claims that she couldn't adequately provide for their son were one-hundred percent right.

"I can't lose him," she murmured to herself only a moment before a fresh flood of tears arrived.

And running into Tripp in the wrong parking lot was just icing on a really ugly cake. The man called to her very soul, and it had been very hard for her to push him away. Every time he got a little too close, she'd put the brakes on their relationship. She didn't need another man walking out on her. Another man proving to her how unlovable she was. Another man trying to tell her how to live her life, what to wear, how to be.

She opened the pre-stamped mail chute and put her pathetic packages in. Only six this week, and that meant she'd only earned a hundred and twenty dollars. She couldn't afford much with that, because half went to buying the supplies she needed to make the necklaces.

"Look," a man said, and she turned to find Tripp Walker standing there. He was dark, stormy, and beautiful. She wanted to run to him and let him hold her upright. Whisper in her ear that everything would be all right. Kiss those lips she'd kissed before.

"I don't know how to do any of that stuff you just said," he said, taking a step closer, those sexy cowboy boots making a clunking sound on the hard floor. "But I'm not going to just let you walk away when you're so upset."

"I'm fine," she said, though she was anything but fine. In fact, fine and Ivory weren't even on the same continent at the moment.

"Let me take you to lunch," he said.

"Liam was in the truck."

"Liam knows how to order his own food."

Ivory's stomach cramped with hunger. She wanted—no, *needed*—to eat. And if she were being completely honest with herself, she wanted to be with Tripp.

"I don't think so," she said.

"Why not?"

"Because I don't want you getting the wrong idea," she said, going for snappy truths again. "I'm fine. I just needed to mail my packages." And now she needed to go home, make a pancake out of the giant, ten-pound bag of mix she had, and figure out how to get more people buying jewelry from her online store. What new pieces could she make with the supplies she already owned?

What do people want? she begged. She'd been asking God the same question for months, but so far, He hadn't struck her with any inspiration.

"Let's go to lunch with Liam, then," Tripp said. "I can't get the wrong idea then, right?"

Ivory considered him, thinking of the gossip mill in town. The Walker brothers were a little removed from it, but Ivory wasn't. She'd heard plenty of talk at the salon, while she got her nails done, and at the boutiques where she liked to shop. Well, when she had money to do all of those things.

Nails, hair, and shopping had all been cut from her life, the same way the cable had been.

"Come on, Ivory," he said, clearly exasperated. "I stood

over there and watched you have an anxiety attack. One meal. I won't text you afterward."

Ivory wished she could tell him why she'd gotten so scared and cut him out of her life a few times. But she hadn't dared then, and she didn't dare now either.

"Fine," she said. "One meal. With Liam."

"I'm texting him now," Tripp said. He looked up a moment later. "Ready when you are."

Ivory gestured for him to go first, and instead of walking out, Tripp reached over and took her hand.

"Tripp," she said, but he didn't let go. Outside, the sun had heated the air beyond tolerable, and Ivory felt the sweat start to slide down her back with the first step.

He released her hand when he was obviously satisfied that she wasn't going to run away. They walked over those decorative rocks again, and the silence between them made Ivory's nerves strain.

"How have you been?" she asked.

"Not fair," he said, not even glancing at her.

"What's not fair?"

"You asking me how I've been," he said. "That's not fair."

"*You* asked me to lunch."

"You don't seem fit to drive right now," he said. "I want to make sure you're okay."

"I told you I was fine."

"And I've heard you say that before, when you weren't fine." He looked at her then, and Ivory's steps slowed. "I don't know why you've pushed me away on three separate occasions. I really don't. When we've been together, I've had a great time. I like you." He drew in a deep breath, his frustration like a third person between them.

He looked at her, clearly expecting her to say something. "I'm sorry," she said. "I just...needed a break."

"Must be nice," he said, striding forward again. "To take a break from your life whenever you want one."

Fury moved through her, and she stared after him. "You have no idea what you're talking about. I never get a break."

"That's because you refuse to ask for help." He tossed the words over his shoulder, the length of his strides broadcasting his anger. "Have a good day, Ivory." He touched the brim of that sexy cowboy hat and continued toward the entrance of the restaurant.

"I guess I'm uninvited," she said to his retreating back, nowhere near loud enough for him to hear. She watched until he disappeared inside the surely air conditioned restaurant, and then she sighed, running her hand through her hair.

It felt tangled and messy, and she hated that he'd seen her like that. She hurried to her car and turned on the air conditioning. "I took a break from *you*, Tripp, when you were getting too close to me. When things got too real. When I was afraid I'd fall in love with you, only to have you break up with me."

Ivory hung her head, everything in her wrung out. An

alarm went off on her phone, and she sucked in a breath. Pulled everything back inside. Laced it tight.

After all, it was time for her to pick Oliver up from school, and he deserved a mother that wasn't one tick away from a breakdown.

———

"Ollie," she called from the sliding glass door. "Come on, baby. Dinner's ready."

Her son left his toys in the sandbox and skipped toward her. "Look, Mama. I can skip." He grinned so wide, his whole face shone with joy. He had no idea she'd spent too much at the grocery store that afternoon so they could have sausage with their pancakes that night.

"Good job," she said, stroking her hand over his silky hair. "Are you ready for summer?"

"Yeah," he said. "Dad said he'd take me horseback riding."

"Yep," Ivory said as cheerfully as she could. Daniel had moved to Amarillo after their divorce, but he came to Three Rivers twice a month for his son. And he'd take Oliver the day after school got out for half of the summer.

"Pancakes again?" Oliver asked, and Ivory flinched.

"That's right," she said brightly. "With your favorite— sausage links." She put the plate in front of him as he climbed up on the barstool. She'd added water to the syrup and heated in the microwave, stirring it all together. It was a little thin, but Oliver didn't say anything about that.

She flipped the pancakes on the griddle and served two to her son a minute later. She kept her smile on her face as she ate, but she could barely gag down another bite of pancake. She'd bought hot dogs as well, and she'd definitely have to switch up their diet tomorrow.

Helplessness filled her, but she held back the tears until Ollie finished dinner. "Bath time, bud," she said, her patience for this day almost gone. And she'd have to see Daniel on Saturday, look him in the face, and pretend like he hadn't turned her world upside down with a few pieces of paper.

Oliver didn't get up and skip down the hall to the bathroom. He never did. She didn't have the energy to fight with him tonight, so when he got down and went into the backyard instead of to take a bath, she said nothing.

She sat at the kitchen counter and stared at the watery syrup. The empty plate which had held the sausage links. The pancakes she hadn't been able to swallow.

"What am I going to do?" She tilted her head toward the ceiling. Her parents lived in Tennessee, and she had absolutely no desire to call them. She'd left for college and never gone back, as her father had a drinking problem and turned mean when he drank.

Daniel's parents lived in the Texas Hill Country, and she hadn't spoken to them since the divorce, three years ago.

They'd never offered to help her, but they may have made arrangements with Daniel.

He paid his child support, and without that, Ivory would've been in much worse condition than she was now.

She exhaled, determined not to sit here and cry. Her jewelry-making wasn't working out. So she'd get a job.

With an ache in her bones, she got up and went to the back door again. "Ollie, come on," she said. "Bath time."

"Mom," he whined, and Ivory gestured to him. He argued a little bit, but he eventually came in and stomped down the hall to the bathroom. Ivory cleaned up the kitchen, glancing at the small cowboy figurine on the windowsill above the sink.

Ollie had made it for her in school, and for some reason, Tripp's handsome face appeared in her mind.

If he was her husband, she'd have plenty of money....

The thought waltzed through her mind so slowly. She really had time to think hard about it, ultimately dismissing the idea.

"You're not even talking to him," she muttered to herself as Ollie started singing down the hall. And marrying him?

Wasn't going to happen, even if he did say he wanted to help her.

———

TRIPP is available now in paperback. Get it here by scanning this QR code with the camera on your phone.

Rhett

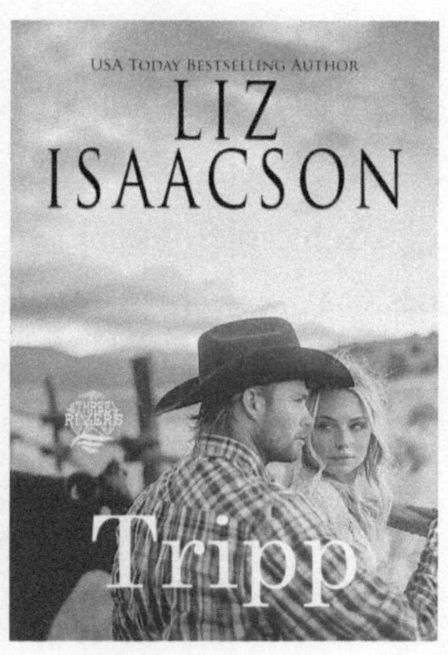

Tripp (Book 2): She needs a husband to keep her son. He's wanted to take their relationship to the next level, but she's always pushing him away. Will their trivial tie take them all the way to happily-ever-after?

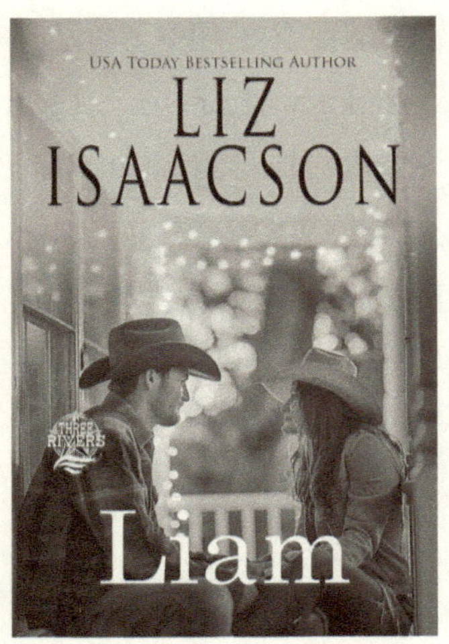

Liam (Book 3): She's desperate to save her ranch. He wants to help her any way he can. Will their invented I-Do open doors that have previously been closed and lead to a happily-ever-after for both of them?

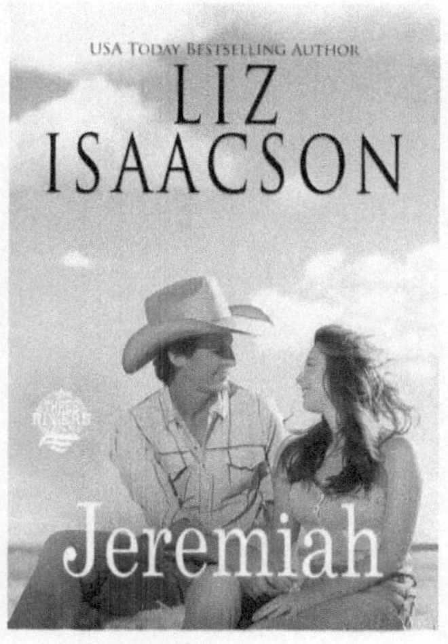

Jeremiah (Book 4): He wants to prove to his brothers that he's not broken. She just wants him. Will a fake marriage heal him or push her further away?

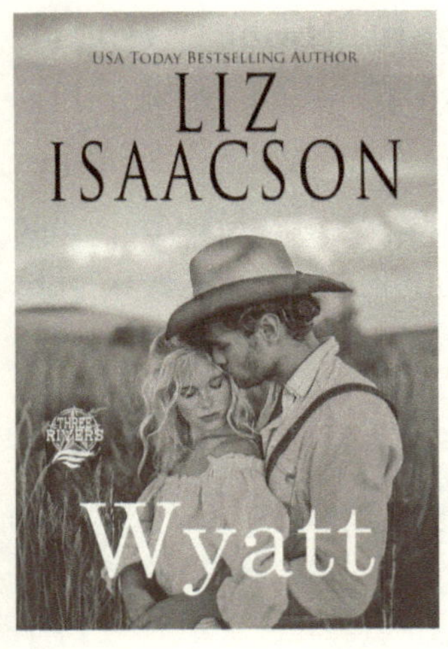

Wyatt (Book 5): To get her inheritance, she needs a husband. He's wanted to fly with her for ages. Can their pretend pledge turn into something real?

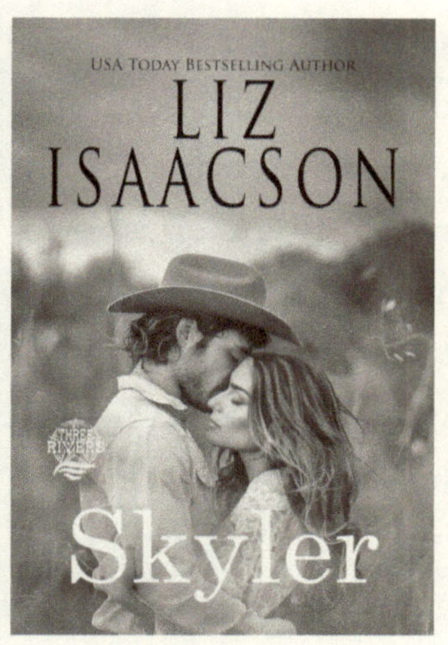

Skyler (Book 6): She needs a new last name to stay in school. He's willing to help a fellow student. Can this wanna-be wife show the playboy that some things should be taken seriously?

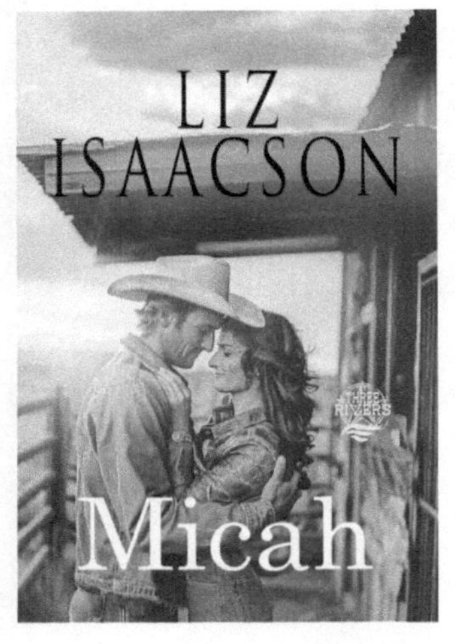

Micah (Book 7): They were just actors auditioning for a play. The marriage was just for the audition – until a clerical error results in a legal marriage. Can these two ex-lovers negotiate this new ground between them and achieve new roles in each other's lives?

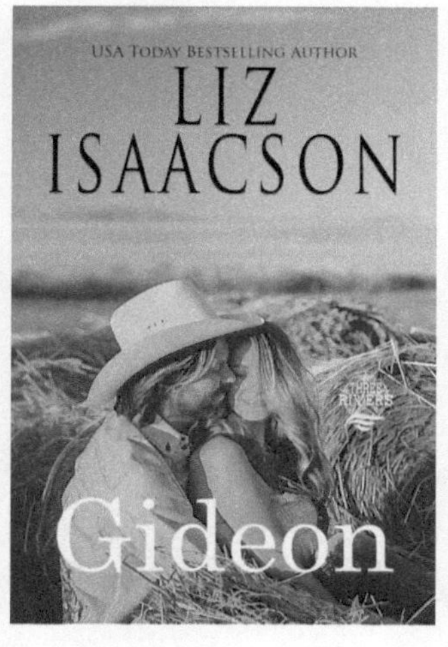 **Gideon (Book 8):** It's 1971, and Gideon Walker is on the cutting edge of all the technology coming out of Texas. He has big dreams and wants to make something of himself. Then he meets Penny Aarons, and everything changes. He only has eyes for her, but she's got plans and dreams of her own...

Read this origin romance for Momma and Daddy from the Seven Sons series today!

Three Rivers Ranch Romance™ Series

Escape to Three Rivers, Texas for small-town charm, sweet and sexy cowboys, and faith and family centered romance. You'll get second chance romance, friends to lovers. older brother's best friend, military romance, secret babies, and more! The Three Rivers cowboys and the women who rope their hearts are waiting for you, so start reading today!

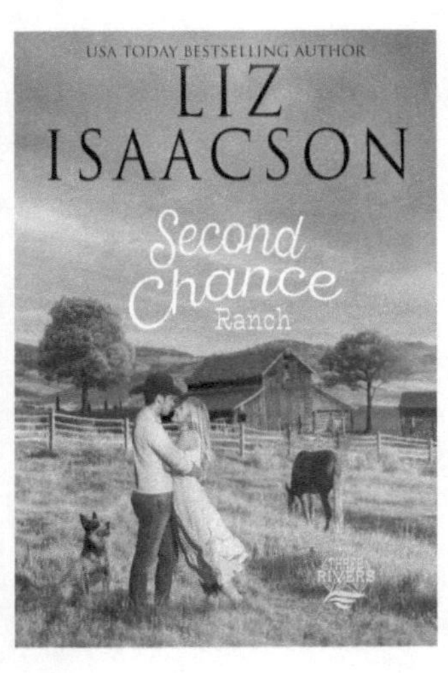

Second Chance Ranch (Book 1): After his deployment, injured and discharged Major Squire Ackerman returns to Three Rivers Ranch, wanting to forgive Kelly for ignoring him a decade ago. He'd like to provide the stable life she needs, but with old wounds opening and a ranch on the brink of financial collapse, it will take patience and faith to make their second chance possible.

Shiloh Ridge Ranch in Three Rivers Romance™

Meet the cowboy billionaires in the southern hills outside of Three Rivers! They love God, horses, the land, and family, and all 12 of them are looking for love in the small Texas town where they grew up. Start this Christian family saga romance series and spend time with people you'd be happy to call YOUR family too!

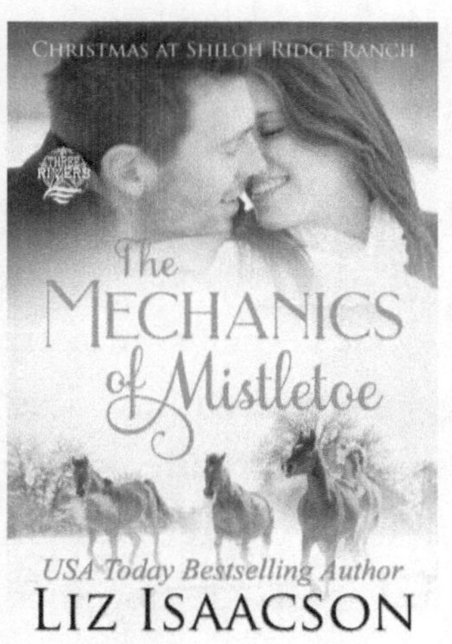

The Mechanics of Mistletoe (Book 1): He can be a teddy or a grizzly. She's a genius with a wrench. Can the pretty mechanic tame this cowboy's wild side, or will they both be left broken-hearted this Christmas?

Second Generation in Three Rivers Romance™

Step back into the heartwarming small Texas town of Three Rivers! Get ready to experience a small-town saga like no other, where the legacy of the past meets the promise of the future. As you journey through these heartwarming stories, you'll not only fall in love with the next generation of cowboys and ranchers but also have the joy of revisiting beloved characters from Three Rivers Ranch, Seven Sons Ranch, and Shiloh Ridge Ranch!

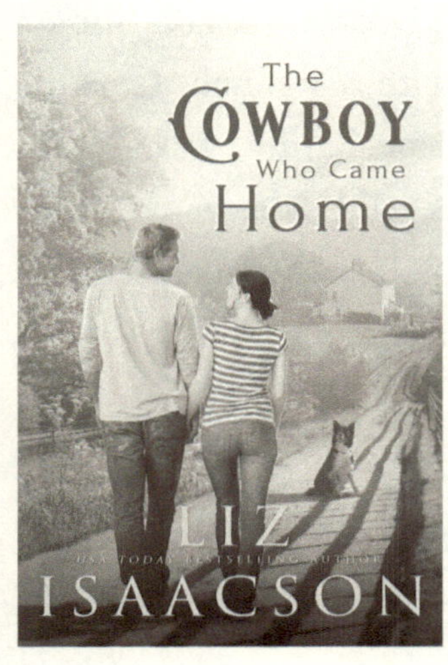

The Cowboy Who Came Home (Book 1): He's been serving in the military for a decade. She's been quietly grieving a devastating loss. When Finn and Edith reunite in small-town Three Rivers where they grew up together, can their second chance romance provide hope, healing, and the happily-ever-after they both crave?

About Liz

Liz Isaacson writes inspirational romance, usually set in Texas, or Wyoming, or anywhere else horses and cowboys exist. She lives in Utah, where she writes full-time, takes her two dogs to the park everyday, and eats a lot of veggies while writing. Find her on her website, along with all of her pen names, at authorelanajohnson.com

www.ingramcontent.com/pod-product-compliance
Lightning Source LLC
Chambersburg PA
CBHW050505110726
47899CB00005B/1336